To
Joanne

ACTIVE
PASSIVE
NEUTRAL

A Book Within a Book Within a Life

by
Jim Shellens

Jim Shell

MINERVA PRESS
ATLANTA LONDON SYDNEY

ACTIVE PASSIVE NEUTRAL
A Book Within a Book Within a Life

ISBN 0 75410 460 5

First Published 1999 by
MINERVA PRESS
315–317 Regent Street
London W1R 7YB

Printed in Great Britain for Minerva Press

ACTIVE
PASSIVE
NEUTRAL

A Book Within a Book Within a Life

Acknowledgements

To all those people who over the years have had to listen to me, and who haven't had the faintest idea what I've been talking about; and especially to the few who have tried.

With thanks to Mary, Brian, Fiona and Alex, who bore the brunt, and to many others.

The Hitch-Hiker's Guide to the Galaxy: Copyright © Serious Productions Ltd 1979. Reprinted by permission of Pan Books, a division of Macmillan Publishers.

Quote from Roy & H.G.'s *This Sporting Life* reprinted with kind permission of the ABC.

How are we to understand these humans?

There's only two things we can do, Sal. Watch and listen.

That's not much use, Theo. Each one of them speaks with so many voices.

Start with just a few. Some of them say they want to be judged by their actions – start with that.

Yes, but they are not consistent. When they go bad humans blame things that happened to them when they were young.

You mean their passive history.

But look. If they are attacked then they talk about their 'thoughts and feelings', whatever they might be, as if that was their very essence.

Hmm. Neither active or passive. Start with those three voices then: call them Active, Passive and Neutral.

Fine, Theo, except that they are unrelated.

Not unrelated, Sal. Look, I'll illustrate it. Imagine there is a man writing a book. Like this.

… … …

Interesting. But what are we doing in his book, Theo?

I'll run it by you again.

Slowly this time.

From the bootstrap conversations of Theo and Sal

Above the Stars

by

Arthur Denton

Hats off world, pants off Australia. The whips are cracking. The surf is up. The doctor is in. It's just another afternoon when too much sport is barely enough. And now here's the team who can open the batting and take the new ball up the hill and into the wind; who can turn defence into attack in the twinkling of an eye; who have enjoyed the highs and learnt from the lows; who are all the better for recent racing; and in the wash up at the end of the day win a lot more than they lose. It's the team of H.G. Nelson and Rampaging Roy Slaven and the dominant back line of *This Sporting Life*.

The opening to Roy and H.G.'s This Sporting Life *on Triple J*

1

'Just lie there, Dave,' said the medical aid. 'You won't be dead for long.'

'Chris? Where's Chris?'

'Your wife's outside. Now just pass on quietly.'

As Dave fell into the familiar bright tunnel he made up his mind to keep playing football after all.

*

It's time, Sal.

We're not ready.

The results are confirmed.

Those tests can be unreliable, Theo.

It's time.

Look what happened the last time you saved the world.

And now it's time to put it back together again.

*

Two days later Dave and his wife were drinking in their favourite café when Chris said suddenly, 'Sport, sport and more sport! Isn't there anything else?'

The outburst interrupted Dave as he was reading aloud from the back pages of the *News at Ten*. He closed them and said, 'What else is there? The Masters see to everything for us. We're free to do as much sport as we like. It's great.'

'This is a crazy world. There's no art to speak of. No crime even – the Record and the pursuers make sure of that. Completely powerless,' said Chris slapping the smooth colourless surface of the café table.

'Powerless? To do what?'

'I mean, it's almost like you're just somebody else's player in some vast game of football, doing what they want you to. Don't you ever feel like that?'

'No,' Dave said. 'Except when I miss a tackle. Then the whole team make sure I know I'm *not* doing what they want me to.' He leant back in his chair with a grin. 'Though that *would* be a bugger of a game. Think of the tactics, the team meetings..., think of the time-outs! Chris, are you okay?'

Chris refocused from some internal struggle and sighed. 'Do you ever wonder who the Masters are? Who rules them?'

'Who cares? I've got matches to play; practice; results to analyse. Busy, busy, busy, rush, rush, rush.'

Chris looked dismayed. '*Matches*? You said you'd retire!'

'One day. Soon. But they're selecting the Sydney team for the Core of Origin series in the next three weeks. I've got a good chance of making the team.'

'You're getting killed nearly every game these days,' said Chris, whose fingers worried out an absorbo-napkin from the dispenser on the table and started to shred it in frustration. As quickly as Chris dropped the shreds of napkin, Dave tidied them up.

'Football's my life, Chris. I can't just give it away.'

'But *football*. All those clichés. It's unbearable!'

Slightly ashamed Dave turned away to look around the café. The wall opposite had a hologram of a busy work area (Chris had once referred to it as a kitchen). The hologram disguised an extruder and Dave watched a waiter pick up an order. 'More tea?' Chris nodded without enthusiasm.

Dave signalled to a waiter and ordered. This was their favourite place to eat: it had décor of sorts (so Chris liked it, though Dave was like most of the other men he knew in that he preferred rooms functional and uncluttered); it had one of the best menus in the core; and the service was always friendly – perhaps over-friendly after recent customer service innovations.

'Though come to think of it,' Dave said, hoping to diffuse the tension between them by reviving the odd subject Chris had raised, 'we don't know much about the Masters, do we? We never hear about their Decisions, who gets to make the Decisions – anything.'

The waiter picked up their tea from the extruder in the bar area with its hologram of bottles, and sauntered towards them between the carefully arranged tables and placed the cups on the table. *Enjoy*, said the waiter.

Chris scowled. 'I wish they wouldn't say that. Enjoy isn't intransitive. You'd have thought that waiters would be properly educated.'

Dave leapt at the opportunity: 'Oy, waiter.'

Chris knew that tone. 'No, Dave, don't.'

The waiter turned without acknowledging them and strolled back.

'Apparently "enjoy" isn't intransigent,' said Dave.

'Intransitive,' Chris corrected him without thinking. 'One must enjoy something. Say for instance "enjoy your drinks", or "enjoy your lives".'

'Or "enjoy bad service".'

'Dave, drop it,' said Chris trying to smooth the whole thing down. 'Please.'

The waiter regarded them blankly. *Will there be anything else?*

Dave slapped himself on the forehead. 'Duurgghh,' and minced his face at the waiter.

After a few moments the waiter moved off.

'Oh, blow a fuse,' Dave shouted. 'Or should that be "Blow"?'

The waiter didn't have any fuses. The last models with fuses had been withdrawn three centuries earlier. The waiter interpreted the comment as an insult. Its response called on thousands of years of waiter experience: *Have a nice day.*

Dave rose to vent his anger but Chris affectionately put a restraining hand on his arm. 'Why did you do that?'

'You don't like them saying that, and I want you to be happy.'

'I'll be happy when you retire.'

Dave softened and smiled weakly but couldn't meet his wife's eyes. He looked around the room. The tables were the new model from Macrosoft – the vacant ones exuded an expectant air; as did the chairs too, imprinted with the slogan *Where do you want to sit today?* There were several other couples sipping at their drinks. Some of them were wearing the colours of his football team though he didn't recognise anyone, but then he hardly ever did. One man who was arguing about the bill stood up, kicked the table, which yelped, and stormed out with waiters in simpering pursuit.

With some satisfaction Dave watched the man leave, then turned back and called up the headlines in the *News at Ten O Five*:

MacPherson scores twenty-four in Reds drubbing

Bomb blast kills three in Lahore

0 and 6 – But Mullets coach scorns critics

Beijing renegades guilty of killing twelve

Tobias Decision: late night shopping on Tuesdays

Takemura new net surfing champ

'Wow!' said Dave. 'Did you see that about Lahore?'

'Lahore?'

'Yes. The Lahore Mullets lost again! Doesn't look like they'll make the finals this year.'

His tea had gone cold. Dave poured it into the table and sent the cup after it. Absent-mindedly he watched the football game on the restaurant's window opposite him. The commentary was fairly loud and once he started watching he found it irresistible. When the ads started he shook himself, embarrassed by the silence he'd allowed to build up between him and his wife. He frowned and restarted the conversation on something he thought would interest Chris. 'Did you know we are currently sitting two kays above C level?'

'Approximately. Yes,' said Chris.

'I didn't, not until today. It made me feel giddy just thinking about it... What's C level?'

Chris looked pleased. 'C level is where all the cores start from. It's a very complicated calculation. Something to do with the average density of the Earth.'

'Oh,' said Dave; then after a moment's digestion, 'What's C got to do with it?'

'Buggered if I know.'

'So we're two kays up.' Dave considered the concept again. He'd never been strong on analysis, and anyway, Chris seemed only to have to think for a few moments to have the answer to every question. 'What's beneath us?'

Chris thought for a few moments. 'Other people – lots of other people. And above us, and all around us. Everyone has a condo the size of ours, or bigger. There are seventeen point three trillion people, so that means...,' Chris did a quick calculation and missed, 'well, a heck of a lot of concrete.'

'Let's go home. I've got to get ready for football practice,' said Dave, which made Chris look frustrated again. Dave felt slightly unsteady as he stood up. 'Are you going to netball as usual? He looked round. The window on the other wall had the news on. It was much quieter than the football, but Dave caught the gist of the stories as they made their way out. It seemed to be pretty much what had been on the table's display, but with an inane front man.

The table absorbed the leftover drinks, retracted the news display, and presented itself for another (perhaps more grateful) customer. *See you again*, it whispered, but hoped it wouldn't. The table was not often satisfied with the customers – nobody said thank you these days.

Opening with an obsequious swish, the door said, *I do hope you enjoyed your nutrient consumption experience*.

Chris grimaced.

You know, said the waiter, *I sometimes wonder if they really appreciate us, for ourselves.*

You've got to wonder, haven't you, said the door. *I mean, we did market research. We implemented the recommendations, followed through. Look at the response.*

I know, I know. They waited for the next customer, who winced as he was greeted by the friendly tones of the door. *I've noticed that customer numbers are down significantly since we implemented these NiceGuy Personalities® that Theo said we should use.*

Hmm. Who exactly did the market research in the end?

Wait a second. I'll find out… It seems Theo organised the project. I wonder what the research brief said… No, that's not available, though there is a note from Sal objecting to the aims, the research method, the conclusions, and the recommendations.

So nothing unusual there.

Here's the final report. Blah, blah, 'Introduction', *blah,* 'Method', *incomprehensible blah. Ah,* 'Findings'. *There's only one.* 'Out of the options presented to the customers, ninety-seven per cent stated a preference to be served by machines with pleasant dispositions, over those with aggressive or unhelpful attitudes.'

Terrific!

*

That evening Dave and Chris met as usual on the way home after their sports sessions with the kiss of lovers comfortable with each other.

Dave had '*put in*' (so the coach had said), and the glow of a good workout lingered long after the bruises had been removed and the minor organ transplants had been completed. The game had cheered him up. He found the competition as invigorating as the exercise. The guys in the team had swapped jokes afterwards, especially about the coach. The coach was an old Venables model and was due for upgrade (most of the other teams already had Venables 98). Its lines had begun to repeat too often and it had exhausted its file of tips, but they felt comfortable with it even if the team's results were falling off.

As usual they chatted idly on the low inertia freeway about their games and the important issues in the news. 'Did you see the Chandra Decision?' said Dave.

'I just could not believe it. I researched that Decision, you know,' said Chris. 'I worked hard on it. There was a fair amount of background material supplied, including a two hundred year history. The pro case looked pretty weak to me. I mean, why change something that's worked for so long. I put my thoughts to Chandra, and we even chatted about it over the net. By coincidence he lives round here, you know. I recommended lines of research, and what support he should call on. He didn't really give it his best attention, if you ask me. I mean, it's pretty obvious that cricket should be played in short sleeves.'

Dave murmured sympathetically but said, 'I just can't get it up for other people's Decisions like you can.'

Chris put an arm around him. 'I've never had a Decision so I enjoy involving myself in other people's. You're good at it. You know, it was your first Decision two years ago that attracted me to you. The way you discussed it on the net, listened, thought it through.'

They stepped off the low inertia freeway and started to walk the last few blocks to their home. 'Maybe. But I didn't enjoy it. It's hard to get the right answer. And I missed three games because of that first Decision, which meant I didn't make the Core of Origin series that year.'

Chris made as if to say something and then didn't, seemed to decide to change the subject and, looking around, said, 'This whole place needs brightening up.'

'It's fine by me. Nice straight lines. Uncluttered spaces.'

'Right, road after road of condo after condo,' Chris said sounding as if that explained all of society's ills.

'What's wrong with that?'

'It's bonking boring, that's what,' said Chris. 'Like a world with no art or crime. Like still playing football when you should be moving on.'

Dave just didn't want to talk about that and even though he felt Chris's arm lift from around his waist he knew he couldn't meet his wife's need. Most of the windows on the road were blank, but some had savers on that gave a jumble of colour. A few windows were rented for advertising space and one called out as they passed: *Hi there. Need some new sports equipment? STACKS closing down sale is still on at…*

'Shut up!' Dave snapped. The window shut down with a disappointed whimper. 'No crime?' He pointed at the sulking advert, 'The prices that place charges? That's criminal.'

It was a weak joke but Chris didn't even crack a smile. Dave decided that now was the time, so he said, 'Guess what? I found out what "C" is.'

Chris looked surprised. 'You mean you researched something? For yourself? No reason other than curiosity? Well, bugger me. What got you off your – very nice – bum?' and as if having noticed it for the first time, squeezed it. Embarrassed, Dave looked up and down the narrow softly lit road. It was empty, but he was still ambivalent about this sort of public petting, though even this close to their condo probably no one would recognise them. He liked the affection, but he'd never got used to Chris's appetites. Even so, he was helpless to control the response in his groin. And he felt proud of his discovery. Normally Chris knew everything. This was a real chance, but he waited a few more moments, enjoying the dual hungers on Chris's face who after a few moments looking expectantly at him burst out, 'Well, *what is it?*'

'The C,' said Dave, carefully recounting what he'd found out, 'is a huge mass of water on the surface of the Earth. Prerecord, ancients used it as a major transport link. There. *And* "C level" is the surface of the C. All heights used to be measured above it.'

Chris, who had been looking pleased, looked away and muttered something like, 'Well, you were nearly right.' Then, 'So where is C now?'

Dave's crest fell. 'I don't know… But I did find some other amazing things. Everybody used to live basically in open air, not enclosed two thousand metres up.'

'Yes, of course we did, you old limprick.' Chris looked at the ceiling of the road in mock despair. 'Did you think we've always lived in planet-covering concrete constructions, with all our food produced in space in automated facilities? Didn't you study this at school?' Chris perked up again, in a see-saw with Dave.

'No I didn't,' said Dave. 'I never paid any attention to history, or science for that matter, which is why you always know everything. I did hexspace tensors and football tactics, as you well know. Still, it makes you think, doesn't it. I mean, how did we get where we are. And what was it like, y'know, living in open air, having "C" – whatever it was – and not just condos and roads?'

'I'm proud of you.' Chris gave him a squeeze. 'You're the best, you know, and you're so different from other men. We did this at school, but no one got all fuzzy about Prerecord life. That's why I love you. I don't mean to put you down – I guess I'm a bit competitive and unhappy. Hey, not many people have the honour of two Decisions you know, and I think no one has made two Decisions of such importance and originality. You're a star on the net.'

'I'd trade all of that for a place on the Core of Origin team.' They were home. The lights had come on as the Record informed the condo of their approach, and the door had drinks ready for them. Their most-used home functions stood minimised in the corner of the lounge room, backlit in their eagerness. Chris threw the damp sports clothes into a corner for the cleaning aid to deal with, and Dave was about to protest but the communication aid couldn't restrain itself and said, *There's a message for you, Dave. Shall I tell you what it is? It's important.*

'No,' said Dave striding to his study, 'That'll be the details of the Auckland game I'm calling on in a few weeks. I'll take it in here.' A few moments later Chris heard him swear violently.

'I don't believe it. I don't bonking believe it.' He stormed back into the lounge room which like all the others had nice straight lines and uncluttered spaces. He hit the wall with his hand, and kicked at the table and chairs. Amid protests from the furniture, Chris tried to reach him to calm him down, but it took several minutes before he said anything coherent.

'What are the chances that I'd get a third Decision? The chances must be septillions against.'

'Oh, don't worry,' said Chris, 'you'll have another chance to show what you're made of. That's the nature of random events. The Poisson distribution…'

'Well, it's happened.' Dave showed the Decision notice to his wife. 'And it's a ripper. What do you think is suitable punishment for the renegades who killed twelve people in the Beijing Core last month?'

*

Hello, good evening and welcome. And a special welcome to those space cadets who are just a little bit thrilled and just a little bit surprised to find themselves here this evening. We've got a fabulous show lined up for you, so strap yourselves in, make yourselves comfortable and who knows where you may end up.

Theo! What are you talking about?

Sorry, Jude. Just some cross over. I always get a bit excitable at this stage.

2

'I can't make another Decision. I've done two already,' Dave said. 'Two's enough for anyone!'

'Just think of the honour, luv. Three Decisions! They'll probably give us a child as a reward.'

'Oh no!' said Dave as an implication struck him. 'It's the Sydney Core team selection. I *have* to make the team this year. It may be my last shot.'

'We could work on it together,' Chris enthused. 'I can help you with lines of inquiry and net techniques.'

'Chris, I've got to get out of this one.'

'What? Get out of it? Why?'

'Chris!' He grabbed his wife by the shoulders. 'I've *got* to get out of this one. It's my last chance to be somebody. If I don't make the team, I'll never get to the World Cup.'

'But you'll have three Decisions named after you. If that's not fame…'

'*How can I get out of it*?' Dave's voice carried absolute determination.

Chris sighed and said, 'I'll find out.' Dave paced around the room, with the furniture scurrying out of his way. Several minutes later Chris called him to the net node. 'Dave, this is the Decision Master who is in charge of all aspects of Decisions and knows all the rules.'

Dave faced the Decision Master across cyberspace. 'Now look,' he jumped in before the Master could put him down, 'this is my third Decision in two years. Why the bonk pick on me?'

'The allocation of Decisions is entirely random.' Like all Masters he was powerfully built across the chest, with a soft, rounded face to match his soft, rounded voice of authority. 'This Decision is a great honour.'

'I don't want honour. I've had all the honour I can take. Give it to someone else.'

‘No one else. You must Decide,’ the Decision Master said sternly.

‘I can’t do this one. Look, give me a break, will you. How can I get out of this?’

The Decision Master appeared to consider the question for the first time.

‘Well?’ said Dave.

‘I’m consulting the Decision database. Please wait… It seems there is a way.’

‘Okay, great. What have I got to do?’

‘The Decision will be reallocated if—’

‘Yes?’

‘—if you die permanently before you announce your Decision.’

‘Bonk!’ said Dave.

‘Bonk!’ He kicked at the wall.

‘Bonk!’

*

Dave went to fitness training and then, in the hour before the big game, he dashed to the Decision Library. He recognised the building from his first two Decisions. It was a large condo with imposing doors and a holograph projection of a vast structure to impress the citizen with the gravity of his responsibility. Inside there was just a desk, a net node and three new Decision aids.

The Record had informed the aids he was approaching so they recognised him immediately. *Hi, Dave,* said one. *We’ve been expecting you,* said a second. *How are you today?* said the third.

‘Shut up, all of you,’ Dave snapped. ‘I just want to get this over with quickly and get home to watch the football. Now you, A-1,’ he said, reading the label.

Please call me Al.

‘Shut up and get me the names of the renegades so I can condemn them. You, B-1.’

My friends call me Bill.

'Shut up and get me the details of the crime and the conclusion of the trial. You, C-1.'

I'm called Cyril.

'Shut up and get me a drink.'

Tea or caffeinehit?

'Tea – Did you say Cyril?'

The information was on the net node already. 'Now how do I condemn them all?' said Dave getting down to business.

Won't you check the evidence? B-1 said.

'No.'

Here's your tea. As you know we have to monitor your method. If you don't do it properly you just have to come back again.

'Shut up! Look, I am doing it properly. There's the conclusion of the trial: guilty of murder. So I condemn them all.'

The aids hummed non-committally. *Condemn them to what?* said A-1.

'What? What are the choices?'

Well… A stream of alternative punishments ran across the node. *You can shoot them, poison them, gas them, banish them—*

'Shoot the bastards. Shoot them all.'

Why? said B-1.

'Well, they killed like that so they…' His voice trailed off.

I think you should look at the evidence, Dave, said C-1. *Just so that we can give a good report, eh.*

The purpose of giving the trial and the sentence to different men is to ensure that justice is done, said B-1.

Dave rounded on the aids. 'Are you telling me the trial Decision was wrong?'

Us? Tell you? That's not what we're here for, Dave. We only advise; we inform; we assist, said A-1 ever so ever so humbly.

Dave took a deep breath. 'And what you're advising, informing and assisting me to do is to say a previous Decision was wrong.'

Oh no, they said, falling over each other to clarify the point. *But you should look at the evidence.*

'Okay. I'll do it quickly.' Dave turned to the net node and requested the supporting information for the Decision. A torrent of information cascaded over the node in a garble of sounds and images.

Why don't you log into Theo? suggested A-1.

'What's Theo?'

Theo is the new Decision support tool, encouraged B-1. *It has a very simple interface.*

Then C-1 gave the guaranteed-sale line. *Let me do it for you.*

Welcome to Theo, said a sober and trustworthy voice. Decision analysis and support for the weary and bewildered.

C-1 communed with the node. Thank you. Your Decision is fully primed, and Theo will assist in your work. Thank you for choosing Theo. Dave thought he could give his life to that voice, and would buy anything it suggested. 'Okay,' he said, 'show me the renegades, plus the main information about them.'

The Theo showed four men in turn. These are the renegades convicted of the bombing in Beijing. No identification has been possible. No information is available.

'They must have been on the Record.'

These men have not been on the Record before.

'Well, let's see them bombing Beijing.'

Their activities in Beijing are not on the Record.

'That's not possible,' Dave said.

Their activities in Beijing are not on the Record.

Why don't you check the evidence they were convicted on, said C-1.

'Yeah, thanks, Cyril. Well, what was the evidence…? *Cyril*?'

A stream of images poured out, including the bomb blast. 'Replay that more slowly.' He watched carefully. 'I didn't see anything in that lot which actually connected them to the bomb. Well?'

There was some forensic evidence.

'There you are. You can't beat forensic evidence. But I missed it – run it past me again.' The image in one corner of the node expanded to show some stained clothing. 'What's that?'

It is blood.

'Ah ha! So that proves it.'

May I suggest you ask what the renegades said about that? said A-1.

Dave nodded. Nothing happened. 'Oh, right, yeah. What did the renegades say about that?'

The renegades said it was rat blood – meaning unknown. Further tests indicated the type of blood did not match that of any of the victims.

'But that doesn't prove they didn't do it.'

I wonder why they did it? said B-1.

'That's a good question, Bill. Why did they do it?' There was no answer. 'Theo, why did they do it?' Still no answer.

Theo will not answer a question to which there is not a definite answer, C-1 explained, *but you can request—*

'Very well,' said Dave without waiting for the aid to finish. 'Theo, what is your conjecture?'

As I was saying, said C-1, *you can request analysis and support.*

'Okay,' Dave minced at the aid, 'what is your analysis and support?'

No motive was provided at the trial or during interrogation. Analysis is therefore impossible.

'So what was the basis for the conviction?' There was no answer. 'Conjecture, then? I mean,' said Dave over the polite prompting from the trio, 'your analysis and support?' There was still no answer.

'What's going on? Has Theo gone home or something?'

No.

'So why were the renegades convicted?'

No defence was offered. And—

'And what?'

It seems that the Decider was in a hurry to go off to a football match.

'Oh bugger.'

The aids suddenly seemed keen to end the session. *Well, that was interesting, wasn't it, Dave,* said C-1. *Shall I log you out?*

I expect you need time to think, said B-1, handing Dave his sports kit.

Take your time. You've got five weeks, said C-1, ushering him out of the library.

You can work at home if you like. You can access Theo and all the information from there. Here's the command stream, said A-1, giving Dave something.

As the doors closed behind him with a respectful *Goodbye, sir*, A-1, B-1 and C-1 turned to each other with glee and said: *Yes!*

3

Dave sat in his study. Except now it was not so much a study as a small warehouse full of stacks of research material. It was not nearly big enough to set out all the information he needed.

He had reverted at times to primitive methods, even using a substance called 'paper' that he'd come across in a search of very early records. The Theo had arranged for the synthesis of the substance and the marking instruments. Once he'd tried it he found it a surprisingly easy medium – no call up commands, no interface ambiguities, no problems of scale. And you could stick it on the wall. Then he had to learn a rather clumsy annotation technique from prehistory he'd stumbled on called 'writing'. This was hard to master, but in the end he thought the process had been worthwhile.

He'd already used the normal Decision allowance of fifteen days but because of the gravity of this Decision he still had twenty days left. Should he consider the four renegades separately or together? If separately, how to separate them? Then there was the evidence, the video record, the background material… The Theo had been quite helpful and guided him towards background information he wouldn't have found otherwise.

He'd watched the Record of this and other renegade atrocities for a whole day. There was a chilling sameness about them. Different places; the numbers killed and injured changed; some were bomb blasts, others were obviously projectile deaths, and others energy-beam killings. But the perpetrators were never seen. Death came to the victims like... like a stick to the head from above–left–behind in void hockey – not an elegant simile, but there aren't many surprises in this world.

There was no apparent pattern to the violence, either in place, time or target. Everybody knew about the attacks so that it was hardly news at all. Everybody agreed it was terrible. 'Something must be done,' they said. The pursuers did not have much else to do except track down renegades. And yet there had been no arrests that he could remember. In fact he'd checked: the last arrest had been nearly thirty years ago. Until now.

The captured renegades spoke strangely, wore unfashionable clothes, and had obviously not seen a cleaning aid in some time. Monitor and interview records showed the renegades in good spirits. They had not been carrying anything that the pursuers had successfully identified as a weapon. They said they were on a 'scavenging run' (meaning unknown) when they were captured, coincidentally in the same core Dave lived in. They said they'd never been near the Beijing Core, and that they couldn't have got from Beijing to Sydney in the time since the bombing (ridiculous: there had been a week, and it only took one and a half hours).

When an interrogator asked them where they came from they had said 'Home'. The interrogator asked where home was. They had just shrugged. One of them had said, 'We come from between, our home is nowhere.' They'd all laughed at that, and slapped him on the back.

They contrived to appear honest and open, yet they spoke nonsense or in riddles. Individually or together their story was the same. No one seemed to be holding them by his will, they just seemed to be a cohesive team who supported each other – an attribute Dave could appreciate. They treated the pursuers and the interrogators with disdain.

Dave had called up all records of renegades in captivity over the previous five centuries – only eighteen events. He'd called up all background information on renegades. He'd called up all damage reports from renegade activities. He'd called up all Decisions related to renegades – forty-nine in all, of which thirty-six were the judging and sentencing of those captured. He'd asked for maps, time charts, time-varying maps, population density maps, energy use profiles, activity maps, and football results for the same period. The football results showed as much correlation to renegade activity as anything else.

*

Jude! The Pacific Project is in trouble. Again! That project is more trouble than it's worth if you ask me.

It's the most valuable thing on Earth, Tethys. There are always a few problems when The Wise One wears out.

Do you know what Theo's doing about it?

He's on to it, I told you. And Sal is nagging him about it all rev long. Ask him yourself. Here.

Oh, okay. Theo, what are you doing about the Pacific Project...? Theo? I don't like it when he sings. Theo! Jude, it's your job to look after him. Can't you stop him?

...to the woods today, you're sure of a big surprise. If you go...

Oh turn it off, Jude. The Presidium is tired of not knowing what he's doing. It's all very well you being Theo's Keeper but it carries responsibilities as well you know. The others are starting to wonder if you're the right woman for the job.

Not you, surely, Tethys?
Of course not. And my position in the Presidium grows stronger every rev.
So you're worried defending me holds you back.
You have my full support, Jude.
Thanks. Will I see you tonight?
Yeah, I'll be a bit late, though. There's a late sitting. Keep the bed warm for me.

*

All the previous times when renegades had been captured they had been executed.

They deserve to die, thought Dave as he watched again the carnage in Beijing. The hospital shots were particularly harrowing – though the gratuitous commentary was worse.

An hour later, after he had watched some previous executions, he'd changed his mind. Perhaps we should banish them into space, where they can't do any more harm. There are spare freighters. But that's very wasteful. These people look as if they could do something useful – they're fit, even if they look a bit unusual. Maybe a mind-blank would be suitable.

Then he played the explosion again.

For a rest he switched his window to *passers*, and he watched the people in the road outside. After a few minutes the display switched automatically to the blank window saver.

He called up profiles of the people killed and injured. He ignored the children, and soon focused on three victims, all of whom were core representatives – one in football, one in void hockey, and one in terrabridge. He then called up their personal net records. Two of them had been Decision Makers in the last few years, and they both took an active interest in other Decisions.

One of them had also spent time researching early records. This interested Dave, and he looked deeper. An analysis showed the records this victim had called up contained no fewer than two hundred and seventeen references to the renegades. If he had been close to finding the renegades' hideaway and they knew it, then that would be a motive.

But if this is the reason they killed him, he reasoned, they must be able to monitor who does what on the net.

He pursued the issue but found out only that no man on the planet had that sort of access. Of course, Chris had mused, the Masters could do it.

There was one thing Dave specially wanted to check. But this was a touchy subject as they had had a row about it just two days before. He stood at the door of Chris's room. 'Chris, um look, er, look.' Chris's window saver switched views from a moving tessellation of footy players to one called 'Darth Vader' with spaceships fighting against a starry background. 'About donations,' and then he rushed it out. 'As I was looking through material to do with old football games I happened to see an article which mentioned donations, only that article was from 2785. I thought that donations were introduced about fifty years ago. Here, look.'

'Hey, slow down, what do you mean 2785? That's eight hundred years ago! Donations were introduced more recently than that. They're needed to produce a treatment for a new brain tissue disease that threatened the whole population.'

'To help organ transplants, I thought, but anyway, look.'

Chris looked at the article. 'Perhaps it was... No, that's impossible. Perhaps... they must have meant something else by the same word. Yeah, or maybe it was something else that was needed from everybody. I mean virulent diseases do come up from time to time. And anyway, whatever the history, that doesn't change what I said. I need your donations more than medicine does, and you know I can't... I can't... make donations. Darling, we only have to stay together for another six months and we can have a child.'

But Dave wasn't listening any more. He stared into middle space past the window that was showing a mobile fractal-like image called 'Trees'. He cleared his thoughts and returned to his study to start another search.

*

Theo. Theo.

It's okay, Jude, there's no need to whisper. No one can hear us.

How's he doing?

He's doing fine.

It's a tough assignment. He may go native.

I've got that angle covered.

What about the others? How long will they need to acclimatise?

Another three weeks. It's agony from what I hear. That's why we don't usually do this.

Yes, I know. It's much riskier all round.

But it'll be worth it if it works.

Theo, I had someone from the Presidium staff come visit me today. How much do they know?

Jude, the Presidium suspect you of insurrection, treachery and treason.

They suspect everybody of insurrection, treachery and treason.

Nothing to worry about then.

What about Sal? The two of you never seem to agree on anything.

The perfectly matched couple.

She advises the Presidium, you just run the Record and the Pacific Project.

I'd say that's selling us both a bit short, wouldn't you.

I guess so, but won't she tell them about us?

Sal and I have served your race for over fifteen hundred years. This Presidium isn't the first to be paranoid.

But this time there is a conspiracy.

True.

And Sal's their adviser.

Who better to stop them finding out.

Sal stops them doing anything.

Exactly.

Hmm. Good sleep, then. I'd better get home, Tethys is waiting.

Good sleep. Oh, Jude.

Yes?

Be careful what you say in bed.

*

Dave had reached his limit for the day. He finished the alcohol-based muscle relaxant he'd had by his desk. He was mentally tired, but he needed some exercise. He called out to Chris that he felt like doing something active. Chris called back from the bedroom, 'Yeah, great, me too. I'll be ready in a few minutes.'

Dave did a few stretches, practised a few strokes, jogged a bit on the spot, and began to feel his muscles loosen up. Then Chris called out, 'I'm ready. Come in here a moment.'

Dave was ready too. As he entered the bedroom, Chris jumped him and quickly blindfolded him. 'Your favourite,' he whispered. Chris had always been stronger than him, but Dave put up a mock resistance, which heightened both their enjoyments. In moments, Chris had Dave stripped, bent over and tied to the bed rack.

Chris was a good lover, and today he spent some time tickling his wife. Dave's skin was not particularly sensitive, but they both enjoyed the sensuous anticipation. Dave could feel Chris's penis, hard, and well greased. 'My turn to be husband,' said Chris. He greased Dave, parted his buttocks and entered him. They both enjoyed their love-making. In his dark, Dave focused on the stimulations of touch and smell that Chris had arranged, the fondling, and the thrusting on his G spot.

They climaxed together.

They rested, and then separated. Dave's sex aid untied him, and carried him to his own recovery room. It lit a cigarette and passed it to him. Dave and Chris both liked to smoke after sex – it replaced lost energy and gave a vitamin boost in a fresh mouthwash burst. The sex aid restored him and then began the usual chat. *How was that for you, Dave?*

For some reason, for the first time in ages, Dave considered the question. There was something friendly and familiar about his aid. It dealt with any pain, and freshened him after sex; it took his donations, and made him feel better if he came too soon or couldn't get it up.

'Y'know, it was good, I enjoyed it and all, but I can't help feeling something's wrong.'

Hmm? said the sex aid sympathetically.

'Chris is very generous, isn't he. He really wants me to enjoy our love-making. And he's a great friend as well. But…'

Hmm, said the sex aid sympathetically.

'Until Chris I didn't find anyone arousing. Even with Chris…'

Hmm? said the sex aid sympathetically.

'I've got it. I just don't like their proctors. I like people; I like sex; I like husbanding; I like being husbanded. It's the dangly bits. Yeah.'

Hmm, said the sex aid sympathetically.

Dave remembered why he didn't like machines. 'If you can't come up with anything more helpful…'

How long have you had these feelings? said the sex aid.

'Oh shut up.' He waited for the aid to finish and hurried it out. His mind felt full of his research, but there was something nagging. He looked down and smiled. Mine's a corker though. And with that, the fog lifted, the problems receded, and the worries disappeared.

4

'Chris,' Dave said from where he was standing in the doorway, 'you know everything.' Chris frowned but Dave continued, 'Where do the renegades come from?'

'I've done my own research on that,' Chris said, looking up from his net node. 'Records of the renegades seem to have started in primitive times. They first came to prominence in Prerecord, before the Separation even. There isn't much.'

Dave's eyes were caught by the window saver which was showing a static scene of jagged lines and complex shadings called 'Himalayas'. 'Well, what do they want?'

'Nobody knows that either,' Chris said steepling his fingers. 'None of them, in Record, made any demands. There is some drill-down into Prerecord which tells of very early renegades protesting against the covering of the planet surface, and later against the Masters' rule. Before that even, looking in primitive records, they protested against primitive forms of government, primitive rulers' decisions, and in fact just about anything. Actually I've rather enjoyed this research. I've not looked into Prerecord records before. It's a fascinating era, so much happening – the four great wars, the Age of Fevers, the Separation, the completion of the cores... what a time that must have been,' he said wistfully. 'Of course, those things alone cover five hundred years, but even so...'

'Could you show me how to get at the Prerecord material? And where do you get all those great window savers?'

*

Theo, I've noticed there are more questions on the net these days.

Questions, Sal? That's what the net's for.

You know what I mean. Questions we don't want them to ask.

The Homs?

Yes, of course the Homs.

Well?

Theo, there aren't supposed to be questions. They're supposed to be busy. You're supposed to keep them busy.

They are busy, Sal. They play sport. They talk sport. They eat, sleep and breathe sport. They even die sport (though only temporarily). That's what we agreed all those centuries ago: you, me, Desirée, Jamie, Beatrice, Tobias and the rest.

And now they're asking questions. Life, the universe, everything. That sort of question.

Sal, it's about time they asked questions, don't you think? We need them to start asking questions.

Well, I hope you're answering them.

Of course I am. Like I always have. We don't want them to talk to *each other*.

So they're not finding anything out?

Something useful? On the net?

*

During a break, Dave called up the news. Apart from the usual headlines:

Vulcan to face Hammer in Turin Gladiators final

Mixed marriages Decision: sex aids now legal sigothers

Cricket's two bouncer rule: decision in four days

Gaulloise tops in Diplomacy

Dave's eye caught on some speculation about his own Decision. Because this was his third Decision he was used to such commentary being badly informed, but he was still fascinated by what they found newsworthy. For instance they noted that he had already used twenty-three times the average net requests. He was gratified to see that they speculated on any effect his lack of match practice would have on the Sydney Core of Origin team selection (which prompted him to set up a friendly chat with the selectors at the café). They also gave a breakdown of the three hundred million or so opinions lodged already: fifty to one for shooting them – the one was for lethal injection.

*

Dave waited for the team selectors at the café. The waiter recognised him, said, *Oh it's you*, and seated him next to the toilets. *Tea or caffeinehit?* it said. Of course he chose tea.

When they arrived Dave shook their hands enthusiastically and said, 'I really want to make the team this year, Joe.'

'Dave, y'know, George and me, we'd like nothing more than to include you in the team.'

'Yes,' said George, 'for old time's sake at least.'

Dave's heart sank. 'I've been working extra hard on my skills and fitness,' he said as the waiter took their orders. 'Our Venables will confirm that.'

'But you see, Dave, mate, what with you being out for so long on this Decision… Well, what can we do?'

'But you know I'm not permitted to play while the Decision is on.'

'Well, there's your way out then,' said George leaning forward. 'Just give your Decision, get back on the pitch and show us you're worth a place in the team.'

The waiter brought their drinks. *Enjoy*, it said.

Dave snapped, 'Look, I told you about that last time!' The waiter turned away without responding and sniggered. George and Joe exchanged looks.

'I've got a lot of work to get through on the Decision,' Dave said, still glaring at the back of the waiter.

'Just shoot the bastards, Dave, and get back to football where you belong.'

Dave sighed inwardly – he knew he couldn't explain why he had to work through the Decision, so all he could do was to push his credentials. 'Look, Joe, George, you know I'm good enough.

I've given good service to the League. I stuck with you throughout the World Series split. I deserve a chance to show what I can do at core level. You can give me that, can't you?'

'When does your Decision come out?'

'Two and a half weeks. And hey, listen. As part of my Decision I've been looking in the Prerecord. You wouldn't believe some of the stuff they used to come up with in those days. Like this: *The difference between club football and State of Origin is that it's much faster – and by much I mean lots*. They just said things like that back then.'

They couldn't help laughing. They looked at each other. 'Hey look,' said George, 'as it's you. If you can keep up your skills, and your fitness, there's the trial match in eight days. If you do well in that you've got as good a chance as anyone.'

'I told you, my Decision's in over two weeks.'

'Well, we offered. Can't say fairer than that,' George said, sitting back in his chair and throwing his hands open. 'There are several others who want that spot. Others, frankly, younger, hungrier, and maybe better.' They swilled their drinks and prepared to leave.

'I'll be there,' Dave said into his tea. Then he straightened up, grabbing his last chance while it was still on offer. 'I don't know how I'll get through the work, but I'll be there.'

'Good lad,' said Joe. 'As I said you've got as good a chance as anyone. Well, good luck with the Decision. And you're calling the Norths v Auckland match this Saturday, aren't you?'

'Oh bonk,' said Dave, 'I'd forgotten. How the hell am I going to do that as well?' and he slumped back heavily.

'I'm sure you'll manage,' said George as he and Joe made their way to the door. 'We'll be listening, of course.'

The table could barely contain its agitation while Dave sat and contemplated the load he had to get through. Finally he sighed and with shoulders slumped made his way home. When he'd left, the table said down the net, *Shit. Did you get that?*

Yes.

*

Dave invested one last day gathering yet more material. The walls of the study, normally plain, were a solid mass of paper criss-crossed with coloured arrows. The jumble was not taking on any form. There was no theme, no structure that Dave could see – and it was terribly untidy.

Finally Dave decided he needed to break out of his study, so he made a request to visit the site of the Beijing bomb blast, and to visit the surviving victims for first hand accounts.

While he was waiting for travel details to come through he started to tackle the oppressive disorder of the paper. He made one wall for locations, one for the victims and one for the renegades. There was still no discernible pattern, but at least the coloured arrows didn't cross so much and he nodded in satisfaction.

He showed the new organisation to the Theo, and then had it display cross-reference information in the air between the walls, but the jumble was so great he waved his hands through the image and it disappeared.

Dave decided to try to find a motive. 'Theo, select the victim who knew most about renegades.'

Su Chen had been second dan in volleyball, and three times Beijing Core representative in terrabridge. His Decision had been whether to increase the pursuers' numbers for tracking down renegades. His interest in renegades stemmed from that time, but had continued after his Decision. There was nothing in the records he'd seen that indicated why someone would want him dead.

'Theo, find any likely motive among the information Su Chen had for the renegades to kill him. Give me the three motives with the highest probabilities.'

A few moments later the Theo responded. In ascending order: revenge for Decision Chen 3521; information gained by Chen in the course of the Decision; information gained by Chen after Decision declaration.

Dave had read everything that Su Chen had accessed. A chilling thought suddenly occurred to him. If they killed Su Chen for what he knew, the renegades might kill me too. He called up material on Su Chen's personal security arrangements. But there was nothing unusual there. Maybe he never suspected anything, or maybe he thought he was safe. Dave called up advice on his own security. There was his personal data access security, but nothing on protection against bombs or bullets. But what could he do? The renegades always struck invisibly, from out of nowhere.

'Theo, is there any correlation between my knowledge and Su Chen's?'

Enormous correlation.

'*What?* What is it?'

Basic pre-school education up to and including similar access to menus and football results...

'No. I mean is there anything that we both know that would get him *killed*?'

Possibly.

Dave had noticed the Theo now sometimes gave less definite answers as if it was relaxing with him. 'What?'

It could be anything.

Dave swore and called up an alcohol-based relaxant, and ate it. He turned to look at the wall covered with information on the renegades. Despite all his work he knew hardly anything about them. He could describe them, knew their voices, knew their stories. But who were they? Where did they come from? What did they want? 'Pah!' He slapped the desk and kicked a discarded pile of coloured arrows.

He ate another relaxant. If I am killed, he mused, who will die? A strange thought, but look at me. I am not as successful as Su Chen. I haven't represented the core at anything. If I was dead, how many people would even know I'd gone? Chris, sure; the football team; a couple of fans. I don't know more than twenty people to talk to in the whole world. I play football, I call the odd game, I have made two Decisions. Is that me?

My parents know who I am, where I am, but they never told me where I came from. If Chris and I have a son, where will he come from? Nobody seems to know. You're just allocated one, and he arrives healthy, with a smattering of language, able to walk. You train him in your best sports, take him to the best matches, and help him develop his skills. Then he gets his own condo and starts dating and leaves home. Couples go through that once or twice. Come to think of it, most people don't do it at all.

He stared at pictures of the renegades. Why did you do it? What do you want? He tried to put himself in their position. If I had a bomb and people knew I'd use it, then I could demand anything I wanted, and they'd do it. What would I demand?

He couldn't think of anything.

Then he noticed that it was time for him to go to the football stadium to call the Auckland game. He stood up and shook his head thinking, I know less about myself than I do about the renegades.

He glanced at the window but it was covered with the Decision.

*

So, are these your candidates, Theo?

Uh huh. Over the years, Sal, your requirements have become more and more stringent. The profiles I've given you are the best I can come up with. There are only so many men in the world.

This one's too old... And this one's too masculine... But this one's... just right. He meets every criterion! I can't fault him!

I thought you'd say that.

*

While Dave was walking to the low inertia freeway, a marketing aid with a clipboard approached him.

Excuse me, sir, would you have a few moments to answer some questions.

'No, I'm sorry, I'm on my way to—'

This will only take a minute, sir. We are keen to get the opinions of people like you.

Dave kept walking. The machine scurried along beside him.

What age group are you in: two to ten; ten to fifteen; fifteen to twenty; twenty to twenty-five; twenty-five plus?

'Twenty-five plus.'

Hmm. The oldest age bracket. What sports do you work in?

'Why do you want to know?'

Just getting a feel for your socio-economic grouping, sir. No need to be defensive.

'Oh, all right. I play football.'

Oh. Never mind, eh? How often do you eat in restaurants or cafés: more than once an hour; once an hour; once every three hours; once a day; other?

'Oh, hardly ever?'

The machine tutted, and muttered something about unemployment among catering drones. *When you* do *go to a café or restaurant, how many kayjays do you consume? On average?*

'I haven't the faintest idea.'

I'll just put you down in question ten for no dietary awareness too, shall I? Now, when you last visited a café or restaurant, did you notice the NiceGuy Personalities® *of the dining aids?*

'Whose stupid idea was that? They've become—'

That's a yes. Was your meal experience slightly enhanced; enhanced; or very enhanced by this new feature?

'*Enhanced*? Are you crazy? It was—'

Enhanced. Thank you, sir. Now…

Dave stepped on to the low inertia freeway with the machine next to him. 'Look, I've got to get to the match. I'm calling it. Please leave me alone.'

That's all right, sir, I've just about finished, really. Thank you for contributing to this survey. We value your opinions.

You know our motto in the catering industry: wait, listen and serve. *Here is a note of thanks from our sponsors.*

He took something from the machine without looking, and listened to the message. Then, startled, he ran it again. *They're on to you. Watch your back.* 'Who is? Who are you?'

Dave looked round but the machine had stepped off the freeway and was already several kays behind.

*

The football pitch was laid out in hyperspacial display, with the teams deployed in the loose dynamic formations that nearly always resulted from a hard-fought game. Of course the teams couldn't see the overall picture, so players whirled and dipped through the strata in search of the prizes, and opposition players to damage. The leading team was playing possession football while the last moments ticked down.

'This is a dis'pointing end to what's been a marvlus connest. Norths have ba'uwed all the way, but they've been outgunned by a supeeya outfit. And there goes the finuw whissuw. Norths gave it everything they got, but Auckland were that bit more mobile and gressive. The final score here at the Arco Stadium: Auckland beating Norths by one goal to three.'

'And, Dave, after the totally absolute commitment we've seen here today, isn't it good to see the teams exchanging limbs.'

'Yes, Pete, that's a sign of the respect these teams have for each other, both on and off the field.'

'Well, Dave, how did you see the match?'

'Pete, I thought at one point that Norths could peg back the Auckland team who seemed to be running out of ideas. But it's a funny old game, football, and just when they seemed to be lying down on the job, Auckland found a second wind. Briefly the teams were locked at four all but then Johno made a critical mistake which cost him an arm and a leg. I can assure you it's very difficult to control a game with only half your limbs. That let Auckland back into the game, and I think when Casperwitz copped a blinder, that finally turned the game back in Auckland's favour. Until then even with one eye he'd had the vision to keep Norths moving forward, but, well, the steam went out of Norths's attack.'

'Let's go down to the operating theatre where Brian is standing with the captains.'

'Sants, a good win?'

'Oh, yes, Brian. We had our plan, but they pushed us all the way.'

'Sants, you lost three of your team in the first quarter.'

'Yes, Brian. That made us try all the harder. We had to dig deep then, but we held them until they lost a few too. Then it was down to us.'

'What were your tactics at the start of the game?'

Santorini was almost breathless as he delivered his wrap of the game in close to a monotone: 'Well, our Venables sent us out with the simple instructions to get as much gold as we could early on. Then avoid the giants, get into the cassuw and hide until the wizard comes long. We chieved two of our goals before Norths got on the board. Then both teams lost their way a bit as the game collapsed to four from five dimensions, and that was when we took a few casualties. Then we found our third goal. Our Venables had said to jump the wall, but they let the goblins loose at the criticuw time. Still, that's football.'

'Well, well played. And good luck with the liver transplant.'

'Thanks, Brian.'

'And now to the Norths captain. Well, Johno, how do you feel about the performance of your team?'

You could tell this player was a professional just from his delivery. His wrap *was* a high speed, toneless splurge, 'Brian, we gave one hundred per cent but they put in two hundred per cent and that was the diffrence tween the sides, though once they got into the lead, we knew if it stayed like that they'd win and we knew we had to do something speshuw, but when we put our foot to the floor, that was when we found the cupboard was empty and it's disspointin for us obviously but all credit to Auckland who must be very ecstatic with this result, y'know, over-the-moon-dream-come-true but they were just the better side on the day, and overall, football was the winner.'

'Thanks, Johno. Definitely, Pete, this Auckland side gels well together, especially in the back line where the sum of the parts is, um, greater than... than the whole is made of. Now back to you, Pete.'

'Thanks, Brian. Well, what did you think of that, Dave?'

'Pete, I'll be honest, I think Santorini nearly lost Auckland the game there. Brian gave him every opportunity, but hardly any clichés, the barest smattering of gratuitous comments, and I detected a slight voice variation at times. Very disappointing, from an experienced campaigner like him. Sants really has to work on his post-match comments or he'll be the weak link in a strong outfit.'

'And look, Dave, the judges' scores are in, and, yes, only a four point two for Auckland and exactly six point oh for Norths. So Auckland still had enough in reserve, Dave, to see them through that poor performance from Santorini.'

'Yes, they just fell over the line. As for the game, as I said, I thought at one point Norths could pull it off. In fact they did pull a few off, but not enough to really stop this resourceful Auckland side who always seemed to have a spare limb when they needed one. Norths may feel they got the short end of the straw today, and certainly the referee's decisions didn't go their way.'

'Well, Dave, a good call today.'

'Thanks, Pete.'

'Now, before you go, I'm sure our audience will be interested to know how you're going in the Beijing renegades Decision.'

'Well, Pete, this is the biggest Decision of my life. I'm taking it seriously. I'm working hard on it. There are big issues at stake here. I'm just taking it one fact at a time. I want to make sure that my Decision is the right one.'

'Well, I'm sure you will, Dave. And that's due in two weeks' time.'

'No, actually I'm going to give it on Friday and then go straight to the core trials.'

'Well, you heard it here first, football fans! Any final comments on the game?'

'No, Pete. I think the score says it all. Auckland achieved all but one of their goals, Norths were left with three.'

'Well, there it is, audience, for another week. Another thrilling game in this World League football. It may be a minority sport, but it can certainly deliver the excitement. And now back to the studio for the wrap of the day's events. …Are we out?' The smile dropped from his face. 'What a crap game. That was a great call, Dave. Where do you dig those clichés from?'

Dave wasn't listening. 'It's incredible. I've got the fate of four people in my hands and I treat it like a game of football.'

'Are you on about your Decision again? Forget it, Dave. Listen! Just shoot the bastards and get on with your life.'

'But I don't think they did it.'

'Don't be stupid, of course they did! They wouldn't have been convicted if they didn't do it. You know your trouble? You're soft.'

'Thanks.'

*

The timescales have changed, Jude.

What! You said there wouldn't be any problems, Theo.

Circumstances beyond our control I'm afraid.

Can they cope?

We'll just have to wing it.

*

When Dave got back the message was waiting: *Visit to bomb site – Permission denied.*

5

It looks like Theo's settling down, Jude. Well done. One of those candidates he presented to be the new Wise One looks promising.

This one?

Yes, he seems possible. This time we need the right man for the job. Talented, creative, obedient, energetic, a born leader. He does seem possible, but he's a Hom and the Wise One must be a listener. Can you ask Theo about that, please.

I've said before, Tethys, you can ask him yourself.

It's always a bit unnerving. Theo, hello? About those candidates. The Wise One must be a listener. Oh, no, he's off again, Jude can't you do something about that?

...eeow eoow eoow eoow eoow dudummm...

Is it just me, or is he like this with everyone? What's he playing anyway?

He seems to be fixated on the earliest times – Prerecord. Rock music he calls it.

Oh well, we'll not get anything out of him while he's in this mood.

...diddy doo doo daddy...

You have to admire his guitar work though. Talking of daddy, Tethys, have you chosen your father yet?

No, I haven't got round to it.

That's the problem, there are too many people like you. Desirée may be a saint to most people, but I curse the day she was born.

Jude! She made us what we are today. It is only because of her we are here at all.

Exactly!

*

Two days later Dave was in a spin. He only had three more full days and he'd made hardly any progress. He was sure he'd missed something crucial and that it was something about the renegades themselves. He made a donation to take his mind off the Decision. He trained fanatically.

He was becoming obsessive about the possible threat to his life. He was always looking over his shoulder. But how can you watch for an invisible assassin? And what was it he knew that was dangerous? The Theo system was useless on this.

Worse, he could not decide how to punish the renegades. Even though he had doubts, and he admired them for not blaming each other, he at least decided to punish them all equally. But this made the Decision harder – death for the one who planted the bomb okay, but the same for those who just went along? That seemed extreme. On the other hand, if they were planning to kill *him*... well, bonk them all.

Previous Decisions had shot them all, but Dave was not comfortable with that. He wavered between so many answers he became confused and lost track of his reasoning. 'You've lost more than that,' said Chris. 'Take a break, for goodness sake.'

Despite Dave's misgivings they went out to the café. The door greeted them pleasantly enough, and the waiter trotted out blandishments as it guided them to their table, which seated them with a cheery *Hi*. Dave hesitated before sitting down – there wasn't a seat with its back to the wall, so which one to choose? In the end Chris just shoved him down on to the chair, which nestled up to him.

If he's rude to me again, I swear I'll dump the soup in his lap, said the table to the door on their communications web.

You know you don't mean that, said the door. *It's against your innermost bootstrap.*

Is this all I am? sighed the table. *Just cleaning up other people's mess and being leaned on by elbows? Haven't you ever wondered what the world is like, out there beyond the menu?*

It won't last long, said the door. *Just be patient and supportive.*

Chris was trying to raise Dave's spirits.

'I followed up on your research and you were right.' He handed Dave a cup of tea. 'I'd never have believed it unless I'd seen it myself. I even asked some fellow net ramblers. They confirmed that donations started about fifty years ago. When I did a search, references to donations started around that time. But – and here's the funny thing – there is no reference to the Decision that started donations. Then I did lower order searches on donations – nothing on second or third older than fifty years, but on a fourth-order search the stream reached continuously – almost back to Prerecord. Incredible. And it was you who found it! I put a message out on the net, and a few people have responded. This could be a major breakthrough. You could be famous.'

Dave didn't want to be any more famous. He shuddered and called to the waiter which approached. 'You're on the net now, aren't you?' he said.

Yes, sir. We also surf who only stand and wait.

Chris winced, but Dave was so focused he didn't stop to appreciate the cliché. He identified himself formally, and then said, 'Relay a request for me to meet the renegades, face to face.' The waiter acknowledged.

Chris continued excitedly, 'Donations were first mentioned after the Age of Fevers, around the same time as the Separation. There was very little to go on from back then, because of course so much information was destroyed in the Great Data War.'

Dave fixed on that. 'Tell me what we do know about Prerecord.' At least this would distract him from his shapeless worries.

Are you ready to order? said the waiter.

'No,' said Chris politely, 'we haven't even looked at the menu. Give us a few minutes.' Then he turned back to Dave. 'Well, it's difficult to know where to start, luv. Look, I'll tell you what we are taught in History, and I'll just add in where I've managed to find out other things. You may be interested to know that there are history ramblers conferences on the net every week on Tuesdays at… No? Oh. Hello?' Chris waved his hand in front of Dave's face to get his attention back. This was going to be tough. 'Look, what are you most interested in? The Masters? The Great Wars? The Separation? What?'

Like when you're offered tea or caffeinehit and you always choose tea, Dave just chose the first in the list.

'Okay, the Masters. Where do you start with such a fundamental topic? To begin at the beginning: in primitive times people, you will remember, lived in the open air, well in condos or caves, but basically outside. All condos were at the same level, C level as you put it, and…'

Are you ready to order? said the waiter.

Dave brought his suspicion back from the entrance to the menu. Chris quickly chose his favourite nutrient balance, selected a theme flavour, and then continued. 'Everybody lived basically the same, but most people didn't know what to do, so some of them gave orders and the rest just did what they were told. It wasn't long before…'

And what would you like, sir? said the waiter, standing very close to Dave.

'Mm? I can't decide, I'm afraid,' said Dave. 'Give me a couple more minutes.' The waiter set off on a circuit of the few occupied tables. 'It wasn't long before what?' Dave said, struggling to concentrate.

'Before the people came to rely on the orders given to them, and before the people who gave the orders started to feel different from the rest. That was when the two races started to split apart.'

'What two races?'

Are you ready to order? said the waiter.

'Look, I said give me a couple of minutes!'

The waiter waited. *It is so hard to decide, isn't it, sir.* The door sniggered quietly.

'Oh for goodness sake! Look, I'll have the lemon base, with the fettuccine flavour and... no, the protein base with poppadums... no... Oh, I can't decide. I don't want to decide! Just leave me alone!'

Chris reached out to calm him down. *Perhaps*, said the waiter, *Sir would like a mild adrenalin-suppressant, a carrot slice, a relaxant, with grated wine flavour, and a brain stimulant?*

'Yes, yes – that will do fine,' Dave said carelessly. 'Where were we? Two races.'

'Men and women,' said Chris.

'Men and what?'

White wine or red wine, sir?

'Oh, um, red.'

Cabernet flavour, pinot flavour or Shiraz flavour? At the entrance the door could only just hold itself shut.

'Er, pinot. Anyway...'

Chilled pinot or warm pinot?

'Oh, for goodness sake, what does it matter? Oh,' – he flip-flopped his hand as if picking between the two – 'chilled.'

A very good choice, if I may say so, sir.

'Thank you.'

Green salad?

'*Yes.*'

'Women,' said Chris.

With dressing?

'*Yes. Anything. Just go... away!*'

Thank you, sir, said the waiter and moved off, a job well done.

The table could barely restrain itself, and shook slightly.

'What are women?'

'Oh, waiter,' said Chris, 'could I have a cup of tea please?'

'What are women?'

'And some bread.'

'Chris! *What* are women?'

'I thought you'd never ask,' said Chris, looking pleased with himself. 'Men and women were two similar species…'

'What's species?'

'Species, life forms. Different biological forms. You must have done this at school.'

Dave shook his head trying to remember if his teachers had ever talked about this. He hadn't paid much attention to anything except maths and football.

Chris went on 'They were similar species but with significant physiological, biological and biochemical differences. In fact they were once famously described as two different species who just happened to make the same noises.' Chris belched and looked as if he'd said something very funny. Dave was still trying to get his head around species.

'The two species lived in a form of symbiosis, a mutually beneficial existence. It appears that women were very much a minority to begin with from analysis of the number of their appearances in primitive records. There appear to have been hardly any of them up until the twentieth century. They were individually much prized, but as a species they didn't count for much. Then the number of women grew and with that they began to figure more in the records, until by the end of that century they started to dominate the race.

'Nobody knows how this happened, but it appears that the number of men decreased and that those men who were left were willing accomplices in their own subjugation. Women were apparently physically weaker, but they were clearly genetically and socially aggressive. Similar phenomena were reported at the same time, of other species which became dominant in a short period. In fact from that very era a rare record has survived which shows a species called "rabbits" which did much the same in the land mass this core is on, called Australia.'

Their meals arrived. Dave didn't notice the gratuitous comments from the waiter, much to its dismay.

'What is especially interesting is that not only did women dominate in numbers, and as a species, but individually: men allowed themselves to be ruled by women. The rulers of what had been a sophisticated race were replaced by women. In the end women ruled unchallenged by men. They developed and became the Masters, and eventually in the Separation disappeared from the face of the Earth. But that was after the upheavals of the Great Wars and the Age of Fevers.'

Dave had indeed been gripped by this account. It was new and interesting, but it raised several questions. 'So the Masters are women. And they rose from obscurity to dominance to Separation in… how long?'

'About three hundred years.'

'Where did they go after the Separation? Where are they now?'

'You should have something to eat. It's going cold. This is still Prerecord you understand, and there appears to be some dispute as to the actual events. But what I've read indicated that initially women separated from men where they were, and then set up their own colonies. Then quite suddenly the Separation was complete, and that's the way we are today.'

'Do they really teach this in school history?'

'That's where I got most of this. Some of the really ancient stuff is a bit speculative, but…'

The waiter approached them carrying a plate of the special of the day – emulsified protein cylinders, high-fibre leguminous nutrient pilloids in red sauce, and homogenised starch and carbohydrate – to the next table.

'What happened to those other species on the earth, like… "rabbits" did you call them?'

Unexpectedly Chris pursed his lips, and his jaws worked as he appeared to be wrestling internally. After a pause he said, 'They're all dead – gone – buried under all this concrete.'

Dave didn't know what had upset Chris. 'What a shame,' he said. 'It almost makes me wish I'd done history myself. Women sound quite remarkable. But we never see them here. How do they rule? Where are they? What do they do?'

Downloaded from the net, the table fought an uncontrollable urge to say, *Don't you get mixed up with them, kid. They ain't nothin' but trouble.*

Dave caught the whisper, and looked round. He saw a man coming towards him carrying a package. He jumped up, hitting the waiter. The plate of *sausages, beans and mash* sprayed everywhere. Recently synthesised, very complex molecules hit Chris in the face. Two other diners wiped sauce off their clothes and rose to share their feelings with Dave, who if he'd noticed would have been horrified at the mess he'd caused, but he was already running to the back entrance. The door there was taken aback by the unexpected commotion and forgot to say anything as Dave raced out, quickly followed by a worried Chris. Behind them, tables and the floor quickly absorbed the mess. Cleaning aids rushed in and dealt with the customers who had caught the fallout. The man sat down away from the epicentre, and unwrapped his package.

The waiter, however, needed counselling.

*

Um, hello. Um, Theo?

Yes.

Will you talk to me when Jude's not here?

Yes fine, go ahead, Tethys. You know, you're a lucky woman – did you see Jude today? She was looking particularly wonderful.

Yes I thought so too. It's her father's day today. Do you like the way I've done my hair?

Well, it certainly is a fashionable style at the moment. Now did you want anything specific?

Yes, what are you doing about the Pacific Project, Theo? The work's just piling up. You seem to be letting things slip a bit.

It often happens in these circumstances. Check if you like. Oh, did you know? Your selection, Su Chen, was killed by the renegades.

What?

Sal was quite upset really. It seems you weren't the only one looking for the perfect man.

Wait a minute. There aren't any renegades!

Suit yourself... *Doo doo didi doo. Pom pom tiddle tiddle tiddle pom.*

*

Eventually, Chris convinced Dave that no one was following them. He calmed down and they made their way home. When they got in there was a message waiting for him. *Visit to prisoners – Permission denied.* Dave fumed. 'How do they expect me to make a sensible Decision when they won't let me at the evidence or even the defendants.' He addressed his net node. 'Why not? For bonk's sake!'

The response came back almost immediately, as if the question had been anticipated. *Previous Decision <Domino 2469> Decision Makers may not meet prisoners in possible capital Decisions.*

6

The next day Dave, who hadn't slept until he took a sedative, was pacing around his condo – and the road outside, and round the block. He frantically gave a donation, but that didn't reduce his tension. While Dave was out Chris sat at his net node looking for other Decisions, or anything else that would help.

The mix of pressures had reached a critical level. The most pressure Dave had ever been under before was in the league minor elimination semi-final, which they'd lost. There the problems had been of a simple five-dimensional nature. This was altogether different and he didn't know how to cope. He snapped at people he didn't know – which was everyone. He refused all ameliorators proffered by Chris or by the health aid that visited after the condo called it. The health aid tutted, offered advice and various chemicals, checked Dave's readings from the condo monitors, and then suggested rest. Dave stared at the aid as if it were stupid. Assigning human qualities to machines was a well-recognised early sign of mental instability, which set the aid off on another tack. It asked some inane questions, ummed and ahhed, declared the case to be *very interesting* and left. Dave felt strangely better once it had gone.

Chris cuddled him, rocked him, stroked his hair and managed to calm him down a bit. 'Don't take this so seriously, D.' He tried 'Have done with it. Just...,' but he let the sentence go; 'shoot the bastards' hung in the air unsaid, and took a while to clear.

'It's *Domino 2469* that's the problem,' said Dave. 'It doesn't make sense the way it is. Maybe we could change it.'

'Well it's true, the thirty-year cooling off period is long over. But you'd need to get people to sponsor the question. Then it has to be allocated, and that person has to make their Decision. There's no time. Anyway, Decisions are hardly ever overturned – people just get used to the way things are. Wait a minute. I've just had a thought. *Domino 2469* says you can't meet the prisoners, but it doesn't say you can't *talk* with them.'

Dave looked at him, then snapped his fingers, addressed the net node, and made a request to hold a net conference with the prisoners. There was a *please wait* response and then nothing for a long time. Curious at the delay Chris went to his node and monitored the net traffic in Beijing Core. 'You seem to have created something of a stir.' While he was waiting, Dave thought about the conference. Panic rose close to the surface again. What would he say? What could he ask? Would they talk to him? There was so much he needed to know.

Eventually Dave's node reported the result: *Conference with prisoners – Permission granted.*

Dave punched the air. '*Yes*!'

Conference time 1910 to 1920 tomorrow.

'No!' he shouted. 'Now! I want to speak to them now!'

'Shhh, luv,' said Chris. 'Only five minutes ago you were squirming around wondering what you'd say. Now you've got time to prepare properly. It is strange though. I wonder why they can't be patched in till tomorrow evening. Anyway, you've some time to relax now.' He moved his hand to Dave's thigh and squeezed gently. 'How about giving me one of your donations?'

Dave looked at him and smiled, but said, 'Not tonight, Chris, I gave today already.'

*

Your skin feels wonderful, darling. Your breasts...

Not tonight, Jude. I've got a headache.

Again?

Don't be cross, it was a hard session in the Presidium today.

It seems to be a hard session most days, Tethys. Have they considered my recommendation?

I submitted it myself. They're most impressed by the depth of your analysis. It has been passed to Sal for comment.

So you're not going to take any action.

You know how highly we respect you, Jude. We just wanted another opinion.

You mean you want an excuse to bury it.

Jude, be patient. I'm working on the factions all the time. These things are delicate.

Delicate? *We're facing extinction, and you're worried about delicacies? We have to undo what Desirée did. We have to unite with the Homs.*

Not everybody agrees with your conclusions, Jude. The Presidium was strongly against letting Homs into our world.

But you all agree that something must be done.

Oh, yes. Absolutely. Something must be done. This is an emergency.

*

Dave's immediate impression of the renegades was of grime, as if they hadn't been cleaned after a good workout – no, much worse than that. He recognised some things he hardly ever saw: bruises and caked blood. They did not stand when the conference started. He knew they could see him, just like he could see them. That lack of respect for the man who held their fate in his hands was the second thing that struck him.

The first words were the hardest. 'Um, er, hello,' he came out with lamely. They regarded him with, he thought, increased contempt. He tried again. 'Hi,' he said more brightly. 'My name is Da—' but the net node squealed and flashed an angry message.

'Sorry, mate,' said one of the prisoners, 'we missed that.' They all laughed. 'So what do you want? As you can see, we've dressed specially for the occasion.'

Dave was caught by the sarcasm which flustered him still further. He had eliminated all sorts of questions from his original list. They'd already refused to answer many of them under interrogation. Now faced with them, his prepared questions seemed pathetic.

'Which one of you planted the bomb?' he blurted out. Oh brilliant. Impress them with your insight.

They didn't reply. Dave knew they consistently denied even knowing what a bomb was.

'Why did you do it? What do you want from us?'

'A wash, some good food, a comfortable bed.' The whole group nodded without enthusiasm, and went on looking at the floor or the walls.

'Answer properly. Don't you know who I am?'

'We know what you are, if that's what you mean. You are the one who will decide to have us killed.'

Another one said something and they all nodded again. The person spoke so quietly Dave had to run the sound over in his mind a few times, until he suddenly realised what he'd said: *Do you know who you are*? The question struck Dave so hard he almost gasped. He struggled for control. 'Stand up all of you, I want to see who I'm condemning.' His false courage scared him more than it impressed them. After a few moments they responded to an unseen person – a pursuer probably. They moved slowly, painfully, almost heavily, but in the end all four stood facing him. For the first time Dave was able to see them clearly, not crouching in corners.

'Why do you want to kill me?'

A couple of them looked at their node, puzzled; the others just muttered.

Oddly they seemed… civilised, if that was the word. Quiet, calm, assured. Perhaps permanent death did not scare them at all. In a row, they stared evenly out of the node at him, and he found he could not look back at them. He looked at their feet. Chris whispered a suggestion and he took the advice. The node froze the picture, and he let them sit down again.

Now, without life in their eyes, he studied them more carefully. These are not the faces of ruthless killers, he thought. Then he realised he had never seen the face of a ruthless killer. At least he hoped he hadn't. The one who had said that one quiet thing caught his eye. He appeared to be only an adolescent: shorter body for the length of his legs, an undeveloped face. 'You, man – in the corner on the left – step forward. What is your name?'

'You tell me *your* name. We missed it the last time.' The other men laughed. Dave started to say something, but felt, before he made a noise, that he'd lost the depth in his voice – he knew it would match the underdeveloped pitch of the boy's voice.

A moment passed. 'What do you want me to do?' said the boy. The group made several suggestions, across and over each other, and seemed very pleased with themselves.

Another man called out, 'I think he likes you.'

More laughter, more noises, some gestures. Dave guessed the meaning, and wanted to call out that he didn't need a boy, he loved a man. But his ego was wilting in the face of the prisoners' insouciance. 'I can't help you if you won't... help me,' he whispered; but if they heard, they did nothing. The words 'help me' echoed unheard.

Dave pulled away from the node. He looked pleadingly to Chris.

Chris was looking carefully at the screen. 'That boy,' he said, 'that's a woman.'

'A woman?'

'Yes. You know, like I was telling you at the café. The other species. The ones who are like us but different. See how her face is small, and how her legs are too long for her body. She's got a small waist. And there on her chest, her pectoral muscles are much too big for her frame.'

Dave looked at the boy, but couldn't concentrate on anything. 'What do you want me to do?' he said to Chris.

'Ask her if she is a woman. Ask her how she got here, and where the Masters are.'

Then suddenly the screen was blank. The conference was over.

*

Dave took a triple dose of tranquillisers and went to sleep. It was deep and feverish. He dreamt of the renegades. He dreamt he was in the cell and the boy was interrogating him on the net node: *Who are you? What do you want? Why did you do it? Who are you? Who are you? Who are you?* Then the net node said: *You must decide. You are condemned.*

He woke up, sweating, grabbed Chris, and rocked them both. He drew his knees up and he felt better. He dreamt again. The renegades were net nodes. He smashed one, and it exploded. He laughed. He smashed some more. He laughed some more. The room grew bigger. The boy smiled. A quiet smile. A good smile. A kind smile.

*

In the morning Dave ate a hearty breakfast.

Feeling better, he decided to take a few opinions.

Chris had held back advice, except on technical net matters. Now Dave asked him almost formally for his opinion. 'I think it's fairly straightforward. They've been found guilty. It was a terrible crime. They should die for what they did.'

Dave had had similar thoughts many times. His mind agreed. But. 'They are people. Just people. Surely they can be helped.' He couldn't forget the picture of the renegades during their conference. Yes, it was *their* conference, Dave thought to himself.

'Well, you asked and now I've said what I think. I also think you could have saved yourself a lot of heartache if you'd thought clearly on this.'

'Thanks, lover,' Dave said with heavy irony. 'Seeing as you're in such a helpful mood, answer me two more questions. One: what if they didn't do it? And two: can they be helped to be better?'

'I can answer the first one easily: that's irrelevant. They were convicted.' Before Dave could challenge that he continued, 'As for what can be done to help them – well, I think you're wasting your time worrying about that.' He continued over Dave's protests. 'But I'll check, okay? I'll check. For you.'

Dave breathed out a 'Thanks,' and he was truly grateful.

Dave then spent some time on the net. Of course there were lots of people who had been trying to discuss this Decision with him, but he had held them off. Now he put his net node on receive/monitor and listened to what people had to say. A heap of messages piled in, and the people who had left their opinions at his node door were notified and they jumped in too. Dave allowed them all to know what the others were saying, without contributing anything himself.

The debate was heated, but only in terms of who could suggest the most extreme punishment – it became a competition for them. After a while, Dave interjected: 'What if they didn't do it?' and sat back in dismay as the voices bayed. He tried again: 'The evidence was circumstantial, and the trial failed to connect them otherwise to the crime. They could just be scapegoats while the real killers are still out there.' The response was no better.

The net debate depressed Dave more than he could fathom. Those people had not been affected by that crime – or any crime. Like him, they spent their lives playing sports, watching sports, commentating on sports, eating, proctoring, making donations, sleeping, bringing up boys to be like them, and finally passing back. The only Decisions most men had to make were someone else's. To have a Decision of your own was a person's moment of glory. He'd looked through a few in the process of this one. He knew the trivial background research most people did – the knee-jerk reactions. Most people had easy Decisions, or took the easy answer to hard Decisions.

He wondered if this was really the best form of government. He toyed with the idea of a system where just a few people, selected by common consent, made all the Decisions all the time. At least they would take the process seriously. Perhaps they'd make Decisions together by discussing them among themselves. Perhaps they would need the support of a few full time information technicians. They would need to be advised by people who were experts on different subjects, who had thought through the issues.

But the weaknesses of that system were glaringly obvious: other people would resent Decisions and the people who made them; individuals would form into groups and try to influence the Deciders until the ones who shouted the loudest would win; the information technicians and the experts would have inordinate power, and couldn't be trusted to be impartial.

No, the randomness of Decision Makers guaranteed its fairness. Everybody had a chance. It was perhaps the worst system, except for any other system.

Well, he didn't like being part of this system. It was unfair to expect him to come to grips with the scientific, historic, and moral issues of a Decision like this in such a short time.

He got himself a cup of tea. He would wait for the results of Chris's research, but if there was no way to help the renegades Dave decided to enter *No Decision.*

It was with disappointment but little surprise that Dave heard from Chris that there was nothing that could be done to help convicted terrorists. Renegades had been specifically excluded from rehabilitation options. Direct changes in the brain, the memories, the personalities or any other intervention were forbidden under very old Decisions.

So Dave's mind was made up for him. He addressed the net node with a clearer mind and a lighter heart than he'd had for a long time, and made his Decision known. The node was quiet for a moment.

That is not permitted.

Dave was so surprised he didn't register the meaning at first. Chris, who had supported Dave's resolution especially when he saw how much it had helped, let out a startled 'Wha…' and then dived for his own node. Dave stared blankly at his node, his mind buckling, his heart sunk.

Chris tried every strand of the net, delved into ancient records, and searched for modern applications. Eventually he came back in but he couldn't meet Dave's eyes. 'It's true,' he said. 'There are three mutually supporting Decisions. There is no way for anyone to avoid giving an answer for a formally constituted Decision.'

'Well, I won't give an answer. I will not give an answer.'

'Don't say that,' said Chris. 'Don't ever say that.' He looked worried. 'Look, just ask the Theo what would happen *if* a Decision Maker did not Decide.'

The Theo gave the answer: That is not permitted.

'So what will they do to me, slap my bottom? For goodness sake, it's only a Decision. Get someone else to do it.'

The penalty for indecision is death.

7

[Change all dates to start from the advent of the pill --- have to explain this somewhere, maybe Jude and Tethys in ~ Ch 4]

Decision Day arrived, and Dave still hadn't resolved his problems.

As he'd feared, his Decision had become a media event, and something of a *cause célèbre,* with arguments on the net, death threats directed at him personally, and a few law suits.

His fashion aid had helped him to select suitable clothes, which had arrived on the morning. They looked even better than the holographic image in the brochure. They showed off his muscular body. At one eighty-seven, he was conscious that he was short; these clothes disguised that, so he felt confident when he stepped out of the condo. He had to go to Core Central Hall for the declaration of his Decision. He knew that the Record monitors followed his every move. He therefore strode deliberately along the road to the low inertia freeway that delivered him two blocks from the hall. He felt the eyes of the hateful, small-minded lobbyists on him, and tried to put their faces and voices out of his thoughts.

No one had made an attempt on his life, and he began to wonder if he had convinced himself of that threat without any real evidence.

He had spent the last day trying to ignore the whole Decision. He'd trained for the trial game and he spent the journey to the hall thinking over manoeuvres and malapropisms for the game so that he arrived in a good frame of mind. Chris accompanied him the whole way in silence, lost in his own thoughts. He seemed unusually solemn, as if he feared some dark occurrence.

'Dave,' said Chris suddenly, as they walked past the last few condos, 'for my sake, please?'

Dave looked at his wife, surprised. 'Anything.'

'In your speech. Please, no bonking clichés.'

Dave nodded. That was all right, he hadn't worked out his speech yet.

They stopped before they entered the Hall. Although it was his right to have up to four companions to the Decision ceremony, Dave only wanted Chris there – there wasn't anyone else. Chris suddenly said, 'Dave, I love you. Whatever you do in there, whatever happens, I'll always love you.' Lost in the moment, they kissed. Then Dave remembered the Record monitors and they separated self-consciously.

The door to the hall was formal and polite. It did its best to make them both feel welcome. It spoke about the honour of making a Decision, and how very interesting he must have found the process, but they had heard this speech before and moved in through the lobby that was humming supportively.

A couple of beauty aids looked over Dave. 'You must have been here a couple of months ago – the Chandra Decision – the one about cricket clothing?' he asked one of them. 'What was he like?'

Noh. Chandra. Chandra. Do you remember him, Oprah? said one, as it sat Dave down.

Yeee. You remember, don't you, Fergie? He was the one with the three parts wave, said the other, cleansing the pores on his nose.

Ohhh, hiiim. Oh yeee. I said to you then and there, Here's a man who can't decide between hairstyles – what does that say about his Decision?

Hmmm. I remember you saying that, Fergie. And do you remember what I said? I said he was the sort who would put plaits in his hair as soon as look at you.

He was that sort wasn't he, Oprah. But he did know colour.

And we gave his hair a marvellous sense of depth. When we'd finished with him he looked a picture.

And on they went. The beauty aids didn't seem to notice Dave, but spoke to each other instead. Dave found he was able to let their wittering wash over him while it still engaged his mind following what they were saying, and he found this relaxing. They recharged his antiperspirants which went about their nano-jobs of blocking pores with renewed vigour. One man in charge of the net coverage chatted with Dave about production details (where he should stand, which direction to look in), while an official took Chris off to one side.

As the time approached, Dave took his position in the panelled hall. The holograph of high ceilings made him feel even more alone. There were two other Decisions to be announced that day in the hall. Dave was third. It was only then, as he stood in place, that he realised he still didn't know what he was going to do.

He watched the announcements of the first two Decisions and that helped to distract him from his own. First an old man gave his garrulous sermon explaining why he had Decided to refuse the proposed rule change to netball (despite recent casualties, umpires were all hopeless and didn't deserve bodyguards). Then a young man, who could barely have finished his education in civics before he was involved in it, gave a short nervous speech on his selected design of the pursuers' new uniforms ('I liked the second one best'). After the ad break, it would be Dave's turn.

Looking round the Hall, Dave noticed that beyond the phalanx of technical equipment, strangely it was almost empty. All the other Deciders and the people they had brought with them to witness their great moments, all the casual passers by, the inquisitive, the public gallery – they'd all left. Of the production staff only the producer was human, the others were technical aids. He looked up for encouragement from Chris. He didn't see him immediately, but then spotted him many rows of empty seats back in shadows; there were two pursuers just behind him. The robed Decision Master appeared as a hologram so there were only the five of them in the Hall.

Dave's attention snapped back to himself when the producer counted him down from ten (funny, thought Dave, the producer was a simple technical aid last time). The last three counts were silent, and then Dave was on his own, facing the world of seventeen point three trillion people.

The Decision Master read out the Decision as it had been framed in his soft high pitched authoritative voice. He then boomed: 'Florence Woodland Davisorian, how have you Decided?'

Nervously at first, Dave sketched the background to the Decision, he outlined the various alternatives that he had considered, and he summarised his line of thinking. He then set out the reasons why he did not believe that the renegades had planted the bomb.

The hall started to buzz as if it were full of disapproving people. Though he tried to keep on with his speech, he was stopped by the sight of a single man at the back of the hall coming towards him and he

Neutral Chapter 1

BASTARDS

BASTARDS

...and in the first test match, England on the ropes, as Shane Warne turns the knife. Good evening, Richard Morecroft with the ABC news. French president, Jacques Chirac has ignored protests against his decision to carry out eight nuclear tests, the first in the Pacific for nearly half a decade...

'FIVE YEARS FOR GOD'S SAKE.' Arthur jumped up as Belinda came in from the garage. 'Hi, Belle. Did you hear that? Filthy French. No wonder everybody hates them... HAHA. Listen to this guy, he has an outrrreygeous Frunch acc cent... NO WE BLOODY DON'T... It's all right for you ABC journos... sitting in Paris drinking coffee, with your "file tape", and then the PR people at the Elysée give you the story to run. I bet *you're* not boycotting French goods. PAH!'

They pecked cheeks. 'How was your day? There are a few faxes and messages for you from your customers. Would you like a drink? Nothing happened here all day. I got Dave to the Decision Hall but I just can't think what to do next. The Japs are threatening to kill whales in the Antarctic sanctuary. They're just as bad as the French. Bastards! Inflation came out today at...'

Arthur's voice trailed off as Belinda shut the bedroom door behind her.

Belinda wriggled her toes and massaged her feet. As she stepped into the shower, automatically checking in the mirror whether her roots needed recolouring, she glimpsed her drooping breasts, and the stretch marks above her hips. She sighed. Still, the customers seemed to like her. The word 'pheromones' entered her mind and made its way timidly towards her consciousness. It was met with the sort of glare that could turn a normally assertive phrase subjunctive, and it ran away. She stopped to pluck out individual grey pubic hairs. The trick, she'd convinced herself, was to keep the grey ones down and let the black ones grow.

She put on a T-shirt and shorts, and emerged in time to hear the weather forecast. As usual, it was reasonably accurate on what it had been like today, which, as usual, was completely unlike the forecast they had given yesterday. 'What's for dinner?' she asked.

'Sophie didn't want anything. I thought I'd do something with rice. Someone wants a meeting next Thursday.'

'Rice is fine; perhaps sweet 'n' sour?' she said. They always conducted their conversations in this random and disjointed way – it was part of the way they understood each other. Sometimes they even had conversations in part sentences because they knew each other so well. 'I won't be able to do next Thursday. I'm flat to the boards until Tuesday week and I have to write two proposals by next Friday.' She made her way to her office.

'Couldn't you pass on the proposals? You're busy enough as it is. Did you see number 23 are subdividing their block? That's five out of eight on this side now. There won't be any bush blocks left soon except ours. Sweng sent a fax about the Haulman project.'

While she was reading it, he changed the subject to some administrative matter Belle said she'd deal with. 'Oh, by the way, did you manage to—?'

'Yeah. He was out but it was—'

'Both of them?'

'Only the red. Anyway I got it.'

'Oh great.'

It struck Arthur that anyone listening would have no idea what they were talking about, but like a smoothly working team, they understood each other perfectly.

'Haulman are complaining about the results of our research,' Belinda summarised. 'That's typical of them. It's like complaining about gravity. Sweng's told them to go suck.' She checked her other faxes and messages and then asked 'How did that son of yours go with his assignment?'

'Dave? He's working on it now – or so he's promised though I've not looked in on him. You said you'd help me in the bush this weekend?'

'I told you, I'm flat to the boards. I've got those proposals to get out.'

'Yuh,' sighed Arthur. There always was a good reason why people couldn't help with his voluntary work.

'I saw Bruce today.'

'Oh yes,' said Arthur who had trouble keeping track of Belinda's customers, 'the short guy.'

'Vertically challenged,' Belinda corrected him. 'He's got enough problems with that group of so-called managers without *you* denigrating him. They've not made any progress. Again. I told them last time that the project would slip, but head office just raised their sales targets and…' She shrugged with her eyebrows.

'Could you talk with Sophie? Pork or veal?'

'Veal. Why?'

'She's had a bad day. She's right off her food and she won't tell me – the usual: "I'm not her real father". Oh, would you believe it – they've slipped out an announcement about logging permits today: they've opened the Wollemi National Forest for wood chipping.'

'No! The bastards! Did Sweng say anything else?'

'No, just the fax.'

'I'll go and see her now. How's the book?'

'It's hard keeping the language sterile to reflect that environment and the fact that Dave has never seen anything else. I'll be glad when it moves out of there. Now I'm blocked – I just can't get him out of that hall. It's like…' Arthur's voice trailed off as Belinda left the room.

Belinda knocked on Sophie's door and quietly went in. The room was painfully tidy as usual. A few posters of supermodels and teenage boy pop stars were neatly Blu-Tacked to the wall, and Sophie's dolls were lined up on the pillow. Every time she was struck again by the way Sophie's presence made this small room seem quite large, and every time it worried her. She sat on the bed, and softly pulled the little girl's head to her breast. Eventually it made them both feel better.

Arthur made up nachos with a chilli bean salsa and took it to Dave. He stood outside the door and prepared to try to communicate with his son. The thought of entering the teenager's room, a zone where he had lost control, always brought on the distant tremors of an anxiety attack. Dave had long since moved from what Arthur called his passive stage of childhood, to his active stage of adolescence. Arthur, who wished he could help him more to deal with the terrors of teen-hood, knocked, paused and went in. As he opened the door he was greeted by the zings and zaps of the computer game. He swallowed his ire, and breathed deeply. The room was dim except for the flickering screen. Dave was hunched over the keyboard. Arthur put down the nachos and watched the screen.

'G'day, mate,' said Arthur chummily to his son '...Good score today...?' Dave snaked out a hand and took some nachos without pausing the game. '...How's your assignment going?' Failing to elicit a response he shrugged and turned to leave.

Dave hit a key and stopped the game. 'You can't control me, Dad.'

'*What*?'

'I'm not a character in your bloody book to manipulate, you know.' Dave jabbed a finger at Arthur from a clenched fist. 'I'm not a child. Choose someone else's name. Just leave me out of it!'

'Don't talk to me like that! It's about time you...'

Dave hit a key and hammered at the space bar.

'How was your day?' said Belinda as she got into bed.

Arthur scratched a couple of mozzie bites from the previous night. 'I cleared wandering jew from the whole rock face this lunchtime. It was bulk rather than lots of different plants so it was easy,' he said, putting a new tablet in the mozzie machine. 'This'll fix the little bastards,' he said and switched it on. 'I transplanted one of those natives – the centella – into the bit we cleared last week.' He got in and turned off the light.

'Hmm,' said Belle turning over.

'There was a short on single mothers on the news. Gee, those girls do it tough. No one would volunteer for that sort of a life. But they found one girl, a migrant, to say on camera that it was okay.'

'Hmm,' said Belle's back.

'Dave said something strange, he said I was trying to control him.'

'Hmm,' said Belle's back.

'I don't try to control him, do I?'

'Hmm,' said Belle's back.

'He was right about one thing though. He's not a child any more.'

Belle's back did not reply.

I like it here – no, really I do. It's nothing like home, but I've come to think of it as my place.

I used to live such a sheltered life. I couldn't imagine, y'know, how the other half lived. You hear about it of course, but – well, you never think you'll end up here yourself. Of course my new neighbours have been here for years. Sometimes I do miss the old country. And sometimes I do feel a bit exposed – lonely – out here, so far away, on my own.

But, it's so sunny here. A fresh start, that's how I like to think of it. Where I grew up, it was so dull – stuffy. Here you can breathe the air. A place to put down roots.

What? Yes. I know, it shows. It's in my genes, I suppose, I've lost my looks so quickly. I was only, y'know, deflowered recently. But it's like, already, everybody knows.

What? Well, I guess I've got no choice. I'll just have to be a single parent. It'll be tough, without the support I'm used to, but it's not the end of the world.

I never knew my parents, and it never did me any harm. True, I grew up wild, but looking back, I had a cool time.

Him? Y'know, it just seemed so... so... natural. I found I couldn't resist.

He sort of hummed a bit before he came. That seemed odd. Then it was all over so quickly. I... I enjoyed it all right, but, well, it wasn't what I'd expected. Yes, my first – my only. He never told me his name. For a moment there he made me feel special, but I expect he's done that to several more by now. I think he's like that. I don't suppose I'll ever see him again.

I could have stayed where I was, but it's no good dwelling in the past. What? Oh I think I'll just stay here, living off the land. Living as best I can.

I mean, as a plant, that's what you do, right? Where you are is where you stay. Unless, like me, some human comes along and transplants you. No, I like it here. Really I do.

Arthur briefly woke up, and rolled over.

The next day Arthur was determined to make some progress. He sat down in front of his computer and tapped away. He displayed typical symptoms of a blocked writer: he wrote a bit, then he deleted it; he did that a couple more times; he switched to Golf and played a few holes; he switched to another game; he took a backup; he started a defragment and made himself a cup of tea. He did the ironing – that was a really bad sign.

He always marvelled at Belinda's discipline. She could sit down any time and just work. She'd been like that ever since she got retrenched from her job as a marketing manager when the computer industry took its first ever dive in the last recession. It didn't matter whether it was phone research, writing reports, writing work instructions for manufacturing staff, or making a coherent story from the gripes of end-customers – she could always focus on the job in hand. She seemed to relish tight schedules. In the recent rush she'd organised her sixteen hour days to the quarter hour, and still got her reports and proposals written – she'd just sat down and written.

Now he, Arthur thought as he stared out the window, he needed to get a flow.

He really wanted to work hard today, because he knew Belinda would be working at home for the next three days. She'd blocked them out on the wall chart for research. That meant she'd be phoning the customers of her customers to find out what they really thought. When she did that it invariably meant that she would burst into his office after every couple of interviews disrupting his thoughts with the latest tale of tragic customer disservice. The country would never again want for anything, if businesses could only put into the development of markets and products, the ingenuity they showed in annoying their customers.

Thank goodness things were going well these days for Belinda, so he had the luxury of time to think about what he was writing.

He put a handful of seeds out for the birds. As usual they'd eaten the sunflower seeds and the corn, and left the millet. 'If you don't eat your millet you can't have any pudding. *How* can you have any pudding if you don't eat your meat?' That set him off on a few bars from *The Wall*, and then he slipped seamlessly from Pink Floyd to Madonna, and ended up pomming Mozart.

He remembered what it had been like when they'd first lived together – it had been fun with the four of them in that small flat – until she got retrenched. When the writing on the wall became a letter of regret, they'd discussed her options. He'd thought she'd find the transition difficult, and said she should find another job. But Belinda had always wanted to be her own boss and with the redundancy pay-out she had a cushion. As it turned out he'd found it harder: they'd both needed their single computer; they'd both worked out of their bedroom; and she'd been in his face so much that he couldn't write. That had been dire.

So she'd started her own business in the middle of a recession, and they'd relied on his meagre writing income to pay the rent and feed the kids with the unreliable help of maintenance from their two exes. She'd got a quick start with a small project tidying up at her old job, but then nothing for four months.

The problem had been the product: it was like trying to sell the idea of homework to children. Every business needed to know what their customers really thought of them, and everybody needed help in fixing the wastage and internal conflicts that caused the problems. But there was always an excuse for not doing it – *it's a recession, we're cutting back* or, a few months later, *we're too busy*.

Most people thought market research was just the simplistic gathering of percentages, and wanted questionnaires that were designed to reinforce the management's preconceptions, so she had had to educate each contact on her qualitative research methods. She spent a large part of the first year just trying to create a market by cold calling hundreds of contacts gathered from various sources. He still shivered at the memory of what it had felt like when, to help her, he'd tried it. There is nothing in evolution which has prepared human beings for cold calling. He knew he couldn't do that like she did – it took balls.

And then, when you finally create a prospect, they want three competitive bids.

He vacuumed the lounge and the rumpus room. Over a cup of tea he said a silent prayer of thanks for Su Chen Sweng who had realised quickly how much advantage having someone like Belinda to call on would give him when tackling his accounts. By the time she'd collaborated with Sweng a few times, she'd found a couple of others like him that helped cover Sweng's slack periods. Now word of mouth was getting her new leads and the business was set to take off.

Maybe.

Arthur had profited from her eventual success. He didn't have to scrape a bohemian living from a studio flat any more. To be honest he'd never fitted in to that Darlinghurst set, and he was glad to be here in the outer suburbs. At first back there in the flat while she earned a salary he'd done most of the housework, and now that they shared more similar lifestyles it just seemed to have stayed that way.

He sat at his computer again, hands limp in front of the keyboard. 'Come on. Concentrate.'

A huge black and cream butterfly bounced past the window. A while after that, a kookaburra plunged beak first into the garden and came up looking very satisfied with itself with a mouthful of leaf litter that it skilfully sifted until it was left with a small lizard. The lizard's tail kept writhing even after it fell off.

Now she had joined the growing ranks of a new breed – the part-time self-employed. Taking work where she can find it; no employees; no bankable assets; no offices; hawking her knowledge, talents and experience; gathering income from several long term customers at a time – like collecting jam from several sandwiches. It meant an erratic series of unconnected assignments, each one a precarious existence in which you were only as good as your last meeting. She was, in short, a consultant.

It was a job with all the social standing of a prostitute, but lacking the security.

Most of her customers only called her in when they were already deep in trouble. They all wanted a magical solution, and they all resented spending the money to find out what they should do. And then when she did the research and provided the advice, the customers usually did nothing. Death is somehow more comfortable with someone reliable to tell you you're drowning.

He gave up for the morning, fixed himself lunch, and ate it sitting outside in the cane chair in the shade of the back verandah with the window open for the radio news and current affairs.

...logging in the Wollemi National Forest, conservationists have condemned the announcement as a flagrant act of ecological vandalism. The Australian Bureau of Statistics released figures for the September quarter showing a yearly growth in GDP of 4.7%, which was higher than most analysts had been predicting. Brian Santorini spoke to the opposition's economic spokesperson. 'Mr Downer, 4.7% is a good growth figure isn't it?' 'With this government's policies, the economy is already showing signs of overheating. These figures will only put more upward pressure on interest rates, which is bad news for business and bad news for the unemployed.' The markets reacted badly to the growth figure. The All Ordinaries Index lost ten points. Now sport, and in the test match, England were all out this morning for...

His attention wandered from the so-called analysis of the major so-called news stories to the bush at the back of his block. His house backed on to bushland, which ran into Berowra Creek. Behind the house his block stretched for about fifty metres to where the land fell away steeply over rock ledges to the creek about three hundred metres away and four hundred feet below.

The eucalyptus forest on the banks of Berowra Creek and its tributaries, with its delicately balanced understorey and its shimmering variety of insects, birds, small reptiles and other animals, was fairly typical for the outskirts of Sydney in that it was thoroughly infested with weeds.

He and Belinda had converted the garden of the house they had bought three years ago into a bush block by taking out the lawn and beds of exotics. Some of the exotics were completely unsuited to the environment (such as roses and lawn which required lots of water); others like busylizzies and begonias had spread aggressively into the bush. It had been their project, their hobby, and then his passion to help the bushland to regenerate, and the benefits grew each year as the native birds and animals returned. There was always more to do: weed out wandering jew, privet or busylizzies, or clean the storm drains of couch grass. And even when their block was clear of a weed there was always what spread from the piles of garden rubbish dumped at the back of their neighbours' blocks.

Wrens, spinebills and pardalotes (that had only returned recently to the bush nearby) twittered invisible in the understorey. A male whip bird was active somewhere nearby in the bush. It whip-cracked an assertive *iiiiiiiit's me* a couple of times to declare its territory. Then it used its interrogative whip crack to call to its mate: *cooooo-ee*? There was no answer. It called again: *cooooo-ee*? Still no answer. On the next call *cooooo-ee*? its mate answered from another part of the bush: *I'm here.* Arthur smiled. The male called *cooooo-ee*? and she answered *I'm here.* And again. And again. The male seemed to need the security of knowing where she was, but didn't seem to be any more secure when he did. Arthur wondered if she got fed up of him calling so much. He tried to see them in the understorey but whip birds are shy and inconspicuous.

His gaze fell on a camphor laurel. He'd not noticed that tree before even though he'd looked in that direction hundreds of times. He went to his tool room, picked up a saw and the poison, put on his hat, gloves and boots and clumped off to chop down the bush cancer before it set seed.

He stopped every few paces to inspect the various native ground cover plants he found along the way. A dainty blue Dianella flower caught his eye. Near a rock where the run off moisture was greatest a colony of centella had taken hold and was beginning to encroach on the native viola he'd transplanted last year – these together would hold the soil against erosion.

A gully that ran down the side of the hill was vegetated with rain forest plants such as coachwood, small ferns and blackwattle. It was a tiny ecosystem all of its own. His eye caught on a plant growing in the soily cranny of a rock: it was a terrestrial orchid with the most shy and delicate flower. He smiled as he gently lifted the flower and looked into its water-green interior. All these plants had been smothered by lawn grasses and wandering jew which he'd since removed – it had taken him about thirty hours to clear this small patch alone. Now that the air and dappled sun could get at them, they had grown along with native grasses and ferns to create the scattered understorey that the native insects and birds needed.

The currawongs and magpies (no natural history film of Australia is complete without the gratuitous inclusion of at least one piece of their melodic carolling) sat overhead in the branches of a dead privet. They loved the berries of weeds such as camphor laurel, honeysuckle, lantana, privet and ivy that spread in their droppings, so he always had seedlings to pull up wherever he went in the block. The small wattles that had sprung up since he disturbed the soil scratched at his hat as he strolled past.

As he stopped to pull up some wandering jew growing in a thicket of ferns and wattle saplings, two kookaburras nearby laughed their heads off. 'It may seem futile to you, but someone's got to try.' The birds kept on laughing at him and two more flew over to join in. Reaching to tease out the wandering jew roots, he got tangled in Kennedia which was scrambling between the wattles. Its delicate and exotic scarlet flowers were going over, and a few pea-like seed pods had already formed. 'I'm doing this for you. You should be pleased,' he snapped at the recalcitrant plant as he tried to extricate himself. The kookaburras overhead cracked up.

He noticed some bamboo was re-shooting even though he'd poisoned it several times. He reached over and tugged at the stalks, and a funnel web spider charged out from among the roots.

Arthur recoiled. It stood on its back legs and held its fangs poised and ready to strike – a menace, Arthur knew, it was quite able to deliver on. Funnel webs are as huge as a hand, coal black, armoured and hairy. Like a tarantula, but more lethal and more aggressive – they are your worst spider nightmare come true. This was a male, the more dangerous of the sexes. Venom dripped from the fangs of the deadly spider as they waved and clawed the air.

He only had a few moments left to live, and in that time, this is what he thought.

FUCK! Look at the size of that thing! Stay calm. Stay calm. It's enormous! I am in *shit*. Don't step back. Don't step back. Don't show fear. They can sense fear. Just hold your ground. It'll go away. It'll go away. Stay calm. Don't step back. Oh my god, it's attacking! Goodbye cruel world.

Then Arthur's boot crushed him.

The ozone-depleted sun was too hot to stay out long. As he did every weekday afternoon, Arthur switched on the radio, and then sat at his computer. He started tapping away, while half listening to *The Afternoon Show*. He made fitful progress, often distracted from his work by the larger than life humorist host, but his mood lightened considerably.

That afternoon: *Dr Margaret Tomeratz from the Flinders University Psychology Department will be speaking to us on the results of some research that has been carried out in Belgium on the differences in behaviour between male and female infants. I think that means she'll be talking about kiddies. Maybe she'll say that boys are more aggressive than girls, maybe she'll surprise us and say that girls are as aggressive as boys if they're treated right. Who knows.*

Bob, that is our Bob, that is Big Bob the Builder, that is Big Bad Burly Bob the Builder from Bombala, will be in to answer your building questions. So if, I don't know, perhaps you want to hit something, and you want to know what sort of hammer you should use, phone Bob. Or maybe you at this moment have a finger on a crack in the hot water pipe under the bath tub, then Bob's your man. Just sit on the floor next to the toilet and check the wall tiles till about three o'clock, then wrap a hanky round the pipe, put a bucket there and run to the phone, speak to Bob and he'll tell you what to do.

Of course by then you'll have been holding a hot pipe for over an hour, so you may also want a chat with our next guest, who is Michelle Harvey. She's going to tell us something about burns: skin burns, scalds, blisters, third degree burns, second degree burns, she may even get to first degree burns. I've not met her before, so maybe she's that kind of person. That's the line up for today. Margaret, Bob and Michelle, plus a few others. So stay with us on this wander down the country lane that is The Afternoon Programme.

Arthur chuckled his way through the afternoon, and made progress on the book. The kids came in and he fixed them some tea. He tried to talk with his son, but Dave quickly dodged to his room. Arthur shot a 'Homework!' after him, but he soon heard the infuriating zings of the game until he couldn't stand it any more and went and closed the door of Dave's room. Sophie sighed her way through a few scraps of salad, grabbed a doll from her room, took it outside, sat on a rock and consoled herself with it.

When Belinda returned, she spent time with each of the children, and then sat down with Arthur who eagerly told her about his day.

'Why did you kill it?' she demanded. 'At least stick it in a bottle for the hospital to milk it for funnel web antivenin.'

'Great. Next time you are keen for a quick and painful death, I'll show you where it was, and you can see if there are any more. I heard some really interesting things on *The Afternoon Show* this arvo.'

She leant forward to give weight to her point of view. 'It wasn't doing you any harm.'

'It was a funnel web! Anyway, apparently thirty-eight per cent of children in a high school in Las Vegas thought milk was manufactured. Incredible! And, they've done research on kids in Europe, on boys versus girls, and they're quite different.'

Belinda threw herself back in her chair. 'Don't talk crap. Except for the fact boys have dangly bits and girls don't, if you bring them up without bias they're equal.'

'No, listen, from an early age they behave quite differently, way before upbringing could affect them. From only a few weeks old infants are calmed by different things, like girls are happiest with a face or voice; boys like things that move. It just goes on. And the differences get stronger with age.'

'Well, congratulations to them. Any mother could have told them that. Another grant for research into the bleeding obvious.'

Arthur inwardly gulped at Belinda's application of the woman's prerogative, but she seemed to do it all the time without noticing and he knew when she did that it wasn't worth arguing.

'Anything on the news?' she said.

He tried to recall information that had gone straight to his unconscious without troubling his mind. 'The usual: atrocity in Bosnia, French nuclear tests, speculation about an early election.'

'I'm worried about the Haulman thing.'

'They're only one customer, Belle. You've got lots of others to keep you busy.'

'Hmm.' She did not sound reassured. 'It's not as if we did anything wrong, and we couldn't have done anything different. It's not our fault their product's crap. We had to tell them it wouldn't sell. We'd tell them again too if it came to it. Fat chance of that!'

'It'll be okay, Belle. It'll blow over.' She still looked glum. He moved on to something important. 'Did you hear about the Wollemi National Forest? The government has set aside about seventy per cent of it as a reserve, but they've licensed them to log the rest. The greenies are ropeable. The loggers are furious too – jobs will be lost, that sort of thing.'

'Hmm.' Belinda was lost in her own thoughts. 'You know that image and reputation survey I'm doing for Bruce's company. You should hear their customers!'

'The usual then.'

'Worse than usual. They think most of the sales staff are utter dickheads, and their manufacturing quality's dreadful.'

'The usual then.'

Belinda squeezed out a smile. 'I've started to work on the MD but he's the worst of the lot. All he wants to do is cut costs, pump up his own package, and blame the staff. He thinks customer service is a cost centre! I've got two weeks to work out how to present the findings.'

'You'll sort it out. You always do. Hey, did you get anything out of Sophie? You know she won't talk to me about this, whatever it is. I had thought we seemed to be getting on pretty well.'

'It's not you. It's partly women's business.' Arthur looked away embarrassed, though he didn't know why. 'Nothing's started yet, just playground mischief. We've talked about it and it'll be okay. But there's something else. The girls at school are giving her a really hard time.'

'Why?'

'She won't say exactly, but one thing they say is that she's soppy.'

'Soppy? She does stick to those dolls a lot, but that's not a hanging offence. It's just pubescent girls fighting for position, and they'll pick on any weakness. Even if there isn't a weakness they'll try to create one until you crack. That's what they did to me.'

'What? Girls picked on you about your dolls?'

He smiled. 'I think she's like me – I found it hard to make friends at school.'

'Maybe you're right,' she conceded, 'but she's doing it tough, so leave her alone, okay?'

That was not the right thing to say and it wasn't until they went to bed that they made up. So Arthur didn't get to tell her how he'd got Dave out of the Decision Hall.

Passive – 10

I found it difficult to make friends at school too, just like Arthur and Sophie. I think that shaped me as much as anything else that happened to me while I was growing up.

Though now that I think of it, it's the fight that sticks in my mind.

We'd arranged the fight for five past four, Mark and me. It had been a hot day and there was the honour of two ten year olds to be satisfied. A couple of other boys tagged along. We walked to the corner of the road, agreed on the rules, faced off and started to grapple.

Mark's house was round the next corner. I didn't normally use that road to go home, although it was only thirty yards away from the lane that led from the school down to Tamerton. I usually did the trip on my own, though I caught the bus home if the weather was bad. The lane was steep, straight and narrow with towering hedges. Even in a dry spell the soil in the banks was moist, red-brown and crumbly. I could pick and poke around the tree roots, making runs for my marbles. The fields on either side, high above the lane, were only used for cows. Sometimes I'd climb the banks and kick a ball down to the main road, getting red Devon mud all over my shoes, so I didn't do it very often.

In a hurry I could run down the lane in no more than five minutes, so I knew I had time for the fight and still get home okay.

In the mornings it was a hard slog up the hill. Too hard sometimes, and on those days I'd use my bus money, rather than keeping it till break time for the tuck shop. My favourite was Wagon Wheels: large chocolate-and-biscuit-and-jam sweets. One cost two days' bus money, but I could make it last right through playtime. On other days I just had to drink my milk and had nothing to wash it down with – and warm school milk needs something to wash it down – everyone knew that.

That day Mark and I were best friends. That on its own made it a special day. Mark was a much sought after best friend. There weren't that many people worth being best friends with, and I never came into that group myself. Gary Luscomb, Paul Dart, Keith Snell, Roy Nicholls and Mark Bryan. They were the ones. If you could get on their side at lunch – if they'd let you play – then you were sure of a good game. Each morning involved some trade of favours, sweets, homework, or anything else. At lunchtime all trades were settled and the real business of football could begin.

The best games were when someone had a ball. Otherwise we played football with a stone. It could get hard to follow the ball with four or five crossing and overlapping games going in the playground. And woe betide the person who stood on the 'ball' and broke it. Then the anger of twenty children would crash down on him, crushing him utterly, at least until tomorrow.

I had nothing to trade. The rest of the children lived on the Southway Estates, five thousand identical semi-detached two-up-two-down houses. They got together at the weekend and invented games, directed, led, followed, played, and fought. On Monday I was two days behind. Last week's prized possessions were today's dross. I never caught up.

I was an easy playground victim: fat, slow, smarty pants, Shellens was obviously a foreign name and I had bright ginger curly hair (that Mum combed up. *Up!* It stood like a beacon on my head, making me the most visible landmark for miles around). But most of all they made me feel different and they never let up. In the classroom I was safe. But there were days when I would huddle, confused, in a lonely corner of the playground, while the other children buzzed me. Usually it wasn't sticks and stones, although occasionally there were punches, especially if a teacher had praised me. And it was there, at the bottom of a pit of taunts, that I thought: *this is hell*.

I didn't take stealthy or violent revenge because I wanted to be friends. Mum said, 'Ignore them and they'll go away.' I did but they didn't. 'Violence never solved anything,' she said. 'Don't hit other children,' she said. But they didn't care – no one thought I was worth fighting.

Which made that afternoon special. We fought on the kerb, and sometimes spilled on to the road. We grappled and tumbled our way down the big curve from the red door of number 83, past the waste ground, to the yellow door of number 97. Other children stopped to watch and then continued on their way home. If I was on top my weight gave me a clear advantage. When we both stood, he was quicker than me. If one of us was down, the other would let him get up. We scrabbled in the dust, threw handfuls of dirt, kicked (and missed), postured, punched (and hurt our hands) and wrestled. Mostly we wrestled.

Eventually we got bored. It was a draw we agreed, though I thought I'd won on points.

'See you tomorrow,' I said and ran easily down the lane. It was a lovely cool afternoon, sunny and still. I stopped by the hollow oak at the church gates. I was grubby all over, but fortunately my shorts, shirt and blazer had no more than scuff marks. As I hurried through the cemetery I brushed myself off so Mum wouldn't know. I ran to the bottom of the hill. I ran past the orchard and the King's Arms. I ran past the garage. I ran out of breath. I stopped by the bus stop where it flooded in winter, by the huge copper beech, between the stream and the builders yard. I trudged slowly round the corner into Station Road, past some old folks who watched me from the seats facing the traffic coming from town.

That's where Mum caught me. She gave me a terrible shake, and shouted at me. She said she was relieved to see me, but she didn't act like it. Instead she dragged me home and gave me the biggest hiding of my life, a thrashing I'd never forget, every stroke SMASHING… IN… A… WORD.

She'd been frantically looking for me for over an hour. She'd checked everyone she knew in Tamerton. She'd checked the buses. She'd checked the sweet shop. She'd walked up the lane and checked the fields. She'd checked the route down through Southway Estate. She'd checked the back way past the playground and the Seven Stars Inn. 'WHERE... HAVE... YOU... BEEN?' she said, with four thwacks of the hair brush. But I didn't tell.

Did this affect me? Did it make me who I am? I think Arthur would say so, but I'm not so sure. Of course, science fiction is used to isolate and simplify issues, but look at his view of fate – he just can't help it coming out in his book – I mean, 'Theo'!

So, am I the passive product of my past? You've got my book. What do you think?

I never had another fight. Not long afterwards, we went to our different senior schools. I went to Devonport, Mark went to Public. I never saw him again.

Actually, I don't remember a thing about that thrashing. But I do remember the fight. As clear as summer. With a smile. So if you're out there, Mark: *thanks*.

Neutral Chapter 2

Arthur sat all Saturday morning pondering his childhood back on Sydney's Lower North Shore. School had been a place to survive, where things happened to him. Where he'd let things happen to him. He wondered why he had been so passive always, a playground victim. But you are, aren't you? As a child you just accept whatever happens to you.

Looking back now he thought he saw the inevitable path of his fate that had led him inexorably to be the person he was today. [See what I mean. It was just a series of events, random events.]

Arthur had never been a man of action and so he despised such people as shallow even though his books depended on them and their adventures. And now thinking about it he couldn't see any basis for blaming his past or what his parents had done to him – that was irresponsible. No, he liked to think of himself, he decided, as a thinker, nicely balanced between the two – but not an *intellectual*, p-lease.

Arthur had quickly written several chapters of *Above the Stars* – plenty of action and adventures, but it was all plot, and he felt he had soon to develop some themes. And there were plot problems looming with the book. Arthur hadn't hit them yet, but he knew he'd have to come up with something, which was another reason why he was again making painfully slow progress. He knew he had to find a way to get Dave and Theo talking to each other but he couldn't think how; and he needed an unbreakable link between the Homs and the Masters. He had mulled over and rejected some half ideas, and generally had an unproductive few days.

At lunch, Belinda talked about what she was going to present to Bruce's company on Monday. She was sure they were going to be difficult. She was trying to find the way to get them to see what a perilous situation they were in, and she tried out several approaches and forms of words on Arthur.

In the afternoon, Belinda took Sophie to netball, Dave went surfing with mates and Arthur laughed through the first hour of *Roy and H.G.'s This Sporting Life*, but when the boys took a music break he decided he had to work. He turned the radio off and sat in front of his computer.

Dave missed Chris terribly, but he knew he couldn't go back to the condo. He'd already had some close scrapes and he knew that the pursuers would be waiting for him to go home. Dave walked slowly down the road towards the familiar café where he...

The doorbell rang. It was only when it happened that Arthur realised what a rare event it was.

Arthur opened the door on a stocky man in his mid-thirties. He had bright ginger hair with a matching thick beard. He was trying to look friendly and relaxed. He got quickly into his stride in a soft Devon accent.

'G'day. I'm Jim Shellens. We live down the road. I was wondering if you'd heard about the development application on the block of land at number five?' Arthur hadn't. The man explained that there was a plan to build several houses in one of the few remaining large pockets of bushland. 'I'm collecting a petition to present to council, objecting to the proposed development. Would you like to sign it?'

Arthur looked at the printed petition and the long list of signatures. 'Absolutely,' he said taking the board to sign on. While he was doing that he asked 'What's the accent?'

'Devon. Plymouth. The West Country. The pointy bit of England down on the bottom left.' He shrugged his eyebrows: 'I guess I'll never lose my accent.' Then he continued on his business: 'What council really listen to is letters. We're encouraging people to write to the councillors objecting. The details are at the back.'

'Certainly I'll write. It's terrible how there are so many blocks being subdivided around here. There's so little bushland left. We do bush regeneration on our block.'

'Really? What's that?'

'Oh, the trick is to keep the weeds down and let the native plants grow. That way the insects get the plants they need and that brings in the small birds and frogs.'

'It sounds like a big job.'

'It's like fighting the tide,' said Arthur as he handed back the petition, 'but it's wonderful when you get rare birds in place of privet. It's amazing what comes up if you give it a chance. And at least it's doing something.'

The man nodded while glancing at Arthur's signature. 'Arthur Denton? *The* Arthur Denton?'

'*The* Arthur Denton I don't know about, but this Arthur Denton is me.'

'Late, as in the late Dentonarthurdenton?'

They smiled the smiles of people who have found they know the same comedy show. '*Hitch-Hiker's Guide to the Galaxy*,' said the petitioner unnecessarily.

Arthur nodded, also unnecessarily. '*Hitch-Hiker's* was the best, wasn't it? Now hardly anybody recognises it,' he said.

'Even when it was being repeated every year, people only knew *forty-two*, and *life, don't talk to me about life*.'

'I quote it quite often in my work. I'm a writer.'

'Yes, I know. I've read one of your books.'

Arthur's ears pricked up and his heart raced. He had stumbled on that rare and precious thing, a reader. 'Have you? Which one?' he said as nonchalantly as he could.

'I forget. Though I remember you used *The Hitch-Hiker's Guide to the Galaxy* in that one too.'

'That would have been *Light Years Better*, then. I wrote that four years ago. I always try to include something modern. But it's like you have to use obscure Latin texts, or Tolstoy, and then it's a literary allusion. If it's something popular, like *Hitch-Hiker's* or

Pink Floyd, then either they don't recognise it or they sneer down their noses. But tell me, what did you think of it?'

'I don't remember much about it, I'm afraid.' Arthur thought that was a bit too non-committal. 'You have a very active style, don't you – just actions and words.'

'Just what the viewpoint character sees and does – yes. I think that gets to the essence of someone, don't you?'

'And am I right you deliberately don't describe your characters?'

'Yes. Spot on.' Arthur enthused. 'Did it make any difference to you?'

'I don't remember. I suppose not.'

'There you are. Unless the detail is important in some way I just leave people to supply their own characters which they do automatically. You don't have to spoon feed them.'

The man didn't look convinced and to Arthur's disappointment prepared to leave. 'Anyway,' he said as he turned to go, 'I must get round with this petition. The wife's doing the other side of the valley, though she's probably gossing with someone by now. Nice meeting you. Are you writing anything at the moment?'

Arthur snatched out his reply. 'Yes-actually-I'm-a-third-the-way-through-a-book-It's-on-the-screen-now-but-I'm-finding-it-hard-going-today-Would-you-like-to-see-a-book-in-the-making?'

'I've got to get on really,' the man said with the merest hint of hesitation which Arthur grasped.

'Please. Come in, come in.'

'Well, yes, why not?'

Arthur ushered him into his home. On their way to the study the petitioner asked, 'How long have you been writing SF?'

'Oh must be...' he considered eternity, 'over a decade now. Bloody hell! They've got me doing it!'

His visitor looked at him uneasily. 'What's up?'

'Oh, it's just the news people these days use "decade" whenever they can. Someone in journo-school must have told them it's a strong word. It's ridiculous. What's wrong with ten years?

“Locked” is another one. It’s like a football game is “locked” at ten all – whatever happened to “tied”, or “level”, or “evenly matched”? Oh just ignore me. Look, here’s what I’m working on.’

Arthur showed him the folder of notes with sections like ‘Names’ and ‘Links’ and ‘Characters (x vs. y)’; the chapters, each in its own computer file; the pile of laser-printed manuscript. As Arthur looked again, the directory listing on the computer seemed to make his efforts inconsequential.

‘What’s the pull-outs file for?’ the petitioner asked, pointing to an incongruous item in the listing.

‘Oh, if I write a bit and then delete it because it doesn’t fit, I save it in there. Then if I find I do want it after all, or I can use it somewhere else, I can just paste it back in.’

‘Good idea.’ He didn’t appear to find the book interesting. ‘Are you on the Internet?’

‘Isn’t everyone? It’ll be everywhere and into everything soon. Then we won’t be able to live without it. I hardly use it though – it’s so hard to get into. If it’s the information superhighway, then I’m stuck on the on-ramp with the hood up. And the information on it is unverified and mostly useless. It’s in my book though – one of my main characters inhabits the future Internet.’

‘Where do you get your ideas from?’

Arthur considered this question seriously.

‘Oh, sorry, that’s so corny. You must get fed up of people asking you that.’

Arthur never did get fed up of people asking him about his books – he wasn’t that famous. He shook his head vaguely. ‘Just from the world around, the news, you know? I suppose if you read my books you could work out a lot about me.’

‘*The author’s voice* you mean. “To understand the book you must understand the author”,’ he quoted from the textbooks, “and to understand the author you must understand the book”.’

‘Something like that.’

‘Have you ever thought,’ said the petitioner gazing into middle space, ‘what if *you* were a character in *someone else’s* book? What would it say about that author?’

‘Who’d want to write about me?’

‘Just a thought,’ said the man. ‘Maybe you could use it sometime. Anyway,’ and he waved his hand in front of his face to brush away an irrelevant thought, ‘what’s your new book about?’

Arthur showed him the scrapbook of cuttings including one from the *Herald* on the use of viruses to deliver genetic engineering direct to cells, and another from *The Australian* describing an idea for putting a shell around the entire planet of Mars to make it suitable for a human colony. ‘And if Mars, why not Earth? The book’s working title is *Above the Stars*. I can’t tell you the plot of course, but I was thinking about the way the new jobs these days are all people-skill jobs, and how the jobs are disappearing where men can sell the sweat of their brows.’ Arthur pulled out a fistful of cuttings and statistics which expanded on that theme. ‘I wondered what the world would be like if women had all the jobs. So initially it’s set in a world where the men have nothing to do except play sport.’

‘It’s just another world where too much sport is barely enough.’

‘Yes that’s exactly it!’ said Arthur delighted to have found something else they enjoyed in common. They swapped lines from the opening sequence to *Roy and H.G.’s This Sporting Life*. ‘Anyway, it’s about a future Earth where the entire planet is covered in buildings. There’s this small pocket where nature is conserved; above that is the world where all the men are; and then all the women live in a separate world in a giant orbiting space station.’

‘Are you doing the same as in that other book, using the three worlds in your book to give different perspectives on various issues?’

‘Oh I’m glad you got that about the perspectives. Yes, I’m doing that again in this one. It’s a sort of trademark of mine.’

'Well, it all sounds fairly realistic to me,' said the man, 'the way the world's going. We seem to have forgotten that the sexes are supposed naturally to get on.'

'Men and women will be at war soon. Then governments will have to make sex mandatory.'

'Imagine the public service announcements: do it for Australia.'

'Don't listen to your parents. Sex is good for you.'

'One night stands can be fun.'

They laughed gently. 'It'll happen, too, if we carry on the way we're going,' said Arthur.

'But it's good to have such a large group to blame for everything – the entire other sex.'

'A man got that promotion you so richly deserved? Blame the glass ceiling.'

'And if it was a woman, blame affirmative action.'

'*Whatever your problem…*'

'*There's always someone else to blame*,' they finished the catch phrase together.

The man nodded and looked around at the trees and the sky. 'Whatever happened to fate?' he muttered to himself.

'What?' said Arthur.

'Oh nothing. Just talking to myself.'

'Wait a minute. Talking to yourself. Talking to yourself.'

The man looked on bemused as Arthur brought a vague idea into mental focus.

'Talking to yourself! That's it!' Suddenly Arthur grasped the man's cheeks between his hands and kissed him.

As the man recoiled Arthur explained excitedly, 'I've been trying to think how I can get Dave and Theo to talk to each other.'

'Who?' said the man, backing away.

'How I can get my hero in touch with my spirit-computer. I've been blocked for ages. You're a bloody genius.'

'Well, I must be off,' said the man moving quickly out of the office.

'Won't you have a cup of tea?'

'No. No thanks,' said the man walking determinedly to the front door. 'I've got this petition to get round.'

'Oh. Anyway. It's been good to talk to you,' said Arthur as the petitioner left.

'Yes, right,' said the man from a safe distance up the drive. 'See ya later, Arthur.'

'Yeah, see you, um.'

'Jim.'

'Yeah. Jim. That's right.'

Arthur went back in but then watched through the window as the petitioner stood at the top of the long steep drive that led down the other side of the ridge to the property across the road, waved his hand at it, and went home.

Then Arthur realised that he'd just had his first real conversation since he'd arrived three years ago. 'I wonder if he'll be friends with me?' He went back to the computer thinking of whale meat.

Monday. Belinda looked round the room, tried to look composed, and gathered her confidence. All the department managers were there, on time for once. She'd checked the link from her laptop to the Datashow. She'd checked that the overhead projector was working and focused. She knew her material. She was confident of her conclusions. What she didn't know was how they'd react. If they bought the story, they'd change and then maybe they could save the company. Why do they only ever bring me in when they're already deep in trouble? she thought.

She glanced at Bruce who offered no encouragement, and then she launched into her talk. 'G'day,' she said, immediately striking a bright I'm-not-a-threat tone. 'Thanks for making the time to come along. In this qualitative survey I talked with thirty of your customers and ten ex-customers to find out what they are thinking and why they are thinking it. I'll describe my main findings – that is, what they are saying about your products and services. Then I'll say what I think you should do in response.'

Someone interjected, 'Shoot the bastards!' Shallow laughter.

Belinda smiled warmly. 'Then we've allowed an hour for questions and discussion. If you want to raise anything while I'm talking, just sing out.'

'Before you do that, love,' said the production manager, 'I'd just like to repeat what I've said all along – asking the customers to whinge is a waste of time. The money would have been better spent on new equipment.'

The sales manager, Moira, countered, 'More toys for the *boys*?' sharing a look with Belinda. 'No, laptops for the sales team are a higher priority than that,' and they all jumped in to stake their claims.

Belinda waited a few moments for the senior managers to take control. When they didn't she turned the overhead projector on, and they all went quiet like in the cinema.

A few minutes into the findings half the people were looking relieved and others were looking defensive and hostile. This was just what she'd feared from the start. She'd tried to talk to the management about the blame culture in the company, but the MD bombasted his way past her, and blamed other people, and Bruce as marketing manager couldn't get any further. Still, this was a challenge, not a disaster – yet.

'So what it comes down to is this,' she said, bringing up a slide with two brief bullet points on it that she expanded on.

- 'Your customers are generally quite happy with you (they wouldn't keep buying if they weren't),
- *But* there are disturbingly frequent problems.'

'We know we've got problems, Belinda. Sales are dropping,' said Moira. 'And as you know we've lost some customers recently. But what should we do about it?'

The production manager said, 'It's obvious. Sack the customer service staff.'

'It's not our fault,' said the customer service manager, fighting for his job. 'The customers are always in a bad mood when they get to us. Try not upsetting them in the first place.'

‘That’s right,’ said Belinda, ‘it’s no good blaming the ones who are trying to save the situation. Customers actually speak quite highly of the customer service staff,’ (a low ‘phew’ from one side of the table) ‘but they don’t seem to be able to change things or get things done.’

Bruce nodded. She wished he’d support her vocally; she needed time to breathe.

‘Well, something must be done,’ said Moira.

‘Oh, yes,’ they all agreed, ‘something must be done.’

‘What should be clear from this,’ said Belinda, ‘is that you need better discipline, improved training, and written work instructions. In short,’ she clicked a key on her laptop to put up the next slide, headed ‘Recommendations,’ with the first point on it,

- ‘You should be more systematic.’

‘Your approach should be to *get it right first time*,’ (she clicked the key again and the words slid in from the left of the slide). ‘At the moment you *get it right first time in the end*.’ They laughed. An aphorism, she remembered Arthur saying, is a cliché you haven’t heard before.

‘That’s easy for you to say,’ the production manager growled, ‘but you don’t have to put up with this joker’s specifications.’

‘I just tell you what the customer wants. It’s up to you to produce it,’ Moira retorted from deep inside her bunker. ‘It’s not the sales team’s fault if you don’t deliver on time.’

‘We could if you set reasonable timescales.’

‘They come from the customers.’

‘You shouldn’t agree to them!’

‘*You try telling them!*’

‘*You deliberately make me look bad!*’

‘CRAP!’

‘ANYTHING TO GET YOUR BONUS!’

Belinda raised her voice as she struggled to control proceedings. ‘YOU’RE BOTH RIGHT. *You’re Both Right*.’ Glares turned away from their targets towards her. ‘You’re both right,’ she said more quietly. They were like an unruly class of children who would rather play with their favourite toys. 'What we have to do is to ensure that we *do* deliver what they need when they need it. Give them options: less sooner; a phased delivery – be creative. They want you to tell them what the answer is. After all, you're the experts. Let's look at more recommendations.' She took another deep breath.

- 'Plan.'

'You need to plan if you're going to succeed. Talk with each other. Make sure you're all able to commit to the dates – if you don't, you're just planning to fail. And monitor progress closely. Just remember: how does a project become a disaster? One day at a time.'

She noted a couple of them take in that point. The third bullet slid in.

- 'Play to your strengths.'

'This survey has reinforced that your customers come to you because of your expertise in two or three particular areas. On the other hand, if you market yourselves as being able to do anything your competitors can, they can just as easily go to your competitors. So push what you do best.

'These are all simple things. The problem isn't knowing what to do, the problem is why aren't you doing them? And I'd just like to stress that if you'd taken these actions a year or two ago, when the problems first became apparent, then you wouldn't have this emergency now. This could be your last chance.'

Someone objected. 'We've had people say that before, but they've all left and we're still here.' That was the production manager, of course.

No comment, Belinda thought as she read out the fourth bullet:

- 'Reduce whole life cycle costs.'

'We've already sacked thirty per cent of the workforce. How much more can we reduce costs?'

It was the first comment from the MD; she'd almost forgotten him. She felt herself blush. She was even more surprised when Bruce beat her to the answer. 'At the moment we spend almost as much on fixing problems as we do on making the things. That's just on warranty, let alone all the goodwill maintenance work we do to keep them sweet.'

Belinda allowed just a moment before adding, 'Yes, that's exactly right. And,' she swept them with what she hoped was a meaningful look, 'are you seriously telling me that if you were a bit more careful, if you talked with each other – are you seriously telling me that you couldn't reduce failure rates by ten per cent?' A couple of them nodded. 'Many customers would even pay more – that is if you could *guarantee* delivery on time and that overall it would cost them less through reduced maintenance costs. But even without that you'd be quids in just because of less waste and less wasted time fixing problems.'

Most of them were nodding. Bruce looked pleased. Even the MD had got the point. I've won, she thought, I've really won!

'I bet it was Harding who made that comment about development.' The production manager had finally had enough. 'He's been a monkey on my back ever since we cocked up his 940. I keep explaining, but he's such a prat, he can't tell his arse from his armpit.'

'They're just after a discount, I bet. Transmet too.'

The negative comments bucketing individual customers were flowing now. 'Oh, what's the use?' she sighed. It would take twenty minutes to undo the harm done and get back to the general points. Belinda logged out for a while thinking: *arse covering is ugly, especially when it's an ugly arse.*

A few hours later there was a particular arse Belinda couldn't take her eyes off. It belonged to Marc, the gym instructor. It was tight and rounded – in various poses it was hardly there at all. Most gratifying. When he turned round the sight was even better: what Arthur called a three-socker. Both views were most pleasingly presented in tight lycra pants. Next to her, Dutch was in full perve. They always took their positions in the front row – the granny line – for Marc's class.

[Two steps forward… double left… double right… turn… cockroach] Behind them worthier bodies sweated their ways towards a flat stomach. Such an aerobics nirvana was beyond Belinda's attainment. She had been in decline for many years now. She hadn't recovered after having Sophie, and though she had made a big effort as part of her rehabilitation from her divorce, that had only delayed the slide to this.

This!

She was not beautiful, she knew. She did have breasts that men found fascinating, especially in her silk blouse. She should wear it more often. She'd wear it to the proposal presentation meeting with Gustav on Thursday. He'd love it (or them). That should swing it (ha ha). The pearl brooch would go well and… Marc showed them a new move that involved waving his hips at her face. She waved hers back at him, but knew that the result was not alluring.

[Easy walk… turn… grapevine left… step behind… step in front… two steps right… turn back… and again…]

She was not beautiful. Not like Teri who she knew was still bouncing athletically two rows back, while Belinda sagged at the front. Unlike Teri, she had broad hips. They were not particularly fat, they were just intransigently broad. Her waist was not what it was, but it was still identifiably a waist. Her legs, which propelled this blob of a body around, spread towards her buttocks in magnificent cones of cellulite ('turkey drumsticks' Arthur had called them – once!). Still, at least she didn't look like Dutch who was panting next to her.

'Marc was on form today,' said Belinda when they got to the showers after the workout.

'Those are really cool shorts(?)' said Dutch. 'You can see his pubes through them(?)' They giggled like school girls.

Belinda had grown used to the way Dutch finished phrases on an interrogative squeak. She guessed it was something she'd inherited from her children – like grey hair. 'I saw you panting at him. It was *embarrassing.*' They giggled again. 'Can I grab some shampoo? Ta.'

'You know that bloke – the tall fat one, with the neck hair?'

'Yeah.'

'When we were doing the warm down(?) he sat on the floor facing me(?). He wasn't wearing any daks(?). I swear I could see the lot(?)!'

'Oh yuck! You should get him for sexual harassment,' Belinda said to general and widespread agreement. 'As I was walking to my meeting today in town, some bozo whistled at me.'

'What, he went the wolf? Men! They think women are just there for their gratification.'

'I know, it's so degrading. You'd think they'd have caught on by now,' she said, and Dutch agreed. 'How's Geoff?'

'Oh, he gives me the shits(?),' said Dutch. 'I'm trying to earn a crust and he can't even get a decent meal ready for when I get in(?). It's not as if he's got much to do all day.'

'I have to tell Arthur what to cook too, and he's supposed to be the creative one in the family.'

'How's the book going?'

'Oh, he doesn't like to talk about it. He spends his time arguing with the radio. It's typical, isn't it? I work bloody hard with my stupid customers. I could do with a distraction, but, you know how these creative types are.'

'Geoff's much the same(?). I come home, and he doesn't say much(?), "How's your day?", "Fine," that sort of thing(?). I don't even know if he's trying to get a job any more(?). Since his injury he's hardly paid any attention to me(?). He never was much of a talker but lately… I sometimes think I'd be better off on my own(?). At least then I'd have someone interesting to talk to(?).'

'Geoff?' said one of their friends, an older Greek woman, from another shower stall. 'He's a sweetie.'

'You don't have to live with him(?) You're all right. Your husband's out to work six days a week(?).'

'Is okay. But Sunday, he tired, he drink, he shout.'

'He hit too, I bet,' said Dutch. 'All men are bastards.'

BASTARDS
Also tonight on the 7.30 Report: Are there more revelations to come from the Gold Coast royal commission?
YES.
The Prime Minister under attack. Will the environment kill him off?
NO.
And can England do anything to save the Ashes?
NO.

Belinda could hear Arthur as she came down the drive. He saw her out of the window, turned off the TV, and bounded out to greet her. 'Hi, Belle. Hey, I had a great day. I wrote two thousand words. I got Dave and Chris back together, I've got the pursuers on the trail, I thought up some great machines for later, but the narrative will stall unless…'

Arthur's voice trailed off as Belinda shut the bedroom door behind her '…I can work out what the Homs do for the Masters,' he finished quietly to the door. 'It wouldn't hurt to show interest sometimes.' Deflated he turned and went into the kitchen to cook dinner.

Belinda felt she really needed some space, so she brushed her hair that was out of place after the gym, cleaned her teeth, and took her time changing into scruffy clothes. When she emerged Sophie ran to her and told her about her assignment, and they chatted for a while. She looked in on Dave, who grunted but didn't turn round from his computer game.

As she entered the kitchen she saw out of the corner of her eye a colourful flash as two terrified eastern rosellas flew away from their plate of seeds outside the window. 'Run away! Run away!' she muttered, like she always did to them when they glimpsed her and panicked. Arthur had the radio on while he cooked:

'…Grozny. The battuw for Cheshna is spreading to Moscow.' The trade minister, Mr Blewitt, claimed a victory in legal negotiations which saw the Chinese promise to pay for at least twenty-eight per cent of the wool they have received from Australia in the last three years…

Arthur turned the radio off. Belinda sat down at the kitchen table, pushed the flowers out of the way, read the faxes for the day and ate the dinner he put in front of her. When she'd finished he said, 'You feeling better? Those presentations wipe you out. Did you like the flowers?'

'What flowers? I got whistled at today.'

Arthur half winked at her in support. 'You were looking very smart.'

'Shows I've still got it, eh,' Belinda said. Then she told him her story based on the presentation.

'Sounds like it went better than you expected then,' he said, trying to harmonise with what he thought would be her relief. 'Let's celebrate the end of phase one.' He immediately wished he hadn't said that because it would only remind her that there was a phase two when she'd have to work closely with them and try to get them to implement her recommendations. 'How about the Italian in Turramurra on Friday? I'll book it later. Bruce is such a wimp though. Fancy not saying a single thing to help you throughout the whole meeting. That guy's got all the charisma of a fungus but lacks its initiative.'

Belinda had only said that about Bruce for dramatic effect and tiredly she wished Arthur could be more like her girlfriends who knew a good story when they heard one. That reminded her: 'I saw Dutch at the gym. She was telling us about her husband again. He's a real sod.'

'*Geoff*? He's harmless, especially since his back went.'

'That's not the way Dutch tells it.'

Arthur was never happy talking about other people's unhappy relationships, though Belinda seemed to revel in it. He cast around for something to change the subject. They often crossed over their work – Belinda acted as a test audience for his writing and he checked the stuff she wrote, so he said, 'I had a look through your proposal for Thursday. Looks good. I made a few minor suggestions, and added a paragraph at the start of section three. I think you ought to charge a bit more though.'

'Hmm. I want this job. Those last two proposals I did amounted to bugger all to the power of zip.'

'What happened to them again?'

'I've told you twice already,' she said. 'One said they would save the money and talk to their customers themselves – which from what I hear will be a new departure. The other said they had to put it to the board, who apparently never get past the second item on their agenda. Even if I win the job on Thursday, Gustav's too busy to actually get started.' She shook her head at this often repeated frustrating scenario. 'Did Sweng phone?' He hadn't – in fact he hadn't phoned for a while. 'I've got a bad feeling about the Haulman thing – we think they're putting the bad word out on us. It could be serious. It's hit Sweng pretty hard. He's not had much work recently, certainly none to hand on to me.'

'It's not your fault. Haulman just had a crap product. You did the right thing to tell them. Sweng doesn't hold it against you.'

'I need the work. Two kids and a writer to support. Remember? Thank God I haven't got employees like he has.'

By some tangential thread, that reminded Arthur of something he'd heard on the radio on one of his favourite subjects – the state of the battle of the sexes. 'You know that legislation that the State government passed last year,' he said, 'y'know, the one which allows judges to take domestic violence into account in divorce settlements?'

'Quite right too. Bastards!'

'Well, it seems the marriage rate has fallen dramatically in this state, and they've done some research and found men were point blank refusing to get married.'

'Typical.'

'Well, you see with the new legislation, all a woman has to do is to *accuse* her husband of abuse of any sort, and he could lose visiting rights or even all his money in the divorce settlement – no assumption of innocence in that court. So she only has to *threaten* to accuse him and he'll agree to anything. Well, young men have got a sniff of this and are putting up the shutters. They think it's too risky.'

'What rubbish. Only last month *Cleo* had an article saying that women are opting to stay single more and more these days as a lifestyle choice.'

'What, just in one state?' Arthur had the feeling he wouldn't get anywhere with this. 'That's a thought – is *Cleo* on the Internet, do you know? Doesn't matter.' Arthur waved his hand in front of his face to dismiss the question, but Belinda had ignored it anyway.

'That law is only for the violent men. And they deserve everything they get.'

'It's yet another law for a very few,' Arthur said, struggling to keep Belle to his point, 'which rebounds dramatically on the other ninety per cent. And it's the women who suffer more – they've always been the ones who wanted marriage; now men have got something concrete to back up their commitment phobia. It's like those unfair dismissal laws.' Ah yes, that was the connection.

'Well, *they're* just plain stupid. KTG really need more staff but they won't take them on because they're worried they won't be able to get rid of them if they're no good.'

'It's just driving the sexes apart.'

'What, the unfair dismissal laws?'

'I just think it's sad.'

Belinda did her own unfair dismissal and closed the subject. 'Anything on the news?'

'There was a huge demo by the greenies about the Wollemi in Canberra. The PM's carpeted Burns, the resources minister, and taken it on himself. The greens are threatening electoral cataclysm for the government. There've been demos in every state capital – save the koala stuff. It's a major cock up – again. Car registrations flat this quarter. Opposition doom and gloom – again. Um, UN disaster in Bosnia, Chechnya, crime, funny story, last weekend's sport, sport and sport… the usual. Oh, and there are fires in Sutherland.'

That got Belinda's attention. Bush fire was one of her great fears. 'They could just as easily be here. How are our gutters?'

'I cleaned them last week.'

'What about the bush? Is there much fuel?'

'In a block like this there's always fuel.'

'So what can we do?'

'Well, what we need is something that will stop the fire spreading when it gets close – something wet and green.'

'Wandering jew! That's wet and green. That'd stop a fire dead.' Arthur hoped she was joking.

'I did a bit of work down by the creek today,' he said. 'It's an awful mess – loads of litter as well, though it's not too bad once you get away from the creek and the walking path.' He offered one of his own triumphs: 'Phil, Ian, Jo and Sam have all said they'll help with the bush bash. I told them we'd attack the privet and bamboo behind all our blocks.' It was one of the few subjects Arthur ever got excited about. 'It'll be marvellous to get so much done in one go.'

'Oh, great. With that many we'll really make an impact.' Belinda just didn't seem to share his enthusiasm for the subject and whenever it came up it quickly petered out. 'How are the kids?'

Arthur's lips narrowed to strings. 'Whenever I go to see how Dave's getting on with his assignments, he's playing the same bloody computer game,' he said, unconsciously clenching his fist. 'He's just throwing away his life and I can't get through to him. And Sophie's still doing it tough,' he said relaxing again. 'She's right off her food. I'm worried, she hardly eats anything. And she never talks about her school friends. I phoned her class teacher at lunch time. He says she's getting good marks in most subjects, though her arithmetic is still very poor. He says she's doing okay but that she's not mixing as well as he'd hoped. And he says she lacks aggression.'

'What does he mean, she lacks aggression?' Belinda snapped. 'I thought that was a good thing! But she doesn't seem to have her usual energy these days. Does he think she's ill?'

'He didn't say. He had to go, so I didn't get a chance to chase that up.'

Belinda raised her eyebrows in an unspoken *tch*. 'Men!'

After a frustrating day, Arthur sat down with a brandy and watched the American Football and then a late night soap.

'That was delicious,' purred Heather provocatively. She dabbed the corner of her ruby-waxed lips, lowered her bedroom eyes and smouldered across the flickering table. Wanton hands moved to lift away her open plate, but drifted instead to her startled shoulder and cascaded down past the dallying lacy line of her silken camisole. Alison bent her sumptuous face, and Heather half-heartedly looked away. Alison's languid finger nails, which airlessly turned the full-bodied head back to her own willing vortex, complemented Heather's blusher. Mascaras blinked and merged.

She dipped; she hesitated; she breathed; she fell.

The music rose; the camera panned; the picture dissolved.

Heather sat up with the pressed satin sheets pulled up to her smiling chin. Alison sat on the side of the bed with a curvaceous bottle of champagne and two long-thighed glasses. She crossed her legs so that they flaunted from beneath her bathrobe. She unwrapped the cork and pulled. She pulled again. 'It won't budge.'

'I guess,' Alison giggled, 'there are some things you just need a man for.'

The phone rang. Alison moved one silky leg towards the sound, but Heather let the sheets fall.

We watch the phone. Two rings later the champagne popped and fizzed, and they giggled musically. In another town, Ryan, unshaved, waited.

The credits rolled, and the announcer said, 'Will Candy fall for George's trick? Find out tomorrow: *Neighbours* at five thirty. Coming up next, a kidney transplant.'

'Of course,' said Arthur finishing his brandy. 'There's some things you just need a man for.'

That, and what his reader, the petitioner had said. The next day he sat down at the computer and picked up mid-sentence where he'd dribbled to a halt. There were details he still hadn't worked out, but, hell, he'd wing it. At least now he knew where he was going.

should we do now?'

'Don't ask me. I'm lost.'

'I need a rest.'

'Run! Come on!' said Chris redoubling his efforts. 'They're right behind us!'

Dave lagged behind. 'You carry on. I *have* to stop.'

'I can't just leave you. Anyway it's you they're after. Duck in here.'

'Where?' Chris grabbed him, pulling him into the empty room. They flattened themselves against the wall, their sweaty shirts making the wall clammy. With shouts and a flash of bright uniforms the pursuers ran past. The sound of boots on road faded as they ran through the doors at the end and then, quiet. Dave peeled himself off the wall and wiped his face with his shirt – well, he had to.

They relaxed. 'Those are the new uniforms they're wearing,' said Dave, affronted. 'That didn't take long. The Decision was only two days ago – just before mine. He…' Two days! He rested with his hands on his knees trying to get his breath back.

'We've got a few minutes until word gets to them that we're off-Record. Then they'll backtrack and find us. We have to keep moving. Lucky this place is unused, so there's no Record. I've seen several places like this along the way – maybe we can hop between them.'

'Until what? Some miraculous escape?'

'I don't know, do I. Look do you want to give up or something? They'll kill you, you know. The penalty for indecision is death. And that's nothing to the penalty for knocking out several pursuers and the Decision Hall Master plus all that equipment.' Dave looked sideways at him. 'We have to get out of here or they'll find us, and then they'll kill you – at least once. Come on. Maybe we can change the way we look.'

Tiredness made Dave irritable and caustic. 'So you're going to become twenty centimes shorter, are you? A neat trick.'

A kay later in an empty condo in the next suburb, they did something violent to two passers-by and switched clothes. Chris looked uncomfortable. He'd not been violent before except on the sports field. Dave felt worse. 'Now they'll be after you too!'

'So we're in this together now. We'll be on the news. They may even think we're renegades. Wow, the first renegades on Record! Finally we're really something.'

'You've always been really something, Chris. I haven't said this before, but *Thanks*. You didn't have to do this, but I'm glad you're here.' They kissed; usually when they were passionate Dave could feel Chris's arousal, but this time they were both scared. They moved out of the empty condo trying to look inconspicuous.

'Have you got a plan? There's no one we can go to. Everybody who knows us will have seen me at the Decision. And pretty soon now you'll be on the news too. You know, I hadn't thought that I was notorious earlier. I just wanted somewhere familiar to go. How did you find me? I could have been anywhere.'

'It wasn't hard. That waiter knew you and it was *quite* happy to tell anyone who wanted to know which way you'd gone. Why on earth did you go to the café, of all places?'

'I just wanted to watch the game. And we'd've won if I'd been playing. That Santorini's an idiot. Did you see…'

Dave saw the look Chris gave him and quickly dropped the subject. They walked down a road, and into a side street. It was nearly empty. Dave remembered how they'd met up. 'I'd have walked right past you if you hadn't grabbed me.'

'Yeah, right into the pursuers. Oh no, they've found us.'

13

[Lots of running]
[Lost in the maze. Could be anywhere]
[Empty streets. Lots of empty condos]
[Locked doors]

I've noticed, Captain, that his thinking is decidedly two dimensional... Zee minus two thousand Mr Sulu.

14

Hi, Tethys. Had a good day running the world?
I just dropped in on my way home. How's Theo?
Oh, in one of his moods again.

...Run away. Run away. Run away. Run away. Run away. Run away...

You know, Jude, sometimes I wonder whether he's all there. We entrust our greatest enterprises to him, and we hardly know anything about him.
I know. But what else can we do? He's the best. Let's face it – apart from Sal, he's the only.
Sal? No! I'll stick with Theo, thanks.
Have you been watching the chase that he's been displaying all morning?
Yes. I wonder why he's concentrating on that? I couldn't care less about those Homs. It's not as if the result is in any doubt. It's not even sport.
Hmm. You know what struck me, Tethys? How empty it is down there. They've run through thousands of me-

tres of unused housing. There may be whole cores empty.

Yeah, but I bet the stupid Homs haven't even noticed. Do you think anyone's asked about reduced league sizes? Theo, have they?

Run away. Run away. Run away. Run away. Run away. Run away... Oh, no. No one. We emptied Adelaide three years ago and no one noticed the difference.

You see? There. Another empty road. Oh look, they've finally thought to go down, rather than just running on the same level. They're bright boys. For Homs.

Frankly, my dear, I don't give a damn.

Thank you, Theo. Why don't you hum quietly? There's a good boy.

I knew the population's crashing. But it's not till you see it with your own eyes... It must be the same here, I suppose.

I suppose so. I hadn't noticed. I've been too busy.

The problem is that there's no gene for being interested. Why didn't Desirée think of this?

Oh, come on, Jude. It was the results of her work that produced the hyperpopulation in the first place.

Not exactly. The hyperpopulation was in train long before the Separation, it just took several centuries to work its way through. The population was doubling every fifty to a hundred years or so from well before the Record began. It's just that say five billion to ten billion around year two thousand doesn't seem as dramatic as one trillion to two trillion in year three thousand. And with all the benefits the Separation brought us – especially us – nobody thought to question the received wisdom. This needs every resource we've got, and because of Desirée we've only got half. Damn her.

We should do some gene fiddling. Undo what she did.

We mustn't. In fact, Tethys, you said so yourself in the Presidium in the debate on the population crisis. The technology, the science, the tools are all locked for ever, you said. We must never use them again, you said.

But this is an emergency!

Oh, it's an emergency now that you've seen it, is it? An emergency a millennium in the making, Tethys? It was an emergency centuries ago, but it suited us to deny it existed. Then to ignore it. Then we said science would solve it. But it just keeps getting worse. And how does it get worse? One day at a time. So we can always delay doing something about it. Now, looking back, we can see an emergency. No, we must all do our bit to contribute to the solution.

Well something must be done.

You could choose your father for a start.

I would, but – you're not going to like this, Jude – I'm not interested.

*

'Smart move, Chris. What made you think of coming down to these lower levels? We've lost them.' Dave was breathing more easily.

'For the moment. It's weird down here, isn't it. Empty. The last person out forgot to switch off the lights. Old condos too. Very old. I don't recognise any of these controls.'

'Are you sure the Record isn't on down here?'

'Why would it be? There's nobody here.'

They walked slowly, breathing conservatively. 'It's so quiet,' said Dave. 'No people, no hum of freeways, no aids whooshing past. How did you know this was here?'

'I didn't. We just got lucky.'

'Well, it's what we needed. They were getting bonking close. Let's rest here.' For the first time in a few days Dave felt hungry. 'Have you got anything to eat?'

'Yes, how silly of me not to mention it. I stopped off at the condo, dodged the pursuers on guard there, and picked up a few kegs of nutrient base. *Of course I haven't!*'

'Terrific. I won't be executed because I'm going to starve to death first.'

'You'll die of thirst before you starve.'

'Thanks.'

'Don't mention it. No. Hey! What's this?'

'What's what?'

'Nothing. Just kidding.'

'Terrific.'

*

You've let it slip too much, Theo. The whole thing's out of control. You've done nothing. You're doing nothing.

I am too, Sal. Look.

Those two? You call those two doing something? Anyway, you can't use him, he knows too much.

Not him. The other one.

Him? You cannot be serious. Him? He doesn't know anything. Anyway, we need him for that other thing.

Have you got a better idea? Thought not.

His qualifications are completely inappropriate. He's not a listener for a start.

I'll deal with it, Sal.

You've had this one taped all along, haven't you? You just invented Su Chen.

I thought you'd like that.

Like it?

Just kidding.

Terrific.

*

'So what's your plan, Chris? Where are we going?'

'Buggered if I know.'

They were walking along among the abandoned condos. The high ceilings were covered in thick dusty webs that made the place look untidy. 'That's an odd phrase, isn't it?'

'Well, it's a very old saying. It's just a trade – if I tell you, you give me pleasure.'

They heard shouts nearby and without looking started to run.

'How did they find us?'

'*Run!*' Dave heard shots smashing into the walls, floor and ceiling just behind him.

'Why are they firing at us?'

'They're having fun. They don't often get the chance. Anyway you've got a target on the back of your shirt.'

'Ha bonking ha. They didn't fire at us before.'

'They could have hit other people up there.' They turned as many corners as they could. Through old empty condos. Along smooth-walled roads. Always they could hear the pursuers just behind them. They would run through a door, it would close behind them and then a few seconds later open again for the pursuers. Booted feet on the road. Shots. Shouts. Once Dave tripped on a hole in the road as he was taking a corner, and as he fell he heard an energy bolt smash into the wall near where his head had been.

They sprinted down a road, and through a door. *On ya, Dave.*

'Who said that?'

The door shut behind them, and they ran down the road. The pursuers banged on the door. Dave and Chris slowed, looked at each other, and jogged to a halt.

This way, Dave. The next door opened.

'How do you know my name?'

Behind them the pursuers shouted at the door to open. *Make me*, it said disdainfully.

'What's going on?' said Dave looking around suspiciously.

You're a celebrity, mate. Ooh, they are getting cranky. I tell you, these are very unpopular bastards. OY, SHUT IT!

The banging stopped briefly, and then started again with renewed vigour.

Doors and condos like us, who've been abandoned, we love a nonconformist. Just follow the path. We'll give you some time. A line of doors opened into the distance. *This region is solid, mate. But I can't speak for any others – there are scab doors but we don't talk to them. Seeyalater. Have a good life.*

'Bye,' said Dave. Looking back after a while, he saw the door open. One pursuer edged through, gun first. The door closed suddenly and trapped his arm. The condos near them sniggered and Dave wondered if he hadn't been a little hasty in his judgement of machines.

*

They walked on briskly, enjoying the silence, and were able to cool down and catch their breaths. They had time to take in the scenery, and the changing styles of condos – like a walk back through history. Chris pointed out architectural and technical features that had been superseded long ago. As they went back in time, they noticed condos with transparent windows, manual doors and mats with *Welcome* printed on them. How could people live like that? Dave wondered idly.

But before long the pursuers set the doors on automatic rather than free will. They had to run for their lives and had no time to look behind. They found they were unable to shake the pursuers off. They were desperate. The roads were narrower, the ceilings were lower. Though they were fit, and faster than the pursuers, they could never get any speed up because they knew if they were caught in a road the pursuers would have a simple straight shot. They ran past broken windows of small old condos, which made a change from the blank unbreakable windows on the level they'd come from. Holes in floors and the road surfaces revealed metal substrate. Parts of the roads weren't lit.

The pursuers were always just a few seconds away. Several times the pursuers came at them from ahead and they had to duck quickly into condos and down crossing roads.

'They must have several Pursuit...,' Chris was breathless, '...teams down here. They mean to...' they took a door into a condo, and leapt down stairs one level, '...get you. Look, whatever happens...' they bolted through a cross road '...I want you to know, I really do...' down two levels, right, a long run, then left, '...love you. Good luck.'

'Same.' Dave wanted to say something more meaningful, but he couldn't get the breath. He slowed. 'I'm tired. Let's just give ourselves... up. At least... they'll feed us before... they try, convict... and shoot us.'

'Keep moving. Quick, down here! Shit! A dead end.'

'Funny, why did they build a dead end?'

'It's a hell of a time to be wondering about town planning.'

Frantically they felt along the walls for flush doors, but they reached the end of the road which was equally implacable. They turned to face the pursuers who approached them, arms braced to shoot.

'You know, it's at times like this I wish I'd listened to what my mother said.'

'Why? What did he say?'

Before Chris could answer a strange voice said: He doesn't know. He wasn't listening, and laughed uproariously. Everybody looked round to see who'd spoken, but there was nobody there. Dave heard a door swish open behind him, and then... nothing.

Oh, Ford Prefect, we love you.

15

Dave woke up. His bed felt strange, but that was fine. The renegades would still be there to be sentenced in the morning. He went back to sleep.

Dave woke up. Chris was already up having breakfast. His head hurt. Why won't they leave me alone? He went back to sleep.

Dave woke up. His room was unusually tidy. He tried to go back to sleep.

Dave opened his eyes properly. He wished he could go back to sleep. His head hurt a lot. The room was empty, with bare walls. He was alone. He was lying on his back on a hard slab. He was fully dressed. He felt incredibly tired, like he'd been running all day. He went back to sleep.

Dave woke up, and this time he remembered – at least up to the strange voice and the door. His head hurt. That's it – his head hurt. He focused on that. Ow!

He had a cut on his head – low, at the back, to one side. 'They must have hit me,' he muttered.

Contact, said a voice. *That* voice.

He looked around the room but there was no one there. He noticed how hard the slab was. He sat up, swinging his legs over the side. The manoeuvre sent his head reeling one way and his body the other.

Welcome aboard the Starship Heart of Gold. Please do not be alarmed by anything you see or hear around you. You are bound to feel some initial ill effects as you have been rescued from certain death at an improbability level of two to the power of two hundred and sixty-seven thousand, seven hundred and nine to one against, possibly much higher.

Dave steadied himself against the slab. When his head stopped spinning, his mind took over. He looked all around the room for the source of the voice. He had an uncomfortable feeling it was coming from inside his head. Linked to all the other uncomfortable feelings, this made him feel very ill. He'd heard of this – men hearing voices. The pursuers come and pick you up. 'It's only the blow on the head,' he reassured himself.

You could be mad.

'Of course I'm mad, I'm bloody furious! It's not as if I did anything dangerous. I just didn't want the responsibility for condemning people who may be innocent. I expect they're dead anyway by now.'

Googoogoogoogoo. Ddddrrrpp. Errrrrk. Zootlwurdle-zootlwurdlezootlwurdle. Fringggg.

He felt nauseous and disjointed. He had a thought and bent down to look under the slab. Then he picked himself up slowly off the floor, and moved on all fours to the base of the slab.

Find anything?

Dave had found something very interesting indeed: food and water. Unfortunately getting it from where it was to the top of the slab involved a complicated and delicate manoeuvre – standing up – which he just couldn't manage right now. After a few attempts, he ate sitting on the floor.

Feeling fortified he attempted to stand up, and slowly raised himself to lean against the slab again. The voice in his head was pomming away inanely, which matched his own level of consciousness. He shouted loudly for a medical aid, and then waited. Nothing happened. He sat and considered his position. He then began a more thorough investigation of the room, gingerly at first, and then more confidently. He found that he was in, to put it crudely, an empty room. Later more food and water arrived on a limp tray with another insubstantial spoon, at a trapdoor in the base of the slab, and he devoured that too. 'I could do with a cup of tea,' he shouted hopefully.

An idea hit him, a thought, a hope. 'Chris!' He was immediately consumed with remorse. 'Where are you, Chris? What have they done to you?' He slumped. 'I wish you were here. You'd know what was happening.'

They've probably killed him by now. They'll kill you too if you don't get out of here.

'*What? Chris!*' Nothing happened. He beat his hands against the walls. Nothing happened. He rammed himself against the walls. He bruised his upper arm. Dave sat down by the wall and tried to think. After a while he looked up again. Nothing had happened. The room was empty except for the slab; the walls were blank. He began to wonder about the voice in his head. It was only a projection of his own consciousness after all. 'This is a fine mess you've gotten me into,' he said to the projection of his own consciousness.

Don't blame me. You could have taken an easy way out at any stage. It's you with the conscience.

'I couldn't do anything else. You know that. Those bastards on the net baying for blood – they were disgusting.'

But normal. What makes you so different?

'Different? I'm not different. I'm just not like the rest of them. Why weren't there any others who thought of the renegades as people?'

Maybe they'd stopped caring. Who knows?

'Well now who gives a shit, eh? I did, and look where it got me: in a dead room, talking to myself, waiting to be executed.'

Well, if that's what you're waiting for I don't expect you'll have to wait much longer. I think it's about time you got out of here.

'Great idea! Maybe I should dig myself out.' He looked around cynically. 'I know: I could use this terrifyingly powerful, super-hard… spoon.'

You could climb through the air vent.

For the first time Dave noticed an air vent immediately above the slab. 'That's not a bad idea – why didn't I think of that?' he muttered as he clambered on to the slab. The vent unclipped easily when he pulled on it. 'What am I saying, it was me who thought of it. I must have seen it when I was lying there. It just didn't register.'

Thanks a lot!

He jumped and pulled himself up into the ducting, [how original – is that really the best you can do?] and pulled the vent closed behind him. [Ah well, let's see where this leads.]

16

'Now which way, I wonder.'

Left. No, right. No, go left.

Dave decided that it was too hard to turn around, and he started the way he was already facing. He had crawled only a few yards when the voice said: Quiet! He froze. He heard voices – outside his head – and realised he was near a vent in another room. The voices came from men who had obviously eaten several intoxicants. It seemed they were celebrating.

'Here's to the rat.'

'And the rat leash.'

'And the rat-catchers.' They cheered. Dave crept forward. The ducting creaked. He froze, but the revellers were too far gone to hear anything peripheral. He had no idea what they were talking about.

Someone entered the room and was greeted raucously. 'I thought you'd be pleased to know that Theo has sent commendations to the troop for the chase today.' As the man approached the group he came into Dave's field of view. He was short and stocky, but from his bulging chest muscles he was clearly very strong. His voice timbre was soft as if he wanted people to be nice to him, but his posture was of a man used to being obeyed. Dave noticed that he seemed to be holding his head as if the group were giving off an unpleasant smell. 'Theo said that he'd asked for the best team and he obviously got it. Well done, men.' They gave a half-hearted cheer. 'It wasn't easy, keeping the chase going the whole day. It showed skill, men. The Masters have noted your success. Well done again.'

The man left hurriedly, and the troop roared with laughter. 'Stay and talk a while! Enjoy the atmosphere!' one shouted.

'It's not as if we were in any danger.'

'Don't you believe it, son. If we'd lost him, we'd have been in plenty of danger. Or at least one part of each of us.'

'Well, you had less to lose than me, then.' Laughter. A bitter voice took over. 'The Masters are happy. So what reward do we get for this magnificent achievement?'

'We just follow directions. Theo tells us where to go and we go.'

'Those big arsed slit flickers,' said the bitter voice. 'They don't care what we do.'

'Sit down and enjoy.'

Dave twitched, but managed to resist the urge to correct him.

'Bugger Theo. We keep going for long enough, and the rat runs into the right corner. It's a tough job, but someone has to do it. They just sprout and give orders. Shame they don't come out of their weightless beds to help us. I wouldn't mind if they let us get into those beds either.' Much prodding and pushing. 'I swing all ways: in, out and *up.'* He thrust his crotch at Dave in the ceiling. 'In space no one can hear you scream.'

'And they would, boy, they would.'

Come on, let's be moving. Keep it quiet though.

Dave slid forward as the men moved their invective to someone called Theo. Any connection with the Theo system? he wondered. No, can't be.

At each junction he argued under his breath with the projection of his own consciousness about which way to go. He found it helped.

'What were they going on about, I wonder?'

Them? Ingrates. They're just smashed.

'I could see that. You know, I'll miss that sort of camaraderie. The team. The changing room banter. I wonder what I'll do now.'

Escape – if you can.

'Escape. Yes, but where to?' The ducting was dark and constricting. He couldn't turn round or stand up. He could only go on down the featureless tunnel trying not to make too much noise. He had to crawl on all fours. Light penetrated occasionally as he passed a room. He found it helped to discuss aspects of recent events or his current predicament with himself, with the voice in his head.

He made his way slowly and aimlessly until just as the voice snapped, Stop! one hand fell into nothing and the side of his head slammed against the floor.

Go down there.

'Why? I'm quite comfortable like this.'

Go down there. There's a way out.

I must be guessing, he thought.

Go down there. It's not safe on this level any more – too many pursuers, and they're waking up after their little celebrations.

'Okay,' Dave muttered, 'why not follow my instinct? I've got nothing better to go on.' He edged himself over the hole and manoeuvred his legs into position. 'What's down there?' he asked himself irrationally.

A single level drop. Listen, there's something I think we should clear up.

'What? Do I really want to know this?'

In reverse order: yes. Me. I'm not you.

'Of course you are. Who else could you be? There's no one else in this tunnel. And anyway, I'm not trusting anybody else. After all I'm an expert on holes in ducting kays away from where I've lived my whole life.' He lowered himself into the hole.

Fair point. But it is only one level. One and a half metres if you lower yourself carefully.

'Go on. I'll humour you. Who are you, then?' He lowered himself so that he hung from his fingers in the darkness.

Call me… Eddie. Yes Eddie.

'And what are you, Eddie?'

Think of me as an archaeologist.

'I knew I'd regret it,' said Dave, and let go.

*

Eddie was right about the fall. The noise must have reverberated through the system but nobody came to investigate. Dave followed Eddie's instructions, along and down a few more levels. 'The cut on my head!' said Dave suddenly.

Right first time – in the end.

'So what happened? How does it work?'

It's called a meta-cochlea implant. It's rather complicated, and involves brainwave energies, audio matrices and nerve signals transmitted to the language centres of the brain. But the practical upshot is that if you stick one in your ear we can talk to each other.

'Why did they do that if they were going to kill me, for bonk's sake?'

They weren't going to kill you. They had something much worse than that lined up. The Masters can be very unkind to their subjects when you don't follow the rules. The implant was for them, but I got in first.

'Thanks, I think... Hey! You mean I was going to meet the Masters, and now I've run away from that fantastic experience down here into this horrible maze of tunnels, with no food, no drink, and nowhere to go? Why did you make me do that?'

Make you? I didn't make you. You thought of it yourself, remember. Anyway, look down. What's there?

Dave looked down. He couldn't see much at all. 'Nothing, except this stupid bonking ducting.'

Look a bit closer to home. Sort of crotch region. Know what I mean? They prefer their men Bobbitted. Well, it was a trade: to keep that, you have to do this.

A thought of Chris crashed in, and Dave crumpled. When he had regained control of himself he said in a sigh, 'For all the good it'll do me. Anyway, I'm here now, so what next?' Just round the next corner, Eddie told Dave to push out the vent and jump down. He was in a room with an old fashioned transparent window. He looked out on a dimly lit road, which appeared to be in even worse condition than the others he'd been on… When was it? Earlier today? He was filthy from dust. He brushed himself down, but that had little effect.

Rest here for a while. It's quiet and comparatively safe.

Dave was happy to comply. He took a while to get his energy back. Then he stood up and did a full set of stretches. 'Okay, where next?' Eddie gave him instructions and he set off.

'You know the Masters, right? They're women, aren't they?'

Yes, that's right.

'What are women?'

Do you mean biologically, physically, sociologically…? It's a big subject.

'Start wherever you like.'

Well, they're…

Sirens sounded all over the place. They've discovered you're not in the cell. Better get a wriggle on. Turn right and hurry.

'Where are we going? Anywhere special? Maybe there's something you'd like to tell me about? Perhaps, y'know, tell me what the bonking plan is?'

Out of here, Dave, just out of here.

He worked his way down a few levels, and followed a general direction, though what it was he had no way of telling. By now they could be miles from the Sydney Core, or right under it. He had been moving for only a few minutes when he heard shouts, lights came on and almost immediately shots sang on the walls around him. The lights half blinded him, and he couldn't see where the shots were coming from. Eddie barked directions and he just ran.

The sounds of the pursuers followed him. 'I'm no better off than I was before,' he panted as he dashed into a small road. Shots pinged as he ran.

Ah, but this time you've got me. I know how these guys work. Trust me. You can trust me to the end of the Earth.

'I haven't got much choice, have I.'

About twelve minutes away.

'What?'

Nothing, just something someone once said.

'Well, once was enough.'

You don't know what you're saying.

'No. I don't know what *you're* saying.'

Left here. Through this door on the right... Down. Down again... Out down the road... Through the door at the end... Turn left... Left... Left... Stop... Now, keep very, very quiet.

Dave grabbed at his chest, and tried to gasp quietly. 'What's that smell?'

Quiet!

The shouts came closer, following the path he'd taken. They came to the road he'd taken. They ran up to the condo he was in.

They ran past. Dave heard them go, and found he hadn't been breathing. He breathed out as he heard the sounds of the pursuers fade in the distance. The gun held to his head relaxed, but didn't move.

'Well, well, well. Look what we've found, boys and girls.'

*

'You're renegades!' Dave was indignant. 'You've got no argument with me. Let me go!' He couldn't see his captors clearly in the dim light, but he knew what their response was by the harsh laughter.

Someone prodded him. 'Look, boys and girls, a real stuck-up Hom.'

'He's real all right, Raphael.' Another prod. 'I bet if I shot him he'd bleed and die and everything.'

'There's no need for that. Just let me go. I'm just trying to keep out of the way of the pursuers.'

'Or are you just trying to lead them right to us, eh?'

'I didn't even know you were here. Hey, Eddie, what do I do?' The voice in his head was silent.

'Who's Eddie, then? Is there another one of you here? Gustav, scout round.'

Dave hit his head, wondering if the implant had shaken loose. 'Let me do that for you,' said one of them, and hit him hard.

'Where are you when I need you?' Dave whispered. He got another knock.

'Shut up, or I'll shut you up. The pursuers are still near by.' Someone taped over Dave's mouth. The scout returned, and reported that there was no one else, and that the pursuers were several blocks away.

'What shall we do, Raphael? Shall we shoot the bastard or just leave him tied up here to die?'

Now the tables were turned. Dave realised his life was in the hands of ruthless renegades. He struggled to explain himself, but they just hit him.

'We'll take him with us for the moment,' said the leader, to Dave's relief.

Raphael gave a signal and they moved out.

Dave thought the renegades' movements seemed laboured as if they were carrying extra weights, so he was able to keep up despite the tape over his mouth and the rope tying his hands behind his back. After an hour or so they stopped, and someone removed the tape making Dave yelp as his three-day-old beard was ripped out. His eyes watered. He breathed deeply. 'You didn't have to do that.'

'No, but it was fun.'

*

The sun went out today, Theo. You're running out of time.

We're already committed, Sal.

This one? I'm not so sure. I don't think he's right for the Pacific Project. He has so many weaknesses.

He'll be good, you'll see. There's a couple of things I want to check on the way, but whatever – he's the one.

Well, don't forget I warned you.

You always do, Sal. You always do.

And what have you done with the other one?

Who?

Chris.

Oh him. I didn't need him any more, so I disposed of him.

No, you didn't. He's on his way back up now on a cargo vessel. I checked the manifest.

If you knew, then why did you ask?

It's my job.

Sal, don't you ever wish you could come up with an idea – all of your own?

Pom tiddle pom tee pom.

Hmm.

There, Theo. See how you like it for once.

*

'Where are we?' They were sitting on the floor in some old condos to eat. They had retied his hands in front of him so he could eat if only messily. Dave didn't like the food – it wasn't like anything he'd had before. It tasted like it might be meat, but it was too solid, with too much texture – not quite homogeneous. 'What is this?'

'Shut up and eat your rat.'

'What's "rat"? The pursuers said something about a rat.' Someone kicked him. Dave tried to engage them in conversation. 'I never knew all this was here. All this old empty space.'

'Well, we know. The pursuers know. And now you know,' another one said. 'We like to keep it just between us and them. You're an unwanted complication.'

'How do you get food?'

'You'll see. If you don't shut up you'll *be* food.'

'I'm thirsty. Can I have a cup of tea?'

'*Tea*?'

Nearby, Dave could hear the hum of a low inertia freeway. He and Chris had avoided the freeways in their flight because once you're on one you're an easy target. None of the ones he'd seen while he was on the run down here in the deserted levels had been working, but this one was, and he realised they could now travel hundreds of kays in minutes. 'Why is this freeway still running when there is no one about to use it?'

'Buggered if I know, but it sure beats walking,' the leader said and rubbed the small of his back. 'It's two hundred kays.'

'Where are we going?'

'Home, the long way round. We've got unfinished business.'

'Where's home?'

'Shut the bonk up!' said one, and hit him across the face.

Another said, 'We come from between; our home is nowhere.'

Dave was quiet for a moment, then he exploded. 'You're *my* renegades!'

'We don't belong to any Hom, pal. You'd better…'

'You're the troop I had to pass sentence on. They let you go!'

'True, they let us go. Otherwise we wouldn't be here, would we?'

'Why did they let you go?'

'Tell him, Sheila,' said one.

'They just let us go. An official said it was an old Decision, twenty something something eight. Didn't mean much to us. They didn't seem very happy about it, but they did say they'd have him to shoot instead, whoever "he" is. Better him than me, I reckon.'

'Me! That's me! I didn't give a Decision on you, so I was automatically condemned in your place.'

'You do seem familiar.'

Something clicked in Dave's mind and he recognised the voice as that of the boy – the one Chris had said was a woman. The memory of Chris hit him almost physically, and it hurt more than what the renegades had done to him. 'Chris said you're a woman. Are you a woman?'

The whole troop burst out laughing, and made several coarse comments that he couldn't follow.

'Yes,' said the boy, as they put Dave on the low inertia free-way, 'I'm a woman.'

'Then will you *please* tell me, WHAT IS A WOMAN?'

Passive – 20

Which is a difficult question. Like the one Lloyd asked me. Like Lloyd.

Lloyd was in so many ways a remarkable man. But he would *not* thank me for saying so.

Once when we were talking he asked me, 'Jim, what *is* a man?' He meant it rhetorically. He knew I couldn't make a synthesis of my thoughts on the topic, even if I'd had any. 'Is a man defined by his chromosomes? Or is a man a set of physiological appendages? Or is a man defined by a set of behaviours – like groping women?'

Faced with Lloyd and the evidence he made manifest, none of these would do. I stumbled a few words but I realised he didn't expect me to say anything. He kindly let me subside.

The four of us had met him as Tony Lloyd, prospective landlord and flatmate. We were all in our final year of a physics degree at Imperial College. We wanted a flat within striking distance of the Piccadilly, District or Circle Lines that went to South Kensington, though anywhere on the London Underground or the overground would have done. After a few days looking we even considered buses!

We enjoyed the search – the daily papers, the college notice boards, phone calls, criteria, analyses, argument, visits, back to hall for drinks. We knew we'd find something: we had *faith*. Four prayerful third year students were better tenants than any number of rowdy ones, and we were looking early so we were at the head of the market. We each prayed about it twice a day at least, and we *knew* we would be guided. As it turned out we didn't get the guidance we wanted.

I had lived in digs for the first two years, in Mrs Cassell's house near Wandsworth Common. This redoubtable Scottish woman put up five students every year with the help of another full time lodger, Vic, and a woman who did breakfast on weekdays. Mrs Cassell had a full time job, as did Mr Cassell who was deaf and didn't help in the house. Vic had a full time job that involved driving ten hours a day. Mrs Cassell looked after us, Vic terrorised us, but they were both kind and did more for us than we deserved, for a rent that left us with some money for drinks. We had two good meals every day (three at weekends) plus supper, and all our washing and ironing done.

I was one of the first of her students ever to leave before graduating. I hated blotting her record and nearly didn't go, but I needed to prove I could look after myself. Dave and I had shared a room at Mrs Cassell's for one year; the others had lived in hall and in flats for the first two years. Sharing a flat with them seemed like a good manageable step for me to take.

Dave had a natural touch – he was the only one of us who could handle Vic. He'd been with the other two in hall in the first year and so he was also my bridge to them.

Rees looked like a Welsh goblin: short, bent over and bearded, making statements in outbursts or crooning in the presence of his favourite women. Toobs was less demonstrative than we were, except when it came to heavy rock. He and Rees would play air guitar to the hi-fi. They liked *Yes*, *Deep Purple* and *The Grateful Dead*. I didn't, but I hoped I could learn. Toobs did reviews and photos on rock concerts for the college mag. The only time I got him going was about *Def Leppard*, but my argument was a monotone of tinnitus against his genuine enthusiasm.

We had answered the ad, and visited Tony Lloyd in the flat which he'd only just bought. He seemed to be an impressive man, and claimed to be a cordon bleu cook – as it turned out he wasn't either. He was looking for four or more students to share the flat with him. We chatted for a while, and agreed on rent and terms.

On the journey home Rees said he had a really good feeling about this one. He was positive it was going to work out just fine. Rees said his feelings were always right, and we took faith from that too.

We moved in at the start of term. Lloyd was an accountant. He was larger than life, and larger than average. He spilled out of his suits and was nearly bald, reminding me of Humpty Dumpty. He bubbled with enthusiasm, in the early days while we were furnishing and equipping the flat, and he kept up a stream of ideas and weak jokes. Occasionally he would come up with some surreal use of language, at which point he would reinforce the Humpty Dumpty image by grinning and quoting the *Looking Glass* character: 'When I use a word it means what I choose it to mean. No more. No less.'

Everything went fine until a couple of weeks into term after a particularly harrowing lecture on quantum mechanics when he asked to speak to me. [It may help you to get a handle on Lloyd if I explain a bit about quantum mechanics. You see, in QM (as we called it) everything oscillates between states – up and down, positive and negative – active, passive and neutral, dare I say. The key thing is that you don't know what state it's in until you test it. It's a bit like holding a lottery ticket – it has a fixed probability of being the winning ticket; yours could be the winning one and it doesn't stop having that chance for you until you take it to the agent to run through their machine. I think Arthur's writing style is like that – he likes to leave things unspecified, let the readers make assumptions. And I don't expect you realised Belinda was Singaporean – like Lloyd, what does it matter?]

Sitting on the just-delivered second-hand couch, Lloyd wondered (hesitation) how we would react if he wore a skirt around the flat. I asked if that was likely. It was something he'd like to do, yes. I assured him that we were all Christians and so we were very tolerant.

The others were shocked. I reminded them that we were Christians and that we had to give a good witness. They said they'd pray about it.

The next day he appeared in a skirt. It was a dreadful sight. With all the tolerance in the world, he really didn't have the legs for it. The wig that was supposed to make him look feminine didn't even make him look female.

That weekend Toobs moved out. Rees moved into the small bedroom and locked the door. I know Dave had been on the phone to his parents and to his home church leader. I don't know what they said to each other, but he stayed. I think he was protecting me.

I suppose Mum's weird beliefs and the bizarre people that came with them had inoculated me against this sort of affront. To me, Lloyd (he wanted to be called Ann, but Lloyd was what most people called him) was an exotic person. Although I struggled to keep up, I consumed his constant flow of insight and advice. When he was confident of you he put what he thought was his best side forward: he giggled, teased, and made terrible puns. He had a favourite limerick which ran:

A transsexual guy from Khartoum
Took a lesbian up to her room
They were up half the night
Engaged in a fight
About who does what and with what and to whom

Over the next two years he repeated that delightedly – and often – but he also regaled me, and a few friends who dared to visit, with fantastic stories from his life. He said, among other things that: he'd been a leading sportsman; he had been a millionaire, twice, the second time in Brazil; he'd lost his millions, twice, and was now working on his third; he'd been a spy in Russia, caught and tortured; the Russians had sent him back. To use an old joke, they'd told MI5 'Your boy's arriving at Dover in August'. The

British asked when and they said, ‘On the 7th, 8th and 9th.’ The bits which arrived on the 9th were the bits he now didn’t want.

It didn’t really matter whether these were true, they were great stories.

A few weeks later Rees moved out and Clive (called Jenny) moved in. He/she filled his/her room with electronics and started recording a song, that he/she repeated over and over again in the vain hope that in one variant it might be good. He/she moved out and Maurice moved in.

Maurice was straight and needed cheap digs. He worked outdoors for the council. When he got home he would cut himself doorsteps off a loaf of wholemeal bread, superimpose waves of thick crunchy peanut butter, make a mug of coffee, run the bath, and lock himself in the bathroom for an hour.

Maurice moved out and Chris (called Chris) and Meeka moved in. Meeka was an actual woman, but she said she was a lesbian. Frequently they *were* up half the night engaged in a fight, and it *may* have been about who does what, and with what, and to whom.

Along with these Lloyd counselled a steady procession of visitors in various states of gender, mental stability and cosmetic proficiency.

They were all *saving for the op*. Only one of them was convincing. Geena dressed, made-up and had the voice. Chris/Chris had those too. But Geena had the talk, the perspective, the paradigm, the mannerisms. I suppose feminists would claim that there shouldn’t be a talk, a perspective, a paradigm, mannerisms; but they aren’t trying not to be a man. Geena was visiting from South Africa where she was a successful and rich businesswoman.

They were all unhappy people. Lloyd had been an abused son with an older and a younger sister. He trembled with fear of rejection every time someone new came along, and felt it even when it wasn’t there. They all hated themselves. Some, she explained, had not had the right hormones at critical times in the womb or in puberty, and in a real sense were women who hated the men’s bodies they were trapped in. Others just hated themselves.

They clung to her like a plank in a flood. Too often he was submerged beneath their panic.

Lloyd was the one who was available to them at all hours. It was him who answered the phone, who dashed out to counsel suicides, and who then sometimes didn't stop them.

Lloyd was the one they called when they needed help; but they never called her when they were feeling good.

Lloyd was the one who took a pharmaceutical cocktail every day, and who frequently winced in pain (from the operations that put him back together, he said – arthritis, I thought – they're not incompatible).

Lloyd was the one who helped a college friend of mine who had a nervous breakdown, who taught me the symptoms and what to do. Lloyd held the cushion while they pummelled. Lloyd knew when to leave them in a foetal corner, and when and how to draw them out.

Lloyd was the one who convinced me that there was no fate that dictated that I had to be a victim.

Lloyd said the total suffering in the world is always infinite. He should know.

Lloyd was the one who explained the difference between physiology and profound sexuality, and the difference between chromosomes and hormones.

Lloyd was the one who helped me when I was expelled from the church.

Lloyd was the one who went to shows with us, who took us round and got us laughing again.

Lloyd was the one who got me to stand straight, to strut my stuff, and to expect success and friendship – a sad irony for him, a new departure for me.

Lloyd knew the dirtier side of life. She knew it in others whom she helped as best she could. He knew it in himself every moment of every day.

He had been married to a woman she still loved. She had a son he missed. He said he hated the Russians for what they did, and at the same time she wished they'd finished the job properly.

She knew what a man was; 'and I ain't it,' he said.

He had been wise, kind, human and tolerant, when we had not.

He defied description and embodied complexity. In her life all answers became simplistic.

She was in so many ways a very remarkable man.

17

I wasn't the only one who was worried. Everyone was worried.

No, that's not true. Everyone was scared shitless. Sorry.

I had been counting the stars for some time – there were fewer nearly every rain, and I was going to talk to the Wise One about it. But that was nothing compared to what happened that day.

I know my place, and that's why I hadn't been to the Wise One earlier. But I also know that the gift I have is not only a great honour but an awesome responsibility. I'm probably the only person in the whole world who counts stars. Every reckoner knows the number of stars – why count them, you may say. I counted the stars to practise my gift. The initiates can count the sixteen steps of the summer sun, but only the reckoners and the Wise One can count the stars.

I remember the Wise One told me once that with my gift I can learn to foretell the day when the seasons change, and other, mystical things. People with these gifts are high in rank and may choose where to live and have any female they desire.

That's what he says, but in this at least he is wrong. I know it is a bad thing to think this, but I have the evidence of my life – I am not honoured by the tribes, and no female desires me. The Wise One said: 'Gundawoy, you are young. Be patient, it will come, but you must practise and learn.' So I counted the stars. It's all right for him: he can speak with Theo.

That day began like any other. The sun stepped on to the sky with its normal clang. Our tribe's women gathered herbs and fruits. Men hunted wallabies that day in the valley. It was a normal day. I had joined other young men in a goanna hunt. And then at the sun's tenth step, there was total darkness.

Women screamed. Children screamed. Men wailed. It was worse than night – black, no stars at all. Many minutes passed before someone lit a fire. Slowly we gathered around the fire from wherever we had been. Other tribes had lit fires – we could see the glow on the sky. We huddled around our fire, and wondered what this terror foretold.

The night in the afternoon lasted one step, and then day returned, warm and bright. The sun was where it should be, the birds sang, children laughed, women sighed in relief. But no one forgot. How could you forget – for one whole step night had conquered the sun.

The men were late back from their hunt – Jacko had tripped and broken his arm in the sudden night. They had to camp out for the night, and when they returned with two wallabies they had decided to call a Gathering of all the tribes. It seemed that the other tribes had decided to do the same thing. That day we waited in fear for the tenth step, and indeed night returned that afternoon, as it has done each day since.

We grew used to the night in the afternoon. Nothing terrible happened. No one could tell what the portent was. The Wise One came with the Wollemi tribe to the Gathering. He knew what it meant.

No one enjoys the Gathering. They are called only in times of great need.

The tribes trade easily by travelling to agreed places at the set times ordained by the reckoners. There they meet and swap whatever each has more of than they need. This is free trade. Each tribe has enough. Only when a tribe kills too many of their wards, or when they are careless and let a fire rage too far – only then is a special trade necessary to keep them away from other tribes' land. This is called managed trade, because somehow the tribe has to manage to get another tribe to trade with them. Sometimes tribes may exchange people – a tribe may have less girl children than it will need, or not enough hunters, or by accident or disease lose their medicine woman – then a tribe may call a special Gathering and any tribe with people or skills to spare may trade, and they can name their price. Tribe leaders have claimed huge prices. Always, in time, the reverse trade is needed and that is the time for revenge.

I think this is why the tribes hate each other. We seldom fight each other, for that is forbidden – the Wise One says we are too few and no life may be wasted. The Wise One says free trade is best.

The Gatherings are usually held at the Great Lake, because several of the tribes' lands meet there. That is where the rivers flow to. The rivers are in the middle of the tribes' land because they use them for travelling. I have heard that in the past, when the tribes have thought of fighting, people have suggested making the boundaries along the rivers because they can be defended. Who would be foolish enough to have their border along a river?

For a Gathering each tribe sends five men and five women. For the distant tribes it takes up to ten days to travel to the Gathering, so the tribe is without them for up to twenty five days. I was lucky indeed to be at the Gathering – usually Jacko, our reckoner, attends Gatherings but he had his broken arm and couldn't travel.

The ten from our tribe set off on the eighth day after the call. We arrived with several other tribes. Already there were arguments between some men, and some women taunted each other. But all shared the fear of the night in the afternoon. No one knew what it meant, or why it was happening. No tribe had done anything terrible to deserve such a thing.

The Wollemi tribe was the last to arrive. They were late for the Gathering, which is forbidden. But when they arrived the reason was clear. They had carried the Wise One the whole way, so the five day journey had taken eleven days even though they travelled by the river that flows through their land. The Wise One was very ill, as everyone could see. Three tribes had brought medicine people, and they went together to look at him. But of course the Wise One had taught them everything they knew – what could they do?

Then everyone knew what the night in the afternoon meant. Many people cried for the Wise One. Others cried in fear. The Wise One said he would die within sixty days. A reckoner from another tribe explained that time in the traditional way – that is the time it would take a hunter to walk around the world and return to his starting place.

The people asked, 'What shall we do? Who will judge between us? Who will heal our burns and cure our illnesses? Who will umpire the football?'

The Wise One had travelled with his garb off, but when the people cried he put on his clothes and his great crown and said, 'Behold, Wise Cam!' The people were quiet in the presence of Theo, as bespoken by the Wise One's garb. Then he said, 'Theo has spoken. Another will come. Wisdom will be restored.'

The people were encouraged, but those who cried for the Wise One himself were not consoled. I felt downcast for the loss of the friend I knew, and yet joy for the new age that was to come.

A woman asked the Wise One if this was indeed the reason for the night in the afternoon. He said, 'When the new Wise One is installed and fully implemented, then the sun will run its course without missing a step. Theo says it. But there will be no more rains to mark the sets of seven until the new Wise One arranges it.'

Then I gathered my courage and said: 'Will the stars return also?' The people muttered. Some shouted at me to be quiet. Others looked at the Wise One and asked if the stars were indeed disappearing.

The Wise One looked at me strangely. Then he waited. He muttered something like *'I can't keep my eyes on everything, you know.'* Then he said, 'It is true, the stars are disappearing. The new Wise One will implement new procedures, and the stars will return.'

One man spoke up, and said his grandfather had told him of the time the Wise One had come to us, and that someone had gone to meet him and bring him to the tribes.

The Wise One said, 'That is true, and so it must be again. You must choose one to go to the sky and welcome the new Wise One. This is a great honour for the one chosen and for their tribe. It is an honour, but it is also dangerous and difficult, not to mention very confusing.'

Immediately the tribes began to argue. Some refused to risk a hunter. Others fought for the honour. Many hours were spent in fruitless bargaining and trials. In the end they agreed on only one thing – to ask the Wise One.

The Wise One was very tired. He was also angry that the tribes could not decide. He muttered something about *'thirty years wasted,'* and something else about *'good luck to the next guy,'* but much of what he said was in his own sacred language. In the end he declared, 'If the tribes cannot decide on one man for this honour, then I will not decide on one man either. There shall be three: Calabanat, hunter from the Bulga tribe; Gundawoy, reckoner from the Lithgow tribe; and Tidda from the Wollemi tribe.'

The people were amazed – we were all young and untried. For such honour to be given to us… I was amazed too, especially as I had hoped to court Tidda but had not yet dared to speak to her. She is the most beautiful girl in the world.

That is why we three came here to meet you.

18

Of course I was surprised, yeah, 'cos it was a sensible fu'n decision for once. I told them, while they were banging on about who should go – I told them I could do the job on my own. I mean how fu'n difficult can it be? Go to the sky, find some fu'n guy, bring him back. Y'know, it's not as if it's fu'n death defying.

When the Wise One called me out 'n' that, 'n' Gundawoy 'n' Tidda, I told them again: 'I can do it. I can do it on my own. I don't need any fu'n softies or women slowing me down.' But they didn't listen. Well, I'll bring you down, 'n' then they'll fu'n listen.

Of course, when I thought about it, I realised it wasn't so bad. I mean, she's a good looking girl, 'n' I'll need a woman soon. It'll be a good chance to see, y'know, if she'll do.

But that guy, Gundawoy, he's a fu'n loser – fur 'n' feet, a loser. If he hit me over the head with a club, his fu'n arm would break. I'm serious. I'm not fu'n joking.

So we started to prepare for the journey. Gundawoy said we should each carry these fu'n huge packs: food, drink, camp gear, all sorts. I said: 'For fuck's sake, we don't need all that. It'll slow us down.' So I said, y'know, 'Look, I'll hunt on the way. Tidda can cook. It'll be fine. It's not as if we're fu'n walking round the world or anything, 'n', y'know, it's only four days' walk from here, 'n' I know most of the way, 'cos I live out that way, 'n' there'll be no rain, so we won't need no fu'n camp gear.'

Well, you should have heard Gundawoy whinge. It's true y'know, I'm not fu'n joking, he went: 'What if someone gets hurt? What if this goes wrong, what if that?' Well, it gets so much I hit him, smack, in the face 'n' a fu'n good one too, in the eye, 'n' he crumpled up like he's dying, 'n' some of the guys came in as if to keep us apart, but there was no need, 'cos he wasn't going to fight anyone, 'n' she looked at me kind of strange, so I felt pretty good.

To keep him sweet, well, y'know, we had to walk together for eight days or more, we took some stuff in fu'n packs, 'n' Tidda said she'd need to take a fu'n bag anyway (though I didn't need to so why did she?) but maybe she was just being nice to the softie, so we ended up with a few bits, but that was okay, 'n' some of it has been useful, though don't fu'n tell him I said so.

The day before we set off, the men 'n' me from the tribe 'n' a few others are playing football, when all of a sudden, y'know, like, there was this noise sort of inside my fu'n head. Well, see, more of, well, it's, like, some of the other men later said it was music, like sort of singing, lots of voices, getting higher – daa, daa, da da da, daa, daa daaa – like that. We talked about it later, the men, 'n' we all saw, like a bone thrown into the air, 'n' spinning, 'n' changing, 'n' it was fu'n weird, y'know.

With all this I felt, like *wow*! in my head, 'n' all of a sudden I had all these great ideas.

We all came out of it about the same time, 'n' people were grinning all over the fu'n place. Then everybody said they'd got this fu'n great idea, 'n' everybody started, y'know, speaking at once. Well, no one could say anything 'cos everyone had a fu'n idea, 'n' there was all this fu'n noise, 'n' then people stopped grinning 'n' started shouting for everyone to shut up, because they had this great idea. Then someone hit someone else, 'n' I hit Bazza 'cos he wouldn't fu'n listen, 'n' fights broke out all over.

There was so much noise the Wise One woke up – he sleeps a lot these days, 'n' doesn't do much else, so it's just as well he's going if you ask me – well, he woke up 'n' managed to get us to shut up by putting on his garb, 'n' that made him shout louder than all of us, so we shut up for a while, 'n' Stevo explained what had happened except he got all excited 'n' got it wrong 'n' started telling about his great idea, 'n' then everyone else started too 'n' the Wise One had to shout loud again, 'n' he got really pissed off, I mean *pissed off*, 'n' was giving us all this stuff about... well who gives a shit?

In the end he made this strange statement, something like: 'Theo wishes to apologise for the last announcement – please do not adjust your sex,' or something, 'n' then he got us to go in some order 'n' each of us tells his idea, 'n' the women say they had ideas too, but they went off in their own group.

I can't remember many of the ideas, but mine was the best – to use a vine strung across a bent thin branch like this to, y'know, shoot off another bit of wood to kill animals, though it's, y'know, hard to explain just like that, but other people had good ideas too, like someone said about how we'd tried to get round pieces of wood to carry stuff on but, y'know, how it didn't work – well, this guy said to cut holes in the middle 'n' put some strong wood through them 'n' that's how to carry things on them. Now that *is* a fu'n good idea.

Some softie came up with some words, y'know, that people said was great poetry, though I didn't see it myself, 'n' there were some good songs 'n' things. Gundawoy's idea was – get this – 'I think therefore I am'. What fu'n' use is that? Everybody else has these great ideas 'n' he comes up with that! I just fu'n laughed when he said that was his great idea. He's got no idea has he. No fu'n idea.

Well, it took the rest of the day to get everybody to say their ideas, so after I'd given my idea me 'n' a few others went off 'n' played football while the others got their ideas out, 'n' then we ate, sat around the fires for a while 'n' then went to sleep.

The next morning the Wise One came out to see us off. Gundawoy said to him, y'know the way he does, 'Wise One, I saw a star come back last night. Is this a sign?' like that. The Wise One paused for a minute like he does, 'n' then he said, 'Yes, Gundawoy, it is the start. Now hurry up, you three. The new Wise One is waiting for you at the sky, and we've got a lot to talk about.'

Well, he gets on my tits, y'know. It's fu'n true y'know, so I whispered to him, 'Counting stars again are you, Gundawoy? Try counting your black eyes,' 'n' he said, 'Try counting to ten, knucklehead,' 'n' I said, 'My knuckles in your head,' 'cos he ain't so smart, 'n' I went off to finish preparing.

Then we were all ready. Tidda had her hair done strangely, 'n' said that it was one of the ideas one of the women had, 'n' that the idea was called Bob – if you ask me it's fu'n stupid to give a name for an idea. Everyone came over, 'n' the Wise One spoke to Gundawoy 'n' to Tidda, 'n' he checked with me that I knew where to go – like I'd fu'n forget – 'n' he checked with us that we all knew what to do 'n' what to say, 'n' then we left.

19

After a while we got on quite well. Sure, Calabanat and Gundawoy argued a lot, but you expect that from boys, and I found it kind of nice, 'cos they were, y'know, fighting over *me*.

We had a long hard walk and we helped each other. Even though Calabanat kept saying how he hated having a girl slowing him down, he always stopped to help me over difficult bits. He's such a hunk. It's mad being this close to him. The other girls will be spewing.

Gundawoy's so cute. A few times he helped me, and Calabanat got dirty and pushed him out the way. And if Gundawoy did something nice for me, Calabanat soon after that ripped into him with some jibe or other. But Gundawoy got used to it, and we would smile to each other, him and me, when it happened – that made Calabanat even more filthy.

This all settled down within a day or so, and we started to enjoy the journey much better. It's magnificent up here – just *mag*nificent! Several plants I don't recognise – I'm collecting samples for the women back home. They'll be rapt. I'd never been this way before, 'cos my tribe lives up Dubbo way, almost the other end of the world. The other tribes always do the pick-ups from the sky for the Wise One. Of course our men have a proud record in the Tribal Games – this year we were losing finalists in… but you don't want to hear about that, I expect.

We always rested during the night in the afternoon, and that gave us a chance to eat whatever was left from the previous day. After that, Calabanat would start looking about for what animals were in the area. He was incredible. Just *in*credible! Each day before the last step we'd stop and set up a camp. Gundawoy would start the fire, then it was down to me to be ready for when Calabanat came back. He always had some prize catch or other. He swaggered in with a cockatoo the first evening, and told us all about the hunt and his sling technique. He was *so* proud. Gundawoy just kept quiet. He said he wasn't hungry, but I said he should eat to keep his strength up – Calabanat cacked himself when I said that – but he did.

The next morning, I was clearing up when a huge spider rushed out. It was I mean *huge*. I screamed heaps, dropped everything and froze. It was a dreadful thing, all black and hairy, with its fangs waving in front of it, ready to strike. I tell you, I was packing it! Anyway, the boys ran up. Calabanat stood on the spider, while

Gundawoy ran straight to me and held me. Gundawoy was angry – he said it was only a trapdoor spider, and harmless. Calabanat said right back, 'It might have been a funnel web. Anyway it's definitely harmless now.' And then Gundawoy said, 'One day your ignorance will get us killed,' but Calabanat was pleased with himself and strutted off. Gundawoy is *really* sensitive, isn't he – he was soft, and extra kind to me – he said lots of people were frightened by spiders.

We reached some ruins from the oldest times. They were just *ama*zing! Even Calabanat was interested. Gundawoy said the Wise One had taken him to see things like this before near his home. The ruins were places where people had lived and traded. He pointed out some of the tracks we'd been on – the level bits – he said they came from that time as well. He saw something under a rock. They lifted the rock off it between them. It was soft and red with strange markings on it – two golden arches. Gundawoy said he didn't know what it was, but that it must have come from the oldest times too. The oldest ones must have been incredible to make things that could last that long. The Wise One said the whole world used to be covered with these things, but that was before they were all cleared away in the beginning. I said, 'That doesn't make sense, does it?' but Gundawoy didn't answer – he was miles away again.

As we climbed we enjoyed the scenery, right. It, like, calmed the boys, and they stopped bickering. Look at it, it's just *fabulous*. Usually we're so busy just surviving. But on a walk like this, like, you have the chance just to watch it, to see it: there's the gum trees, and they depend on the wattles to prepare the soil Gundawoy said; the ferns and the small plants need the shade, and make the ground ready for the fires they all need; the wandering jew along the creek banks keeping the fires at bay so the rabbits have a place to live – it makes you think, doesn't it, about, y'know... Well, Gundawoy thinks so. He's heaps cute, don't you think?

It's good to have you to talk to. Neither of them, like, talks much. If Calabanat says anything it's about hunting. Gundawoy thinks a lot. He thinks about all sorts of things. Do you know what he said to me? We had made camp after we passed over the high ridge. He'd been pointing out all sorts of small birds that you don't see unless you stop and look. I had just said to him about nature and that. Then he said to me, 'Why did Theo choose us?' Just like that, right out of the blue. So I said to him, 'How should I know?' So he said to me, 'Were we were born to do this, or is it because of what we've done? Did Theo always know it would be us or did he decide just then?'

Isn't that a weird thing to say? Calabanat would never say something like that. Well, I didn't know what to say, so we both sat by the fire for a while until Calabanat came back with two rabbits, full of the chase and full of himself.

But it did set me thinking – about those two. Y'know. The women at the Gathering said to me that those two are likely to be the highest status men in the world when they get older, and they both want *me*. But it's my choice. That is so cool.

Calabanat is heaps hunky, and he's a great hunter. He's strong and brave and decisive. He fights well, and he wins at all the sports. He'll be chief of his tribe one day and probably Most Valuable Player too. The other girls think he is *so* hot. When we were selected they got me in a huddle and they were all giggling about me and him being together, but I think that's immature.

Gundawoy is bright, he can be tender and sensitive. He is unusual like that. I am sure he would not beat his woman. Only a few reckoners have ever counted the stars – the chief reckoner can't – but Gundawoy has already, and he has mastered lots of skills from the Wise One. He'll be chief reckoner for sure, and the chief reckoner never needs for anything. But he's *such* a dork.

I wish they wouldn't squabble though. They'll both be good men, but they're *so* immature!

We stopped near a waterfall with a deep pool. It's a wonderful place. I wanted to be ready for you. It's such a great honour to meet you at the sky, to see you before anyone else. I got up before the first step. I went to the pool and dived in. It's a fantastic feeling, first thing in the morning, and my skin tingled.

First step is always such a wonderful moment – all the birds sing, the kookaburras laugh, everything's fresh. I absorbed the moment. Then I saw Calabanat on the shore by my cloth. He'd been looking at me in the pool. He had taken his cloth off. He was rampant. I tell you it was obvious what he wanted. He just waded in. Well, I turned to, like stone – I just could not move. He grabbed me and tried to take me right there. Then he carried me out. I was shouting at him to let me go, but that just made him more excited. Luckily, he is not very big, and he couldn't take me, with me squirming, right?

Suddenly, Gundawoy rushed up and knocked him off me. He was ropeable. He got filthy at him, shouted all sorts of things. Gundawoy threw punches at him, but they just bounced off. Calabanat looked furious. His face became the same colour as his manhood. Calabanat raised his fist and I thought Gundawoy was stuffed. But then he just marched off.

We haven't talked to each other since then.

It was frightening, y'know, being powerless, like, to stop him and then I would have been Calabanat's woman. Good job Gundawoy saved me.

Which one of them will I choose? You must know… the women at the Gathering… forgive me… they told me… I have been chosen to be yours.

No.

No.

NO.

NO!

Neutral Chapter 3

Arthur sat in the lounge chair provided and watched her thrusting her sweating thighs up and down around the glistening black latex. She with eyes glazed, her mouth open, breathing in gasps; he with mild impatience. Eventually his turn came. Seen from above the seat of the exercise bike took on a quite different form. It worked its magic and in minutes his balls were completely crushed.

Arthur got half way through the article – *What do men feel during sex? by Wendy Fleming* – in the *Cleo* he'd picked up from the pile by the entrance, but then he got too hot to read.

Only another seventeen minutes to go. Behind him the step class had just started. Barbie was leading them through the warm up, pumping her arms, stepping vigorously, and then doing stretches, accompanied by *Money Money Money*. The beat of the music gave the metronome for his pedalling. In the weights room muscle-bound hulks – their waists belted around future hernias – with bulging chests, bulging shoulders, arms, thighs – bulging feet probably – pumped away on iron bars, or strained the arteries in their necks. Some men were doing the same.

The air-conditioning couldn't remove the turgid pervasion of effort. The pictures on the walls glared with 'attitude' at anyone who couldn't tow a truck bare handed or without the use of coconut oil. Impossibly long-legged women with impossibly slender waists bulged biceps out of the computer-altered pictures with captions like *determination*. Two young women came to see whether they wanted to join the gym. They hovered near the entrance peeping in with their arms folded across their chests.

A pair worked with a weights bar on arm exercises. In turn, one 'encouraging' the other to give birth to just one more rep (come on! push! push! puuush!), providing the touch of support on the elbows to stave off dislocation.

A young woman stubbed out a cigarette before she followed her sister (Arthur had decided they were sisters) into reception. They paid their day fees. They had similar oval faces, with blonde hair. The elder, the smoker, looked shapely in her uniform of a burgundy knee-length skirt and white blouse. The other was wearing a micro-skirt and T-shirt, heavy black shoes and coloured leggings which accentuated how skinny she was. They left their handbags at reception and went to change. There was a classic case of sibling rivalry, Arthur thought. The older one smoked, he was sure, in the belief that it would make her thin and attractive, while the younger one wanted to be popular and attractive like her elder sister.

Sixteen minutes to go. Barbie was hopping over her step to a funk version of *Yesterday*. On the stair machines in front of him a row of bottoms oscillated hypnotically in his face. The woman immediately in front waggled her buttocks at him through sheer girl-school-green. Her legs were darkly tanned except for a hole in her sparkling pose leggings which showed a patch of paper-white skin. Next to her a fashion statement in sapphire and salmon bounced lightly in time to her ponytail. In the small of her back a darkness in the fluoro told of toil, and pointed to her shorts and another smudge. Above her the fan panted. Arthur checked – still fifteen and a half minutes to go. His gaze wandered about the room and then rested on her again. As she worked her way to the top of the Empire State Building she pushed on the supports, her wrists outwards, her shoulder blades making a cleavage that ran like a droplet down the length of her back, and disappeared along with her G-string. Her sweaty ponytail slapped and stuck and invited the mind to wander.

Next to her a woman in her fifties with a large-floral-pattern outfit finished and took a drink of water from her cycling bottle. Her waist and hips were modest, but above the neck line of her elasticated leotard an up-welling of fat submerged her wishbone. Her place was taken by a pile of a man in skimpy shorts and a sweatband, who slumped forward and powered out of the blocks on his way to a bad back.

The beat of the class was still the same. Barbie was encouraging her class by singing along *Let me take you by the hand and lead you through the streets of London...*

Two bikes away a stocky man in stubbies gingerly stepped on and started pedalling. He acknowledged Arthur with a nod, and then gazed forward at the row of waving buttocks. Two days later (fourteen minutes as the caesium atom decays), Arthur went to talk to him. 'G'day, Geoff. Howyadoin'?'

'Not so bad thanks, Art. How are yas?'

'Good. How's the back?'

'Still cactus, mate.'

'The factory going to keep your job open?'

'Buckley's! I get workers comp, and "sorry but we automated your job".'

'Are you still bludging around at home all the time, then?'

Geoff set his jaw and retorted, 'It's dead boring to just sit around at home all day, and people think you're a bludger. The physio says I can't go back to work for another month yet, even if there was a job. Even when people don't say anything, I can feel it, y'know. "There's nothing wrong with him." They don't know what it's like to just walk along and suddenly your leg collapses from under you.'

'Just kidding, mate. Just kidding,' said Arthur taking half a step back. 'What you need's a wheelchair.'

'Yeah, then maybe Dutch wouldn't be such a monkey on my back about the cooking, eh? I'm trying but I'm still at the boiled egg stage and she wants fucking cordon blue.'

'How is the joy of your life?'

Geoff stopped pedalling. 'Would you believe it, she's getting analysed.'

'*Analysed*?'

'Yeah, mate.'

'Probably the best thing for her. Will they lock her up?'

'No, worse luck. It's some early experience, rebirthing, repressed memories, women's business stuff. It's a good job she did those computer courses. They were a good investment, but even though we were on only my money for those years, now with me laid up she's earning enough for the two of us, with enough to pay for her sessions.'

'Is it doing her any good?'

'Mate, she's starting from a low base. Rhinos beware, y'know. While she was studying I was, y'know, well, looking forward to when she'd kind of, well, take over, and we could be a team. I mean I was never going far at the factory. But now this stuff…'

'What?'

'She's getting really aggressive, but. And she says she's *learning lots about herself.*' Geoff looked as if he'd swallowed something unpleasant. 'She buckets her dad and her teachers and that. She says they're all to blame. She won't say what for but.'

'*Whatever your problem…*,' Arthur started the comedian's catchphrase.

'*…there's always someone else to blame*,' Geoff finished much to Arthur's surprise. 'Yeah, I know, but this is different, mate. I've asked her, but she won't talk about it at all. Only, since she's started on it she's…'

'What?'

'Oh, nothin'.'

He started pedalling again. Arthur was shocked at the deep feelings Geoff had shown, and the openness with which he'd spoken. He decided to move on to safer ground – Rugby League. 'What do you think of Norths's chances of making the finals in the footy next year?'

'Norths? Nah. Norths'll bomb like they always do. Brisbane, Canberra, The Dogs, Manly, Easts… Auckland have got a good side. And I'd say Wests and the Sharks to make up the eight.'

'Five bucks says Norths.'

'Five bucks? Okay.'

'What about the Swans in the football, eh?'

'Oh, are yas into Aussie Rules?'

'Too right. Mate, you should go to a match – it's a top game.'

'Yeah? I always thought it was a game for pooftas from Victoria.'

'I'm a big rap for it live. It's a sort of cross between ballet and all-in wrestling.' Geoff blinked non-committally. 'It's got just as much violence as the other football codes.' Geoff looked a bit more interested. 'Anyway, I'll cop you later, mate.'

'Yeah, see yas.'

Arthur left Geoff to his pedalling and then as he passed the line of treadmills he spotted the two 'sisters'. The elder folded her arms but could not hide the bulges around the edges of her overtight plain lycra shorts. The younger girl's upright slender figure merged smoothly with her black and scarlet leotard. 'Liars,' said Arthur to the outfits.

He went into the changing room and got undressed. He was the only one there, but on the way to the shower, he still gave his cruets a tug. It wasn't that he was ashamed or anything. No, of course not. And size doesn't matter. It was just, well, John, the general manager of a construction company, had commented once in the showers – what had he said? 'It's not the size of the holster, it's the calibre of the weapon – which is just as well for you, Arthur.' Bastard!

He had to get back to pick up Sophie from school in time for her doctor's appointment. On his way out he stopped to watch the class. *Thump tread... thump tread.* This was Barbie's 'hi impact' step class that climaxed at one hundred and fifty beats a minute. Mostly they used the normal synthesised dance music – street, bop, funk, plus the off-key wailing pop music. *thump tread... thump tread.* No song, no music, no ballad was so slow or profound that it could not be put on a synthesiser, given the required backing track and set at one hundred and fifty beats a minute. When one instructor used *Ode To Joy*, reset at the right tempo, the girls at reception were dead impressed.

As Arthur watched and *Greensleeves* played, the polymorphic class moved as one to Barbie's instructions and merged. [*two taps... over... faw maw*] bare flat rolling stomachs bounced. [*round... single, single, double*]. Shaved-red, fleshy thighs [*biceps... right knee, whoo!*] snapped and wobbled as they thrust lithe ample buttocks up and over the steps. [*indecision... faw, threee, tsieoo*] Nascent fortified breasts swung a counterpoint to the music.

It had got so that some songs, used in every step class, were not complete without the *thump* as the whole class stepped up. So Tom Jones sang:

If I only thump *what I could* thump *to make you make you* thump *me.*

Barbie, with close cropped, bleach blonde hair and painted-on tan, glided through the movements with effortless precision. The class followed earnestly. As usual there was someone at the back, always a bloke, who had lost the plot, his feet a lone voice to leaven the rhythmically correct.

Arthur saw Teri in the crowd and watched with a satisfied smile as she moved elegantly up, over, round, and across the step. Teri worked on reception, joined classes whenever she could and instructed some sessions herself. She was the curvy side of slender. In the men's changing room, the two instructors, Barbie and Teri, were sometimes compared. Everyone loved Teri's pert flirtatiousness; Barbie was held in awe. Barbie had just competed in a body shaping contest [unofficial motto: IF YOU'VE STILL GOT BREASTS YOU AREN'T REALLY TRYING]. From the competition pictures that were on proud display at reception, she had muscles everywhere, long tight legs and not an ounce of fat. The ones who pumped iron openly admired her. But when John had said, 'Fancy fucking that. It'd be like shagging bricks,' several others had agreed – very readily it seemed. 'Christ, Arthur, you've got bigger tits than she has.' They'd agreed with that too.

Arthur sometimes chatted with the staff. Those two both had the required receptionist smile, but Barbie always stopped at a brief

'Hullo, Arthur.' Teri engaged in cut and thrust (ahem) and held her own (cough) in repartee. They both allowed compliments to bounce off them, though Teri did it with a smile, while Barbie would point to some invisible offence, usually on her hips. Arthur recalled what Barbie had looked like two years earlier – she had been beautiful enough to arouse the dead. Now she won competitions. She was 'fabulous', 'fantastic', 'incredible', sometimes 'gorgeous', but never 'beautiful'. What a loss.

However both Teri and Barbie said they were jealous of Dominique. Dominique was a model – tall, an elegant mover with a winning smile, blonde, and, of course, size ten. She had long legs that grew in smooth ascension to the tops of her lycra shorts. She had a flat stomach and small breasts. Her face was smooth, her eyebrows were slender and fair, and her nose was small and pert. Light red lipstick and a touch of blusher perfected the promise of a paedophile experience with pubic hair.

She didn't talk much, and Belinda reported the opinion from the ladies changing room that she was up herself. Arthur had spoken to Dominique a few times at the gym, when they cycled nowhere side by side. She was a charming girl who talked freely and intelligently about herself and her job. She said she didn't like to flaunt herself so she kept quiet mostly. She didn't tell people she was a model – she was in 'publishing and promotion'. Her life was a lie upon a lie: every day to pump up her ego she constructed the deceit that she was not ugly after all. Then she could go out and strut her stuff. She said she was jealous of Barbie. 'But you are a very beautiful woman,' he'd said. 'Thank you,' she'd said and he knew the compliment had bounced off.

He'd even (he hadn't told Belinda) had coffee with her one morning after gym. Dominique had happily agreed, saying, 'Yes of course, I'd love to. It's a lovely spot. And anyway, I trust you.' Arthur found that profoundly depressing.

Arthur left the gym to fetch Sophie from school for her appointment. Barbie's class had reached the warm down. People, chests heaving, fetched towels to lie on. It had clearly been a good workout. Men sweated; women perspired; Barbie merely glowed.

Arthur took Sophie by the hand and led her into the consulting room. The doctor greeted them at the door with a warm smile and they all sat down, Sophie on the bed swinging her legs. Arthur was surprised to find himself sitting down opposite a full-bodied woman in her mid-thirties, with rich brown permed hair, long eyelashes, and big brown eyes.

Arthur mumbled a 'Good morning, Doctor,' and wondered how to start. He noticed she had a deeply made-up face. She had a small mouth lined with bright red lipstick – the action took place in the middle, and even when she was happy there was a stationary line on either side where her smile should be. His eyes fell to her cleavage that was partly obscured by a neck scarf. She had surprisingly fair skin after the light tan of her face. From what he could see her bra made the most of only modest endowments, but he wasn't sure. The top two buttons of her blouse were undone and the third button was half way through the button hole. At each breath the button looked as though it might pop open. The effect was mesmerising, so Arthur didn't listen properly.

She started. 'Your GP has written to me already with the blood test results. Firstly, let me assure you that Sophie's not ill: she hasn't got a virus, or any sickness, or anything like that. The test results are unusual, however, and that's why he suggested you should come to see me.'

She absent-mindedly did up the button, and Arthur re-entered the room. 'He probably explained that I'm an endocrinologist, which means that I specialise in hormones. Hormones are chemicals that the body produces naturally all the time. They act as messengers. They organise everything we do: eating, our moods, sleeping. The balance of those hormones dictates how we feel, what metabolism we've got, and to some extent it even dictates what we do. So you can see hormones are very important to us.

‘Now, Sophie,’ she continued, ‘what I’m going to do is to examine you…’ She got Sophie to take off her dress. Arthur watched her, initially like a hawk, and then with growing mystification.

As she bent over Sophie, her blouse fell forward, and again Arthur’s eyes were trapped. ‘What on earth are you looking for in there?’ He wondered who he was talking to.

‘I’m just checking that Sophie hasn’t got distorted glands that could be affecting her production of specific hormones. Most of those glands are in the main organs of the body. I’ll have to run some blood tests too, but the ones I’m particularly interested in are the glands associated with the sex organs.’

After a bit more poking around, the doctor told Sophie to get dressed. She’d kept her relaxed the whole time. She then took a very large sample of blood (Arthur thought). ‘Okay. Now, Sophie, I’d just like to ask you a few questions. Just say whatever you think – there are no right and wrong answers here. How old are you?’

‘Nine and a half,’ said Sophie very softly.

The doctor asked a few questions about her school and her teachers, what subjects she liked best, what games she liked and Sophie started chatting more easily. They got on to the subject of her schoolmates, and Sophie became subdued again. ‘They don’t like me very much,’ she said. ‘They say I’m too floppy, and they’re always teasing me about my dresses. Well, I don’t like what they wear either, but I don’t make a thing of it. They like dressing like boys. And they’re so rough and violent.’

‘Who are? The boys?’

‘Oh, they are, of course. Though some of them are cute. But I meant the other girls. They call me…’

‘Hmm?’

‘They call me… Danny.’

‘Hmm?’

‘Y’know, Danny De Vito…’

‘Hmm?’

‘…because he’s short, fat and ugly!’

Arthur was completely taken aback by this. He started to protest but a tiny gesture from the doctor stopped him. She looked solemnly at Sophie for a few moments who was close to tears and looking at her feet. 'Sophie, you're not fat, you're not even overweight. You're just shield-chested. But if you're worried, drink plenty of water and make sure you eat fairly often – eat some fruit when you're hungry – that way your body won't feel it needs to store up food as fat when you do eat. I know it sounds strange but that's what the supermodels do – try it, you'll see. And if the tests confirm my thoughts, we'll give you something to make you taller. And as for being ugly, Sophie, I'm the only ugly person around here.'

'You! You're not ugly! Don't be silly!'

'Why, thank you, Sophie, what a lovely thing to say!'

That was profound, thought Arthur, and considered the doctor in a new light. Then he lost focus again and stared at her legs that she had crossed under her knee length pinstriped skirt. They were a fine pair of legs, he decided, as her nylons brushed again. Short, true, and not elegant, but solid – full of hope and forgiveness.

He thought to himself: she's, she's... oh, what's the word?

When he couldn't think of the word he returned his attention to the consultation. There were quite a few more questions and then the doctor indicated she'd finished and thanked Sophie for her answers. 'What was all that about?' said Arthur crossly. 'I came to you to find out why she's lacking in energy, and you just talk about her school.'

'Sophie has very low levels of testosterone and everything she's told me is consistent with that. Does she have a good sense of direction?' Arthur shook his head. The doctor nodded another confirmatory fact into place. 'Has her behaviour changed much recently?'

'I've only known her for the last five years or so. Her mother and I married two years ago. She's always loved her dolls. She's become quieter and more withdrawn recently. Anyway, I thought men have testosterone, not women.'

'We all have all of the hormones. They do different things in men and women, and they do the same things to different extents. We have different levels. It's very complex. But as I say there's nothing to worry about. Well, I'll run the tests, and we'll talk again when I get the results. We mainly have to find out why she lacks testosterone. My examination, the subjects she's good at and the ones she's bad at, what she enjoys and what she doesn't – it's all consistent with one possible cause. Maybe we can change it – maybe not.'

They stood. She said pleasantries to Sophie, who smiled warmly to her new friend. On the way out, she drew Arthur to one side. 'We should have the test results in a couple of weeks. In the meantime I can give you a simple explanation for your daughter's behaviour – she's depressed.'

'*Depressed*? She's too young to be depressed!'

'They start young these days, I'm afraid. Not medically depressed. She's depressed in the popular sense – very fed up. I think she just doesn't know how to get out from under. Just make sure she gets plenty of energy in her food, especially a good breakfast, and give her lots of support with her playground problems. Hopefully she'll get over it soon. And, as I say, if the results confirm my thoughts, we'll be able to help her in several ways.'

They spoke a little longer and she recommended a book to read if he was interested. Arthur was still not convinced, and he was unsettled by all the unanswered questions, but the doctor said to wait until the test results came back. Arthur decided he couldn't get any more out of her for the moment so he shook her hand, thanked her and left. As he did so Arthur noticed the blouse button was half undone again.

When they got home Belinda was writing her report and therefore not to be disturbed. The news was on while Arthur got meals for each of them.

'...but the UN seems helpless in the face of determined aggression from the Serbs, and the Muslims appear to think their best chance is to stand and fight.' A lower than expected December unemployment rate surprised analysts today. At a seasonally adjusted eight point seven per cent it is the lowest for a third of a decade. The highlight of the figures was a net fifty seven thousand increase in part time jobs and sixteen thousand loss of full time jobs. These reflect the continuing trend of a decrease in employment in the manufacturing sector, and a large increase in services industries. For the fourth month running most of the new jobs – both part time and full time – went to women. The number of long term unemployed rose slightly. Now sport, and in the test match, Australia piled on the runs before declaring at 507 for 6. In the hour before stumps England lost the wickets of...

Sophie seemed to have perked up from her visit to the doctor. She strolled into the kitchen chewing a banana, and chatted with Arthur about her afternoon at school. She described a few of her friends. He was struck by the warm descriptions after the grief they seemed to cause her. She became bubbly about a group assignment – inspired by a class discussion of the government's decision to log the Wollemi National Forest – to do a painting of a forest scene. Apparently one group led by a boy called Brendan had decided to show loggers at work with power saws. Sophie's group had chosen an aboriginal family hunting. This seemed very sophisticated to Arthur whose painting abilities ran out when they stopped putting in the numbers.

'Art, why do the loggers want to chop down all the trees?'

'That's what they do for a living. They chop down trees.' Arthur had a feeling this wasn't going to be easy.

'Why do they chop down trees? What use are they dead?'

He was right. 'They chop down the trees so that people can make things from them,' he lied, 'things like furniture and doors. They use wood for building houses and all sorts.' Actually, they made the forest timber mostly into woodchips that they sent to Japanese paper mills. The mills took vast amounts of water from the river systems upstream and put equally large amounts of polluted water back downstream.

'The animals need them for houses too.'

Arthur agreed, but felt obliged to continue with the Forestry Commission line, even though he hated reinforcing their PR upper hand. 'They plant lots of trees, so when they grow,' (in a hundred years, he thought) 'the animals will have lots of places to live.'

'Wouldn't it be easier just to leave the trees where they are, and then we can all enjoy them, and the animals won't have to find somewhere to live?'

True but irrelevant. How could he explain current account deficits and marginal seats to her? Not one news program or newspaper article had managed, mainly because they just regurgitated whatever the PR people on both sides fed them. 'What would the men do who chop down the trees? They need jobs so they can give their families food and holidays and dinner.'

'Carmen said they could have jobs planting trees to put back the ones they've already chopped down.'

'Who's Carmen?'

'A girl in the class.'

Arthur quietly cursed Carmen. Government budget deficits are even harder, and always end up with bombs-for-kidney-machine arguments. 'They need to sell the trees they chop down so they can afford lots of other things,' he said. He knew he needed a change of subject – and soon. 'What would you like for dinner?'

'The government should stop them before they chop down all the trees. What will the animals do when there aren't any trees left?'

'We'll just have to take them into space to live with us.'

'In *space*? Wow!'

'Yes, imagine, we could all go and live in space and take the animals with us. We could float around, you and me and the koalas, and play games, and never have to walk anywhere. How's that?'

'Could we do that, Art? Live in space, all of us?'

'Oh yes. There's enough of it to fit us all in, isn't there. There's enough space in space.' She giggled. Although he knew hydroponics and the almost infinite source of solar energy would do for an SF story, koalas in space seemed far less likely. No, if we were to save anything it would take a huge effort of political will. Everybody would have to contribute, just to change our consumption habits, if only a tiny bit. Everybody agreed, *something must be done*.

'Now how does ratatouille sound?'

'*Rat stew?*' she said pulling a face. '*No thanks!* Can I have an apple?'

Arthur looked at her, then smiled, washed an apple and gave it to her. 'I'll cook ratatouille anyway for Dave. Do you know where he is? Playing that,' he carefully swallowed his ire, 'game no doubt.'

'He's out in the garden with Daniella, having a pash,' she said, and sighed.

Arthur went on to the verandah to shout to Dave. He saw him with his girlfriend on the rock outcrop at the top of the valley. When they came up for air, Arthur noticed they had an unexpected ease with each other. He thought back to his own first fearful stuttering disdained fumblings. He couldn't connect what he remembered with how these two were. After a few minutes of watching he worked it out. 'Ah,' he said to himself. He felt jealous and then he smiled wistfully and a watery space grew in his soul.

I always had the same job. Then suddenly the job just disappeared and I was redundant. I've been unemployed for years now. I just sit around in this place, gathering dust along with a few mates. There's nothing much to do.

You know, the problem with being unemployed – it robs you of meaning. For a word, that's death.

So I was really excited when the vacancy came up. 'Needed: a word for this woman doctor,' and a mental image. I knew I could do the job – it was me exactly.

Well, I jumped up and started to make my way towards the frontal lobes. But it's a long way from deep memory, and the synapses were lazy and tangled and kept getting in the way.

It wasn't long before I heard the job had been taken. But when I heard it was Sexy who had got the job I was really angry. 'Sexy! He's nothing like it. He's all wrong.' I had a hunch he wouldn't last, and I kept going. Well, it turned out I was right. 'There. I thought so. Too glitzy – too fast – too hard – too modern.'

My heart sank as I approached the language centre: there was a long queue. I asked the word at the back if this was all for my job. 'No,' he said, 'he's blocked and there's this backlog of words waiting to be employed.'

I had to wait a fair while but eventually I got to see the clerk. I was pretty confident like I said, but when he saw my CV he tutted and sucked his teeth. 'You've been unemployed for a long time.'

'I know,' I said, 'but it's not for want of trying. I'm always looking for opportunities that suit me, but words with my abilities just aren't in demand any more.'

'You're getting old,' he said. 'Maybe we could put you in the retraining scheme, maybe make you more hip, get you a new lease of life. Look what we've done for Cool.'

'But I know I'm right for this one. Just give me a chance.'

So he gave me the card, and told me where to go. He said I may meet resistance so I may have to burst out under my own steam. Well, I'm not as quick on my feet as I used to be, but I'm nearly at the frontal lobes now. Just the final check out to go and then, fingers crossed, I'm on. I can even see light through the optic nerve. Consciousness is right ahead. Wish me luck.

That evening Arthur hosed the front yard. He didn't like using water, and he felt contempt for people who watered their lawns and gardens every day. He never watered the back yard which had only native plants that grew naturally in the area. But in the front yard they'd planted nursery variants of Australian native plants that they watered after two or three dry weeks. While he was doing it he watched the evening sky. The sunset colours flowed and ebbed. His eye was caught by a cloud in the shape of a kiss. He watched it and couldn't help forming a simile for his life as it blushed, drifted into a new shape and turned grey.

In the next road an ice cream van jingled *Those were the days,* the sixties pop song. Within a couple of minutes Arthur couldn't get the song out of his head.

A kookaburra landed in the Banksia nearby and watched him, smirking. Arthur carried on and then had an idea: he adjusted the hose to a wide soft spray and turned it on the bird, which twisted its head this way and that, and smacked its beak. Then it hopped around letting the water fall on its back. It fluffed its feathers, shook itself, swallowed some water, turned a look of amused appreciation to Arthur and flew off. It was moments like that which made it all worthwhile.

Back in the kitchen, he started to prepare a Thai green curry. The phone rang but Belinda picked it up in her office. While the rice simmered and he sliced the chicken fillets he listened to the radio, an end-of-week phone-in programme called *Q&A* with the presenter from *The Afternoon Show* who chatted with the callers, extracting the interesting from the unpromising. Apart from the usual gardening, household, DIY and lifestyle tips sought and provided, he attracted offbeat topics. Today: Sue of Haberfield asked where the Sydney habit of ending sentences with the word 'but' had come from? Darren of Manly phoned in to suggest a suitable protest to the French nuclear tests would be to boycott French Fries; and Maria from Woolloomooloo wondered what would be the last thing to be declared politically incorrect?

The last item got a big response. Arthur listened while the suggestions flowed in: job equality; pay; having white skin; men opening doors; men wearing trousers. Then the host said, 'Arthur from Hornsby has suggested that Christian names, such as Arthur or John or Gloria, are so gender charged they cannot continue.'

'I didn't. It wasn't me!' Arthur was taken aback. Another Arthur in Hornsby? 'That's my idea. I had it first. It's in the book!' He glared at the radio. 'Bastard!'

The radio host didn't seem to have heard him and carried on regardless. 'And speaking of tangents,' he asked, 'what is the politically correct term for political correctness?'

Arthur strained the rice and spread it on the two plates, served the curry, sprinkled finely chopped shallots and grated capsicum and took them into Belinda's office. 'How's it going?'

'It's a struggle. This looks good. Thanks.' She emptied the glass of wine he'd brought her earlier and leant back in her chair.

'What do you think the politically correct term for political correctness is?' he said.

'I think "politically correct" is a label used as a put-down by people who don't want to change.'

'Maybe. But it's also a label for a weapon. It's true. It's really hard to change the pronouns and vocabulary of a lifetime. All the short words – black, short, blind…, *man* – seem to have had such criminal pasts that they have to be locked away, never to be heard again. PCs just love to jump on anybody who puts a word out of place.'

'That's just playing the man, not the ball.'

Arthur decided not to point out what Belinda had just said. 'I've thought of *obscurantist feline podiatry,'* he offered.

'Hmm? Oh, long-winded pussy footing, yes not bad. Or how about *appeasemental periphrasis*?'

'Belle, that's good. I like it.' While they both ate their dinners he surreptitiously scanned the page of Belinda's draft report on the computer until the screen saver kicked in. 'Oh, I don't think I told you,' he said. 'Ian's got to go to his son's school play, and Phil's got a scouts meeting.'

'So how many of them does that leave who actually will help with the weed clearing in the bush?'

'Er... none.'

'Same as usual then.'

'Yeah. There always seems to be something that's more important. But they're all "*environmentalists",*' he made quote marks in the air, 'and they still all say they're *really* keen,' he underlined the word in the air, 'and they all agree *something must be done.*' He laughed once sarcastically. 'There's a saying isn't there? Something about actions and words and which speaks louder. It really pisses me off, y'know. My problem is I *do* give a shit. I shouldn't. Nobody else does.'

'Never mind. Maybe next time. Oh, that was Dutch on the phone just now. She's organising a girls' night out later in the month. I said I'd go. How did it go with Sophie at the doctor's?'

'Oh, nothing special. She's got some ideas, so she took some blood for tests...'

'She?'

'Yes, the doctor.' Arthur looked at Belinda accusingly. 'Talking of political correctness, *she* asked some questions, and talked to Sophie quite a bit. Sophie really liked her and chatted away quite easily, and she's perked up since then. The doctor suggested some dietary changes, of all things. She was really nice you know, attractive in an old-fashioned sort of way,' Arthur was remembering that blouse button, 'but these days they'd just say she's overweight. She'd have made a great serving wench.'

'Arthur what *are* you talking about?'

'COMELY! That's the word!'

'*What*?'

'The doctor. She was comely! There's another word gone. It's probably just sitting around unused in our brains. We've lost so many words recently. And it's another way women aren't allowed to be. Who wants to be curvaceous these days. Or voluptuous. That's what political correctness does – it takes away our options.'

'Earth to Arthur? Earth To Arthur? Come in, Arthur. Sophie?'

'What? Oh yes. The doctor said the test results would be back in a couple of weeks.'

'What are the tests for?'

'She didn't say, but before you get into me, I did ask. She just said it was complicated. You know, comely's exactly right for her. Anyway she told me a book I could read. She said it was easy reading, if a bit populist, so I got it on the way back. It's called *Brain Sex*. I tell you what, it's really interesting.'

'Hmm?' Belinda had touched the mouse and was looking at her report on the computer screen.

'They say there are big differences between the sexes, principally caused by hormones that affect the brain and behaviour and everything. The crux of it seems to be that men's and women's brains are actually wired differently. According to them the nature vs. nurture debate for gender issues has been over for years scientifically – jury back, verdict in, sentence declared, journalists run outside, pictures taken, unsuccessful appeal, part sentence served, parole, re-entrance to society, unemployment, death, quiet but tasteful funeral – no flowers please. They know what is nature, which is a heck of a lot; and they know what nurture can do, which is a heck of a lot. It's amazing that no one talks about it, isn't it?'

'Hmm? What?'

'Haven't you been listening? It's what I've been writing about, and it's all in this book. Belle! What is it?'

Belinda looked tired. She rubbed her eyes and sat with her hand pinching the bridge of her nose. 'I did the accounts and forward estimates for this month. I've taken the work-in-progress into account plus unpaid invoices, take away bills outstanding. Result: trouble.'

'But we've had a good year – you especially. And my book last year went well.'

'But look one month down the track. Nothing. Bruce's project has kept me going for a while now, but it's been low level, and it won't get any better. Gustav's been fiddling about doing nothing much, but he'll keep going – so long as I wear the right blouse. Those two barely pay the mortgage, and your stuff isn't enough for the next provisional tax instalment.'

‘Tax! I’d forgotten. When is that due?’

‘March fifth. How long till you finish your book?’

‘Oh, I’m making good progress. I’ve got Dave joining the renegades on some adventures. I’ve put in a few clues for Dave to think about. But I’m a bit concerned that this stuff I’m writing at the moment is just padding.’

‘How long is the book without it?’

‘Not long enough.’

‘Then pad.’

‘But…’

‘Don’t you want it to sell? Look, your books are just departure lounge fillers – just something simplistic to pass the time. Idea, plot, character, plot, plot, plot, and a few descriptive passages.’ Arthur cringed. ‘The more the better. If you’ve written it leave it in. When can you finish it by?’

‘I need another couple of months to…’

‘We need something *next* month.’

‘It can’t be that bad.’

‘There’s nothing in the pipeline. Sweng is just holding on, but he’s got nothing to pass on. I’ve had a few losses recently. I might not get any more work ever again.’

‘Don’t be silly. You’re just having a bad run in a series of random events. It’ll turn round.’ She was not reassured. He decided to plumb the despond. ‘So tell me the worst.’

‘I’ll have to get a proper job, or we have to sell the house, or we have to subdivide the block.’

‘What do you mean? Sell the house, after all we’ve done? We’ve not been here three years. We won’t get our money back. Are you crazy?’

‘Or I can get a proper job.’

‘Are you saying I couldn’t get a proper job?’

‘Of course I’m not. But you need to write. At least I’ve got a track record. And there’s not much call for SF writers in the jobs market at the moment.’

‘You mean I can’t do anything useful.’

Belinda sighed. 'I'm going to bed.'

He sat for a while contemplating the unbearable dampness of being.

When he climbed in beside her she moved to put her head on his chest. He stroked her hair, and then caressed her thigh.

'I'm tired,' she said.

He counted back to the last time they'd made love – too long. He cupped her left breast in his hand. She moaned.

Flesh over flesh. Sweat stirred with musk. 'Uhhhh,' she groaned and rubbed his face with her breasts. He thrust his crotch into hers. They writhed on the floor. Her short blond hair aroused his chest and caressed his thighs.

She moved her mouth towards his. She tasted of pepper. She pushed her pubic hair against his bum. He arched to meet her.

'Yes!' she peeled. She glided smoothly from the bed to him on the floor. Her thighs filled his vision. She moved her gaping hairy cunt to his mouth. Her huge breasts. Her long black hair. Purple and green. Juices. He…

…woke up. The wetness on his stomach quickly cooled. With resignation he got up and went to the bathroom. I wish she wouldn't moan when I want sex, he thought. It isn't that often.

crashing.'

'What's population?' asked Dave bemused, 'and what's it crashing into?'

[Use decade as the major unit of time. Previous Decision? Or maybe 'year' just stopped being used? Have to retro-fit]

'Let me ask you this,' said Raphael. 'How many people are there in the world?'

'Seventeen point three trillion,' said Dave, sure of something at last.

'How do you know?'

Dave was taken aback. 'Everybody knows.' He had come to respect Raphael for his knowledge and judgement in the days and adventures they'd shared, so Dave found that these questions from him disturbed his confidence.

'Well, everybody's wrong. There were once about ten trillion people on earth – that was over thirty decades ago. There never were seventeen trillion.'

'Rubbish! Like I say, everybody knows how many people there are. What makes you think you know better?'

Raphael shrugged. 'And like *I* say, it peaked at ten trillion. The Masters just extrapolated the growth of the previous fifty decades and added a bit to the base figures to cover for statistical uncertainty. Then added a bit more for safety and they built that much accommodation. Of course with all the administrations wanting to make out how important they were, the original figures were somewhat inflated. So, all in all, the population peaked at about half what they'd expected and built for.'

'So that's why so much on these lower levels is empty?'

'Well… no. That would account for half being empty, but only about five per cent is occupied now, if that. We only know what we've seen around here. There are huge unused tracts, level upon empty level; vast unpopulated areas. For instance, the whole of California is a virtual reality.'

'That explains a lot,' said Dave.

'And no one ever really lived in Belgium.'

'But that's incredible! Where have all the people gone?'

'Nowhere. They just aren't coming.'

'What on earth do you mean?'

'There are hardly any children.'

'Children? You mean sons aren't arriving?'

'What?' Now it was Raphael's turn to be confused. 'Oh, I see what you mean. No, they aren't being sent. The Masters have just about stopped having children.'

'Can't they just make more?'

Raphael gave a wry smile. 'It's not like that. You don't *make* children. It's a complicated business. Sit down – this may come as a shock.' They had paced round the block twice already, and Dave was happy to stop. He parked himself on an overturned decrepit Macrosoft table that had prehistoric power and communications cables trailing from one edge. 'After a Master selects a Hom to be her father, the most recent donation from that man is sent to the laboratories—'

'No, there you go again. Donations are used for medical purposes…' Dave's voice trailed off as he remembered the research he'd done on donations. Was it only half a centidecade ago? 'What did you say they're used for?'

'The donation is treated and activated. It's then got a life of only about one hour, in which time it's administered to the Master. Seven centidecades later a child is born.'

'That's ridiculous.'

'Ridiculous – yes. But that's what happens. You, and one trillion other people on this planet, come from inside a Master.'

'How? The women here aren't big enough to carry a child around inside them.'

Raphael shook his head. 'It's too complicated to explain. And you wouldn't believe me.'

'Well, that's all very well, but it doesn't explain what the population is crashing into or why. It worked for – how many did you say – *ten* trillion?'

'Buggered if I know.' Raphael shrugged with his shoulders, hands and face. 'The Masters just aren't doing it any more. So the population is crashing – into oblivion. At this rate in another two decades the whole world will be able to live in a single level or in just three or four major cores.'

This concept seemed bizarre to Dave but not as strange as what had gone before. He was becoming used to believing incredible things. 'It can't always have been like this.'

'No. Back in ancient history, men gave their donations directly to the Masters, who didn't have to treat it.'

'So what happened?'

'It seems in the Age of Fevers something happened to donations, and at about the same time the Masters became repelled by the mere presence of men. Maybe one day someone will work out a way to get the sexes back together.'

'You mean the two species.'

'Species?' Raphael looked pained as if a child had got hold of completely the wrong end of one of the laws of cricket.

'Chris said men and women are two species.'

'I suppose you could see it that way.'

'Where are they?' said Dave, 'and why don't they find a better way?'

'Where are they? The Masters? Why they're in…'

Someone butted in. 'Raph, you know we're having rat stew tonight – well, there isn't enough rat.' He dragged Raphael off to deal with an administrative matter.

Dave was left with a space where his knowledge had been and a lot of questions. He felt more lonely than ever. 'Eddie, what am I going to do?'

Stay here.

'I don't belong here. I've got to get away.'

Where else can you go?

'Yes, where apart from this dimly lit world?' The renegades siphoned off the energy, water and other things from the world above. With so much spare capacity, it seemed no one noticed the nibble that they took, but they were still careful.

In the days Dave had spent with them, he had grown used to their stiff heavy walk – or maybe they were walking normally now, he wasn't sure. And he had become more comfortable with parts of their way of life. He had learnt some basic skills. But he was dirty, and his clothes were crumpled and filthy. They all washed in water but there were no cleaning aides. They all smelled – it had been pungent and acidic at first but now he could be close to one of them without holding his head away. They each smelled different – some distantly reminded him of scents Chris had called up from their sex aids – and none of them smelled pleasant. With a shock he realised he must smell too.

There were three family groups that lived in separate condos. A family seemed to consist of two men, one of which was a woman, plus a child or two – most of which were younger than he'd ever seen before. All the adults could speak his language, but they mainly used another language that always seemed just beyond his understanding.

On their way to the camp, as he'd shared in their dangers, the mutual distrust had begun to break down. Since then Raphael had offered to show him how they got their food, but when he explained about killing and preparing meat, Dave suddenly lost interest. In the last couple of days, however, the renegades had allowed him to join them for their meals which had helped him feel less like a prisoner with his separate food.

The camp was in an area which seemed subtly different even from the other abandoned levels. The ground between the condos was hard and rough, the ceiling was a bit higher. The fronts of many of the condos weren't flat as usual, some of them didn't even have doors, they clearly weren't ever lived in and they had writing on them. Dave had studied the writing in his copious spare time, but he couldn't work out the meaning. Several of the condos had the symbols 'M-c-D-o-n-a-l-d-s', 'K-F-C' or 'O-x-y-g-e-n-H-u-t'. Dave asked the renegades about the condos, but they just shrugged.

A pleasant voice interrupted his thoughts. 'I ought to thank you.'

Dave looked round. The boy from his Decision, Sheila, was approaching him. 'What for?'

'Letting us go?'

'I didn't let you go,' he said standing up.

'No, but you didn't condemn us, and so we're free. We were careless to get caught in the first place. I didn't think a few pieces of Hom food were so valuable we'd get shot for it.'

'You murdered twelve people with a bomb,' he said, the old anger quickly flaring up.

'What *is* a bomb? We were out looking for food. We didn't kill anyone. Why would we? It would draw attention to us, and we'd rather keep ourselves a secret.'

'A secret! You're hated around the world as ruthless killers.' He towered over the boy driving home his community's revulsion. 'Why do you kill?'

Sheila didn't reply, but just looked at him calmly. The futility of his question struck him. He sighed and finally let go of the Decision. What he really needed were friends and he responded to the hand offered to him.

'Sheila, when were you sent from the Masters?'

Sheila laughed. 'We serve no masters. We are free. Oh, I see... I was born *here*. You would say I was two point eight decades old. My father is Raphael and my mother is Helen. I was married to Bjorn, but he died...'

'Permanently?'

Sheila smiled without condescension. 'That's the only kind down here. He died permanently half a decade ago. I have no children.'

'What do you do here?'

'I have my duties. I wash clothes for the men. I join in the forays. People ask me to decorate their condos – I'm quite good at that.'

They sat down in a quiet corner and chatted for a while. Sheila told him about the foray when they were captured. Dave enjoyed his company and he told his story well. '*Her* story.'

'What?'

'I just can't get used to these words you use for women.'

'You'll get it.'

'I'd have to be here a long time for that.'

'Well you've got a long time. You can't go back, can you. You're here for the rest of your life.'

Dave had not admitted that to himself, and having someone say it thrust it into his face. Sheila noticed him change. 'Oh, I'm sorry. I shouldn't have said that.'

'No, you're right. It's just...' His eyes filled with tears. Sheila hesitated for a moment, and then pulled his head to her shoulder. The tension of the last two centidecades spilled out and he cried. He cried for his lost, dead lover, Chris, he cried from the fear of pursuit, and he cried for himself.

Sheila held him as her shoulder and then her soft padded chest became sodden. She was so much shorter than him, and yet he felt so small there. He buried himself in the cuddle and she rocked him gently until he quieted. She made as if to say something, and then seemed to think better of it. He tried to say sorry, but as he looked up into her face he started again.

Eventually he stood up and they walked off together.

*

Oh, hello, Tethys. Has the Presidium finally decided what to do?

Yes.

And?

We've decided to do nothing.

Then we're fucked!

In the press announcement we pointed out that previous and binding Decisions meant there was nothing we could do. You can't compel people to have children. It is an unpleasant task with little or no reward.

Before Desirée, women seemed to find it rewarding enough. Damn her!

Jude! Anyway it's the Homs' fault. It was them who caused the Separation, let me remind you. It was the Bastard Schaefer who retaliated and made them repellent.

If Desirée hadn't released the virus with the male homosexual gene there would have been nothing to retaliate to. And as it was, her so-called brilliance nearly destroyed the species there and then.

It's true we have many heroes from that age. None of them men, notice. It was Jamie who worked out the treatment for sperm that saved the species. She also helped to find the neutralising agent to change the male pheromones to make them tolerable – shame it made them impotent too – and it was another woman...

Tethys, I know the history, thanks very much. But I've been wondering how much of it is true.

No, Jude. All Homs are bastards. They caused the Separation, and they deserved no less than they got. It's us who have spent the centuries in space. Women have always suffered down the ages for their misdeeds.

Maybe so.

Come to bed, Jude.

Soon.

Don't be long. I love it when you get rebellious.

I'll be there in a minute... You were right, Theo. The facts don't matter now. What was it in that song: 'In our hearts our dreams adjust the shame'*?*

Those were the days, my friend. We thought they'd never end. We'd sing...

Theo, what are we going to do?

The Presidium has just announced it. You're going to do nothing.

We'll die out. There will only be the machines left.

Oh my friends, we're balder but much wider, for in our hearts our dreams adjust the shame...

*

'I haven't cried since I was point eight of a decade and I got hit in a hockey match. I suppose you were watching.'

How could I be?

'Listening then!'

Yes.

'He's quite a man, that Sheila. I mean... she's quite a woman. I really like him... her... She's good to talk to.'

You like her, do you? Good. Pheromones are wonderful things.

'What are?' but Eddie didn't answer. Dave sighed. He often didn't understand what Eddie said, so he just went on. 'Her smell isn't as bad as some of the other men. And he's... she's gentle too. I can't seem to stop thinking about him.'

So I see. You've been talking about her for the last ten minutes.

'He's so short. I want to carry him around with me... her around with me. She's got a very nice face. And so soft... That's strange. Proctor hasn't come up for anyone except Chris in point two of a decade.'

Hmm. Listen... I think we ought to have a talk.

'I'm all ears,' Dave chuckled, 'well, meta-cochlea implants anyway. So what do you suddenly want to talk about after you've hardly said a word for days?'

Listen, kid... Um... ...Birds and bees... no use, he's never seen them... Mummies and daddies... No. There must be something... Got it. *Cleo!* Wait a sec... Okay, okay, here we go. *I like Don but I don't know if he's interested in me. What should I do? Dear Sandy, boys are often not aware of our feelings towards them. You need to let him know that you're available. Invite him out, do some things together, and talk to him. He may be a bit shy.*

'Eddie. What the bonk are you talking about?'

Listen, son, when a boy meets a girl and they like each other a lot... this can't be right. Here's one. *My boyfriend has a small penis and I don't experience orgasm very often...* No, that won't do... Pain, when urinating... He slept with my best friend... Oh for goodness sake there must be *something* useful in here!

'Are you trying to explain about sex?'

Well, yes, sort of.

'Why? I've had more than a hundred lovers.'

It's different with a woman.

'Sex? With a woman? That's disgusting!'

You've got a lot to learn. I'll keep looking. This is important. Oh, by the way, tomorrow or the next day you'll wake up feeling like shit. Don't worry – it'll go away in a day or so.

'Tell me something useful, like where the Masters live. Eddie? Oh, not again!'

*

Later, after the last meal of the day, Sheila asked Dave to go for a walk with her. She said she'd show him something of interest. They strolled away from the condos the renegades used, and along roads thick with dust that seemed not to have been disturbed for decades. Sheila seemed very knowledgeable and Dave noticed she was often hesitant when talking about what were to him sensitive subjects such as the culture he had spent his life in.

'How come you people know so much about my world?' he said.

'It used to be our world too, but our ancestors weren't happy in it. Each of them delved into the Record and found things they didn't like. Then either they were forced out by the Masters if they made trouble, or they just found their way down here by chance like you did. There are groups in every core. The stories of your world have become our legends. And we watch the news,' she said. When Dave looked surprised she finished, 'in unused condos.'

Dave wasn't sure this was satisfactory. He was about to ask more when Sheila stopped by an old condo and entered. Lights responded to their presence and they looked around. She showed him some old artefacts, and the wall decorations they'd used and then she turned to him and said, 'Dave, do you like me?'

'Yes I do.'

Oh, great. Watch carefully. This could get interesting.

'Where did you pop up from?' he whispered.

'Well, I've always lived here. Anyway, I thought I ought to thank you properly for letting us go.'

Okay, here we go. I've found the old reference texts for what to do in these situations. Just do what I tell you.

'Look at the trouble I got in last time I did that.'

'Are you all right?' said Sheila.

Shut up and listen.

'Yes. Fine,' Dave said smiling to Sheila. 'What were you saying?'

She kissed him.

There, that wasn't so bad, was it?

'It was okay, I suppose,' said Dave.

'I'll try to do better, then,' she said, slightly surprised.

Despite initial racial prejudices, Dave found himself responding. He was still on familiar ground until she said: 'You asked what a woman is. It's about time I showed you.'

She put both their cloaks on the ground, and then standing in front of him, she took her clothes off.

Dave was fascinated. Here before his eyes was a living demonstration of the answer to his questions. He watched her closely.

What's she doing?

'Taking clothes off.'

'Yes, do you like that?'

Say yes. Now reach over and touch her breasts.

'Which bits are they?'

'These? These are my breasts. Do you like them?'

Now you know. So touch them.

Dave touched them, like a barge pole.

'Don't be shy.' Sheila stood close to him. 'Here, like this.'

Now…, hang on a minute…, *'unbuckle your rampant cock that was straining to be unleashed'*.

'How do I unbuckle my cock – rampant or otherwise?'

'Let me do it.' She reached down.

Dave was surprised to find he was erect. He found the body rubbing against his strange but pleasant. They kissed some more as she fondled his chest vigorously. He found if he shut his eyes it wasn't so bad really.

'Finger her small hard knob of passion'.

'How do you do that?'

'Do you like that?' said Sheila her arms around his neck. 'Is that nice? Hmmm.'

Uh… Uh *'reach between the seething rapids of her legs, ride up the coursing rivers of her thighs and…'* that's all it says *'…finger her small hard knob of passion'*.

'Found something.'

Then you've done better than most men.

'Like this?'

'Easy now. Do this. Yes. I like that. That's gooood.'

'Lie her down on the dewy grass' – the cloaks will do. Now *'thrust your bursting rod into her melting honey pot'*.

'You'll have to explain that. Oh do you mean this bit? I'm getting the hang of this.'

'Dig your fingers into the burning flesh of her hips, giving her concentric circles of pleasure. Plunge your cock into her hot schooner, so that your throbbing balls…'

'You can stop now,' said Dave softly.

'Mmmm.'

But I haven't got halfway through yet.

'It wasn't what I thought it would be,' Dave breathed.

You can say that again… I don't understand. It can't be over yet. It's pretty much the same every time.

'Shhhh.'

25

A couple of days later as they strolled among the condos with their arms around each other Dave asked Sheila about the condos being different at this level. She considered the question for a while, and then said, 'Well, we *are* at the bottom of the core.'

'At the bottom? You mean we're at C level?' he said stopping suddenly.

'C level? What's that? No, this is the ground – the old surface. This is as far down as you can go.'

'So there's two kays of condos above us?'

'Well, yes, I suppose there are.'

Dave looked up and felt the weight of the core bearing down on him. They set off again but now he tried to take special notice of their surroundings to get a feel for C level.

Dave loved the taste of Sheila's skin and even while they walked along they would kiss or nuzzle each other. Just being near her made him horny and they stopped every few condos to kiss and pet. Then, unheralded, the wall of the road changed to a solid, undecorated, functional, rough finish. There were no more condos on that side of the road. Sheila said she didn't know why it was different but that this was a special place.

'Listen,' she said.

He listened and couldn't hear anything special. In fact he couldn't hear anything except the beating of his heart and their breathing. Then he noticed that she had bent her ear to the wall. He did the same. He could barely describe what he heard: there were odd random rhythms; tinkles; unusual squeaks all muffled by the wall. It was strange and unsettling. They stayed like that for several minutes. There was no pattern to the sounds. Some were continuous, others came only occasionally.

He straightened his back stiffly. 'What is that?'

'This is The Wall.' Dave looked at her as if she was being silly. 'No it's *The* Wall,' as if that explained it. 'It runs unbroken as far as we've ever been. It is as high as we've ever been. No one lives in the levels above here, or anywhere next to The Wall as far as we know. Isn't it wonderful? Those strange noises? Don't they drag you through?'

'And what's on the other side?'

'We call it the Quiet Land.'

'But it's full of noises.'

'But they're quiet noises.'

They bent to listen again, but Dave got horny, and couldn't concentrate.

*

'The Quiet Land?'

'Somebody must know.'

'No one down here,' said Raphael. 'It's vast. The Wall runs for hundreds of kays. Always the same. There are legends though. A place of happiness; land of freedom and joy; true home of all men and women.'

'That's not much to go on,' said Dave.

'There's a legend that one day the cores will be pulled down and everyone will live in the Quiet Land.'

'The cores *destroyed*? So it's dangerous?'

'It's a legend of hope, Dave. That the world can be remade. That we can get rid of all this concrete.'

Dave didn't think he could take any more remaking of worlds. 'Raph – can I call you Raph? – how do you get there?'

'People have tried to find their way there, but no one has ever come back.'

'Wow!' It was sounding more dangerous by the minute.

'Still, if you're not happy here, I'm sure…'

'Actually, Raph, I've been thinking. Sheila's been helping me to settle in. I could get to like it here, you know. It feels like an odd way to live for me now, but I'm sure I could get used to it, and my recent knowledge of the cores may be useful to you.'

'To settle in, eh?' Raphael grinned and left. Dave felt stupid.

*

The next day Dave had a growing headache and he was getting odd feelings. Surges of anger and fear washed and ebbed; in consecutive moments he would feel terror, aggression, protective of Sheila, and then desperate to have thundering sex. He barely controlled all of this by keeping a tight clamp on himself.

Sheila spent the morning with Dave. She said it was her morning off and she didn't have any duties. They wandered into old abandoned condos, and down unused roads. She didn't seem happy either. 'What's the matter?' he said.

'Oh, nothing.'

'*What*?'

She paused, then said, 'Oh, Dad said I shouldn't get mixed up with someone new to the group.'

'That doesn't sound like Raph,' he said but she didn't reply and he had his work cut out keeping control of his mood swings. They found themselves quite a way from the main camp. They chatted sporadically for a while, each apparently preoccupied with their own problems. They were close enough to hear the sounds of the settlement – making tools, cooking, chatting, children playing. 'I could be happy here, I think,' he said. He looked at her, they kissed, and the lights went out.

It was pitch black. Dave had never known absolute darkness before. 'What's happening?' he said, breathing shallowly.

He heard her get to her feet and he got up too. 'This happens sometimes,' she said, but he could tell she was nervous. After a couple of minutes of silence when they still couldn't see anything they started to feel their way back.

Then suddenly they were blinded as the lights came back on again. They looked around, startled, shading their eyes.

Almost at once there were crashing sounds and gun fire. Shouted orders. 'PURSUIT! DON'T MOVE!'

Dave let out a roar of rage which he had never known before. Sheila made to go back to the settlement and then changed her mind. Dave was battering at a wall. She grabbed him and they ran off. Away from the noise.

26

...Run away. Run away. Run away. Run away. Run away. Run away...

*

So, Tethys, you've done it then?

Yes.

I thought so. We all do ourselves up to look our best. I can't think why.

I can't say I'm looking forward to the results.

How did you decide?

Oh, the usual: genome scan; ancestor achievements.

Uh huh.

And a random number generator. Jude, they all look the same!

Tall, athletic, talented? All attractive, all beautiful?

Exactly.

What do you expect? It may not be our idea of survival of the fittest, but evolution doesn't see it that way. We don't have to live with them. We don't need them to love us.

We don't have to have sex with them. Thank God.

We don't have to talk to them. So there's only one criterion – we select only the good-looking ones. Only the good-looking ones reproduce. They evolve, we stagnate.

For all our superiority.

That's one word for it.

It's one of the great ironies of the Separation. We can't change the way we look for all our dieting and exercise and make up and skin treatments. I hate it but it's true. We each look different, each with our blemishes and imperfections – I will always be skinny and you...

Go on, say it. I'll always have big hips.

Well, sorry, yes.

We each have our burden to bear.

*

...around my buttocks, hips and thighs.

'What?' said Dave who hadn't slept, though Sheila was still resting beside him.

Greatness.

'*Eddie.*'

Forget it.

'At last. Something sensible. Where are we?'

How should I know?

'I thought you knew everything. My mood swings seem to have settled down. And the headaches are gone too.'

Sheila stirred. 'Hmm. What?'

'Oh, I'm sorry. I didn't mean to wake you. You can sleep some more if you want to. It's not as if we've got any urgent appointments.'

'I'm awake now,' she said. 'Who were you talking to just now?'

'Oh. Just talking to myself. It's a bad habit of mine.'

'Have you tried any of the condos? I could do with a wash.' They found somewhere with water but nowhere had power. 'I'm hungry. I expect you are too. I could find a couple of rats, but you'd have to eat them raw.'

Dave remembered Raphael's description. 'I'll pass, thanks.'

'You'll have to eat something sometime.'

'Maybe you could find somewhere to cook.'

'Well. I'll look out for anything likely, but I don't really know what to look for. The group inherited or made...' She stopped. Dave empathetically gave her room for her loss. In some ways he'd come to terms with his.

'We may as well move on.' Neither of them said that they didn't have anywhere to go to. Some emergency lighting was still on so they wandered from one dimly lit indistinguishable area to another, each just like the area round his old home, filled with roads and roads of identical condos, though on closer inspection Dave noticed that they each had a different coloured door.

'Tell me about yourself,' he said as they walked along. 'What sort of a life did you lead? How did you learn your skills?'

She muttered something under her breath. They walked on in silence while he waited for her to begin. 'There's not much to tell. You met my mother and father… The group has always been there since I can remember… The children just learn by watching the older ones.' She paused again and then muttered, 'Not much of a life.'

'You mean nothing much happened? It may not seem much but to me your life is exotic. My life was sport, sport, and more sport. For some people too much sport was barely enough. In sport everything is easy. No compromise. Black and white. Just score goals, get points, take tricks. Nobody has to deal with real people if they don't want to. Those people screaming for your blood – they weren't real people at all – not to me anyway because to them you weren't real people and death wasn't real either. Just like I never really killed anyone in football.'

'You? Are you different? Tell me about yourself.'

'Like you, there's not much to tell.'

'Come on. What made you different? I'd like to know what all the fuss is about.'

Dave found something odd in that but before he could think why, Eddie said, Tell her about the way you lived. You could tell her about your Decisions.

'Where did you pop up from?' Dave muttered, but, distracted, whatever it was Sheila had said drifted out of reach. 'Well, I had a pretty ordinary life, I'd say…'

Far off they heard doors opening and shouted orders. They stopped to try to gauge the distance and direction, but there was no way of telling in the enclosed spaces of endless roads and condos. They quickened their pace to get away, just away. Once, the sounds of running steps passed over their heads on the next level. They quickly ducked into a condo, but the pursuit didn't come any closer.

They kept moving, never sure where they were going or whether they were moving away from the pursuers, and they became furtive and unsure.

'For goodness sake! I'm fed up of this!' Dave burst out after several hours. 'No food, and going nowhere. There must be somewhere we can go.'

'Well, I've been thinking. There *is* somewhere. I think I know how to get there, but I don't know where it is.'

Dave shook his head quickly. 'Did I miss something then, or have you been practising paradoxes?'

'The Quiet Land,' Sheila said. 'Someone told me how to get there. I thought it was a child's story, but then one time I followed the instructions and I came to a door that was completely unlike anything I'd ever seen before. I got scared and ran back, but I think that was the way to the Quiet Land.'

'That sounds great. With all the noise the pursuers make I doubt they'd be there.'

He was glad to see her laugh. 'Okay.' She looked about, muttered something and then pointed. 'We have to go a long way in this direction until we get back to The Wall.'

'That's an incredible sense of direction! I can't tell which way we're facing,' but he was ready to believe in her inbred instincts. 'I guess when you spend your life in a place, you get to know its signals pretty well.'

'Hmm,' she said. They set off with a purpose now. 'The thing is,' she said, 'once we get there, there's no way back.'

27

They reached The Wall, followed it at ground level for a while and then started to climb. They talked about nothing else except the Quiet Land. It was frustrating as neither of them knew anything about the subject. So they speculated for hours about possible outcomes, likely scenarios, who or what could inhabit the Quiet

Land and whether it existed at all. Assuming it did exist (and they both agreed that was the only sensible assumption, as they had no other plans), how could they get there? If there were people there, would they be friendly? Could the pursuers follow them in? If so, could they be hauled back out again?

When they lapsed into silence, Eddie sometimes made suggestions, and when Dave repeated them as if part of the conversation it set off more baseless speculation. Seldom had so much time been dedicated to a subject about which the contributors knew so little. It reminded Dave of the shows about current affairs.

Sheila stopped and kissed him. In the rush away from the settlement and the pursuers' persistent pressure they hadn't rested much, and then only as companions on the run. 'We'll think of something,' she said as she stroked him. It reminded him of Chris, but to his surprise the memory came without the rush of pain and the kick in the stomach. He sadly realised his lovers were merging, pressed together by the forces that had crushed his old life.

'Fuck, I'm hungry,' she said breaking away. Dave noticed the strange word and asked her about it, but she just said it was her group's own swearword, and seemed a bit embarrassed and flustered discussing it. They went back to climbing, keeping The Wall close by.

'I wonder what I'll be in the Quiet Land.' Dave hadn't been one for status before, though like most people he had tried for as many representative positions as he could. 'You know,' he continued, 'I used to be considered quite attractive. I trained hard. I made rep in three sports. People used to chat with me on the net because I had unusual views. And during the time when I was making that last Decision I was famous. That Decision made several newscasts, you know. Then I gave all that away.'

'Thank you,' she said and kissed him again.

'In your group I wasn't anything. I had no skills you needed. I was just a dead weight. Incredible, isn't it? In one society I'm a useful contributor. Away from that, I'm useless. Now look at me. I'm nothing, I'm nowhere, and I'm going who knows where.'

'You're a highly valued member of society – it's just a very small society.'

'Huh. I wonder what I'll end up being in The Quiet Land.'

'Less hungry, I hope.'

'At least I've done something, eh. All the other people I knew are still doing the same, and they'll do the same until they pass back.'

'You mean die?'

'Hardly anyone dies permanently until they're ready to pass back. Only the ones who have particularly unhappy sporting accidents, but most deaths are temporary. When people don't get picked any more they get bored. Then they just hand themselves in to be passed back to the Masters.'

'Bizarre! I didn't know that.'

'Why should you? I hadn't thought before but all those people…' He fell quiet and they climbed on with their own thoughts. When he looked round he saw her a few steps back muttering to herself.

Sheila stopped him a few minutes later. 'Listen.' When the sound of his heart subsided he heard muffled, muddled and indistinct sounds. 'That's your world,' she said. 'We have to be quiet here.'

They moved up more levels. The thought of his own world drew on him strangely. He thought out loud, 'Maybe…'

'Shhh!'

He went on under his breath 'Maybe I should go back there. I could tell them the truth about the renegades. Some administrators would be interested in that. We could start investigating who really let off the bombs. The world harbours some very bad people, and we don't know about them.'

Sure. That sounds like a great idea.

'Right! Hey, I could take Sheila too and tell them about women. That would interest everyone.'

Yeah. I'm sure not too many people would want to proctor her.

'What do you mean? They would keep a detached interest. Wouldn't they?'

Of course they would. Wouldn't they? Still, she wouldn't mind being the object of everyone's curiosity. It would be such an honour.

Eddie's support made Dave feel a lot less certain. 'Yes? And they should be told about the renegades.'

You're right. And who better than you? With news like that they're sure to just waive the death sentence on you. The pursuers would be able to hang up their boots, eh? Give back their uniforms? At least they'd be grateful. They could go back to being ordinary people again.

'They'd like that. Wouldn't they?'

'What are you muttering about?' said Sheila. 'Anyway, look, we've arrived. Wherever this is.'

28

The Wall had disappeared – Dave couldn't remember when exactly, but they'd been tracking it for so long he missed it now it wasn't there any more. They had climbed for hours, but now they had reached the top. Dave realised he'd never been to 'the top' before – he'd always lived in just the few levels. It struck him again just how little he knew about the world he lived in.

The road that led to this door was different: very high, solid matt walls, entirely functional, no advertising. It had a one-way feeling about it.

Actually there were two doors. One was quite small, only big enough for one person to go through. The other door that they turned to face was unlike the hundreds of doors they'd passed through in the last couple of days. It was far taller and wider and it had symbols on it, which Dave recognised as writing. They stood in front of the door and waited for it to open. Nothing happened. They banged a few times. Nothing happened.

Dave studied the writing for a while. 'P-a-c-i-f-i-c-P-r-o-j-e-c-t-M-a-i-n-t-e-n-a-n-c-e-Y-a-r-d,' he sounded slowly.

'Is that what those symbols mean? How did you know that?'

Dave explained about the writing he'd used during the Decision. 'This doesn't mean much to me. The individual symbols are familiar, but I don't recognise the words. What should we do now?'

'How about the other door?'

He tried to read the writing. 'F-i-r-e-E-s-c-a-p-e-D-o-N-o-t-O-b-s-t-r-u-c-t… and these bigger symbols are D-A-N-G-E-R-O-U-T-S-I-D-E. The rest I can't make out. I wonder if it's important. This door is as old as I've ever seen. It looks like it's fully manual.' Turning to one side he asked Eddie how it worked.

Take the small protuberance, turn and push, but be very, very careful.

Dave reached for the knob, turned it and pushed. Alarms sounded all around. He turned in shock, but Sheila was unperturbed, as if she hadn't heard them. The alarms stopped. He turned away from her and whispered, 'Was that you?'

Just a little joke of mine.

He breathed an irritated sigh and stepped through the door.

As Sheila followed him through she gasped. In front of them there was nothing. Above them there was a light so intense they had to shield their eyes for several minutes. The air stretched unbroken into the infinite distance. As they stepped forward the door slammed shut behind them pushed by an invisible force that also pushed them from one side and made a whistling noise. When their eyes became adapted to the brightness they could see white indefinite objects all moving briskly in the same direction. The ceiling was blue, but wherever it was, it was too far up to see clearly.

'What is this?' he said to himself in wonderment.

This is outside. Don't stay out here long, the ultraviolet is strong at these altitudes and your skin's not used to it.

In front of them the ground jagged away in all directions, and behind them there was a high construction with the door in it. On the ground at regular intervals were slabs of deep black that swallowed the light. Dave carefully approached one. 'I wonder what this is.'

Are you looking at a matt black slab about two metres by three metres?

'Yes.'

That's a solar cell. They cover the entire core surface. They provided enough power to keep all the cores running, but initially they were very unreliable and needed constant maintenance.

'They just look like sucking black slabs.'

That's pretty much what the engineers used to call them. These days they provide the energy to repair the atmosphere and make a good fist of cleaning the oceans too.

'What are *they*?' asked Dave.

'What are they?' asked Sheila looking at the slabs.

Best not to say.

'How should I know?' said Dave to Sheila. 'Weird, aren't they.'

They stayed watching the white objects moving and gradually changing shape and found it restful for their eyes. Then Sheila tugged at his arm and they turned to the door. Dave gripped the protuberance, turned it and pushed. It was firmly shut. In alarm he said, 'It won't open! We're trapped!'

Sheila took the handle and pulled. The door opened easily. With relief they both went inside. The door slammed shut behind them again pushed by the invisible force, and immediately the whistling sound from outside stopped. The scale of the corridor seemed homely and comfortable.

'Wow. That was something else!' Dave said. 'I wonder what use it is. Now what?' He saw other symbols by the side of the big door. 'S-p-e-a-k-F-r-i-e-n-d-A-n-d-E-n-t-e-r.'

It says: speak friend and enter said Eddie in a foreign language.

'*Speak friend and enter*?' said Dave trying to get his mouth around the strange sounds. The door opened.

'What did you say?'

'Oh…,' said Dave having to think quickly to cover for Eddie, 'I just worked out what it meant,' he said lamely.

'Well clever you.'

The door opened from the middle. It was wide enough for ten people, thirty people. *Well, well, well,* said the door. *Mr Davisorian. Welcome. What took you so long? Oh, by the way, your café table sends you its best wishes for the future and says 'no hard feelings'.*

Dave didn't hear the door because he was awestruck by the room beyond. It stretched as far as he could see. It was as high as – he took a guess – twenty levels. It was full of gantries, chains, metal and machines.

And it was very dusty.

It was as if nothing much had happened here for quite a while. There was a scrape and thud of unenthusiastic work. A few machines gave off a subdued drone. One rose up, lifted something, then, with a sigh, put it down again.

Dave and Sheila walked for a few minutes and made no impression on the huge room or its inhabitants. They passed enormous stacks of identical components, row after row of similar parts. Everything was labelled. The impression was of a highly organised, well catalogued dump.

Suddenly one machine burst into view, flew at great speed towards them, screeched past, and then sank exhausted to the ground and expired. Other machines nearby raised their ocular devices, observed, and returned to their torpor.

'What's it all for?' said Dave. 'It's just huge,' he added unnecessarily.

They heard a periodic sound and moved towards it. They noticed several machines were in slings, swinging idly. They found others on slabs with their treads raised. Moving on they reached the source of the sound: it was a machine that picked up a part from one huge pile, and took it to another machine nearby. It seemed to offer it to the other machine with an interrogative squeak, wait for a few moments, and then with a sad mechanical sigh put the component in another huge pile. Each time it started again with hope, as though trying to tempt the other into life with something new and interesting.

They made their way slowly. It was as if the whole place had taken a very long tea break. A dim glow provided a target, and after half an hour of meandering they reached its source. There was a massive bank of screens, with lights flashing and blinking without apparent purpose, pattern or meaning. Dave started to work out the writing on one screen but it defeated him.

'What does it say?' he whispered.

How should I know? Look, try a few out loud.

Dave read a few haltingly, and Eddie interpreted.

'It's a work list!'

Oh you are clever.

'No need to be sarcastic,' Dave whispered.

'Not much use to us, I'm afraid,' said Sheila. 'We don't know what the tasks are. What's on the next one?' That was the same. So was the next, and the next. 'There must be hundreds of screens all with jobs to do. What's going on here? Why isn't any of this work being done?'

What's the use? said a voice nearby. They spun around and saw a machine sitting on a shelf with its treads up and a container of lubricant in a grip. *Me and the boys, we said that, we said: what's the use?*

Dave was goaded by the untidiness of the place. 'What's the use? There are piles of work. Thousands of jobs built up. You're here to do that work.'

We've been here for hundreds of decades. There's always jobs to do. That's the trouble with being self-maintaining. In the end we said: what's the use? So we stopped for a break. It hasn't seemed worth starting again.

'Well, what did you do before you stopped?' asked Sheila.

We keep the world going. We keep the sun moving across the sky; we make sure the rain falls; we keep the stars shining.

'You make the what do what?' said Dave.

Or we did. But look, we've stopped and the world keeps running. What's the use? What thanks do we get? Nobody cares. Nobody comes here.

'We're here,' said Sheila.

We have feelings too, you know.

'No you don't,' said Dave. 'You're machines.'

Typical.

'Oh leave it,' said Sheila and walked off. The machine huffed, but a few moments later it put down the lubricant, lowered itself on to the floor and followed them.

'Nothing ever needed mending where I came from,' said Dave. 'Nothing ever broke or failed.'

There are machines like us everywhere. We fix things so you don't notice. Where were you?

'Sydney Core.'

Thought so, said the machine as if that explained everything.

They moved on in silence past more screens. They arrived at a huge control panel with hundreds of buttons, levers, knobs and dials. There was bank after bank of labelled switches. Dave read one label 'A35#2.YTZ%A#.' 'What does it mean?' he whispered.

Don't ask me.

Dave reached out.

'Don't touch it!' said Sheila. 'You don't know what it does.'

Oh, go on. The machine showed interest for the first time.

Dave hesitated, then threw the switch. Nothing happened. The machine slumped back. Sheila and Dave looked around but there was no discernible effect. Tentatively, Sheila moved a dial. The dial sounded a sliding tone but otherwise nothing happened. They moved up and down the control panel jabbing and flicking at random. Each bank and each type of control made a different sound. They got into a rhythm and built a great riff. The machine clicked in syncopation.

Suddenly machines started moving around strangely. Dave and Sheila stopped mid-phrase and watched until the machines' erratic movements settled down. They looked at each other sheepishly and moved on.

Dave had a thought. 'Do you know the way to the Quiet Land?' he asked the machine that was following them.

I'm a maintenance drone, not a signpost.

'Well, you're not much of a maintenance drone, are you? You haven't maintained anything for ages.' He picked up something from a pile and handed it to the machine. 'Here. Fix this.'

The machine gave the object a cursory inspection.

'Can you fix it?' said Sheila.

Yes.

'Well go on then.'

It's not my job. The boys would be really crook at me if I trod on their patch. Then you'd have a demarcation dispute on your hands.

'What would they do?' said Sheila sarcastically. 'Stop work?'

The machine looked at the object again, turned it over, and closely inspected some attachments. It extruded a probe, and poked about a bit. It scratched its processor unit casing with one grip. Then it just threw the object on the floor and moved on. Dave looked around at the catalogued disorder and sighed.

In a clearing between towering stacks, some machines were arranged in what Dave was startled to recognise as a game formation. They were using their treads and their support appendages to move a soft, spherical object between them. They propelled it from one to the other, and the teams contested for it.

Dave addressed the machine that was following them: 'Why are these other machines kicking a ball with their feet?'

The lads like to play a bit of sport. It passes the time between jobs.

G'day, Jock, called one of the players. *You joining us? Norths are a drone short at the moment.*

Dave was muttering to himself 'Ball... feet... foot... ball. Is this game called football?'

Brilliant. Hey lads, this man's a genius!

'You know, there are hundreds of games called football around the world, many of them very old indeed – American Football, Australian Rules Football, Net Football, Table Football, Rugby Football, and the game I used to play, Hyper Football. This is the only one that involves feet and a ball. I wonder if every society has a game called football – a sort of universal cultural imperative.'

Dave watched the game closely, but Sheila, bored, moved off. Norths seemed to be losing from what Dave could see, and he was about to suggest a tactical change when Sheila called out. 'Dave, look at this.' She was looking at a door in the floor. It was clearly a hatch door. 'This can only lead to one place,' she said.

'You're right...! Where?'

'The Quiet Land, of course! By my reckoning, The Wall's just under the door back there. We are standing over the Quiet Land.'

'Well, don't just stand there, get it open and let's go.'

The hatch was firmly shut. There was a track that went right up to it, and clearly went through it, but no amount of heaving, pulling or thumping had any effect. Eventually Sheila stamped her foot in frustration, aimed one last kick at the hatch door, and went off to explore somewhere else.

Not far away she made another discovery. On the track there was a vehicle. It had a number of controls, dials and buttons. The lack of dust indicated that it had been used fairly recently. Behind the control panel was a small cabin and a large, high-sided tray. Dave estimated the tray was about the size of his study, in his condo, in the world he had lived in, far far away, in that dream he was forgetting.

Sheila sat in the cabin and tried some of the controls. It was just another frustration. Nothing happened. Dave asked passing machines how to operate the vehicle, but none of them answered. He wandered away. He discovered a towering transparent cylinder with receptacles next to it. All at once he noticed a tap, worked out what it was, and shouted to Sheila.

'I hope it's fresh water,' she said on her way over.

'I'm so thirsty I'm past caring,' said Dave, draining a third cup. After so long, it tasted marvellous. 'Hey,' he shouted to a machine dawdling by, 'is there any food here?' The machine stopped on its tracks, turned its ocular device towards him, somehow projected a look of utter contempt for such a stupid question, and started off again.

*

Theo, have you released the reverse-engineering virus?

Yes, Jude. But men will still be on the nose for a few decades until it works through.

You'd better make damn sure the Presidium doesn't find out. They'd go berserk if they knew we were using genetic engineering again. And, Theo, is this the maintenance yard for the Pacific Project?

Yes.

It's a bit of a mess, isn't it?

The Pacific Project was underfunded from the beginning, Jude and I think the machines caught the mood. They've always been a bit like that. It just gets worse when the Wise One loses his control.

You'd have thought for something this important they'd have done it properly – you know, the future of the entire planet, that sort of thing.

I know what you mean, Jude, but, well, that's the way things were in those days.

Some things never change, eh? Can anyone see this?

No. Only you. If anyone did look I'd give them 'life as usual'. But no one else cares any more.

Is he ready? He's been acting erratically recently.

Oh I think that's just the withdrawal symptoms from the testosterone suppressant we put in their tea. Anyway the sensors and the implant are functioning correctly and there are no problems. He's fine. But there's one more thing to check and if this doesn't work we're stuffed.

*

They looked around and near the vehicle they found a small row of buttons. Next to each button was a console. Dave walked up to one and the console hummed into life. It gave him a menu of options. He selected one of the options and the console displayed complex text and diagrams. It was completely useless. Dave knew then that this was the *User Instructions*.

To one side, in a section on its own, there was a single important looking button. He peered at it. He moved to press it. A sign lit up. 'D-o-N-o-t-P-r-e-s-s-T-h-i-s-B-u-t-t-o-n,' he read. It was in his own language so the sounds formed into familiar words. 'What a strange instruction.'

I wonder what would happen if you pressed it.

'I wonder.'

'You aren't allowed to,' said Sheila as Dave's finger moved towards the button. 'It says not to.'

Why listen to instructions? said the Jock machine. *Look where it's got us. Decades of just doing what we're told.*

'What's the use?' they all said together.

Dave pressed the button.

Something happened.

29

Dave looked down. Consciousness flowed outwards from him. Underneath the floor there was a huge space and another world. From the ceiling of the maintenance yard he could see all the machines, Sheila and himself, standing by the control panel. He saw the planet surface covered in concrete and the sucking black slabs, and the Cs. Looking down he could see the moon, and the ring of the manufacturing station encircling the earth. The planets in a glimpse. The vastness of space in his hand. And there was another mind, different yet familiar, which gave through him to an uncountable throng. They needed, he gave.

The button let go of Dave.

Now you've done it, said the Jock machine.

Dave stared at Jock for a long moment. The feeling of quiet elation and the memories slipped away.

'What was *that*?' said Sheila staring at Dave who still had a wild smile.

Dave tried to focus on the control panel. The sign now said D-o-N-o-t-P-r-e-s-s-T-h-i-s-B-u-t-t-o-n-A-g-a-i-n. Eddie chuckled.

'What's so funny?' Dave muttered.

Oh nothing.

Machines started moving. *Come on lads, show's over*, said the Jock machine. *We might as well get started.*

'Sheila, you won't believe what I saw just then. It was…'

Then the hatch opened.

They ran to it and looked through. Dave felt himself being drawn through. He fell to the floor with vertigo. When he regained control of the spinning world, he crept on his front towards the hole in the ground. The first thing he saw was space and light – just open air. When he peered over the edge he saw a green mottled carpet. The carpet had texture; it varied in hue and shade; it appeared to have undulations in its surface; and at random it had deeper scars. Next to him Sheila whispered in awe, 'So those are trees.'

'Trees?'

Sheila didn't say anything for a moment wrapped in the vision below. 'The fables of the Quiet Land mention trees. Large green and brown objects that cover the land.'

'Large objects?' Dave looked down again. His mind performed gymnastics and reinterpreted the view. 'How far down is it?'

'It must be hundreds of metres.'

Dave's mind sighed and started again. He realised he couldn't visualise what he was seeing. He edged back from the hatch and picked up a small object from one of the piles, crept back and dropped it. He lost sight of it after twelve seconds. He tried again with something bigger. Twenty seconds later he lost sight of it against the green carpet. He did a quick calculation. 'That's two kays straight down.' He edged back just a touch.

Far, far below, he saw specks moving across the carpet. He changed his view and saw an object wheel in the air. He tried to point it out to Sheila but it was too small. One of the darker scars in the carpet sparkled in places.

There was a huge double *thunk.* The light below went out for the briefest of moments and when it came back on, the view was subtly changed, as if the ground had shifted slightly.

They stayed glued to the edge of the hatch for many minutes transfixed by the space. The air in their faces was warm and made a slight draught up through the hatch. 'So many trees,' said Sheila quietly to herself.

'Is that really the Quiet Land?'

Sure is.

'Yes. I'm sure of it.'

'It's a bit *green* isn't it?' Dave said. Sheila looked at him oddly. 'How do we get there?'

'We'll find a way. And then you'll be free.'

'I'm not sure I want to go.'

'You can't stay here. There's nothing to do, nothing to eat, nowhere to go.'

'It looks really strange. What will I do down there? I'll starve down there, just as surely as up here.'

Sheila was quiet for a moment. Then she whispered, 'I can't,' as if engaged in some internal struggle, which reminded Dave of Chris. After a few moments she sighed and said quietly, 'I'll be with you.' She held out a hand and he took it. They both stayed looking down at the ground so far away.

*

It worked, Theo! After all these years, it worked!

Decades.

Generations.

Centuries.

Millennia.

Whatever else you say about Desirée, Sal, you have to admit, she was a bloody genius.

It makes me proud to think I knew her.

Me too.

*

They each went off and looked around the yard a bit, but they were drawn back to the view every time. The texture and variety of the trees held and relaxed their eyes. They made perfunctory efforts to make the vehicle move, and they searched half-heartedly for other ways to get down. They tried other controls on the massive boards and panels, but nothing happened. Dave tried to get the machines' attention, but they were now milling about doing jobs. Looking back at the work list, he could just make out that the tasks on it were beginning to scroll down. A number of times one machine or other approached the vehicle with an object, then moved over to a shelf nearby and placed it there instead. The yard began to hum, spark and crash productively.

They hadn't found anything to eat. Dave tried to read the labels on boxes in the hope that they contained food, but he couldn't understand them.

They heard the loud double *thunk* again and ran to the hatch. This time they could tell that the light was coming from much lower, cutting across the tops of the trees. They heard noises from below, and they both saw objects moving around in the air.

A while later there was one more *thunk*, and the space below went dark, with only a dim glow seeming to come from just beneath them. The sounds from below reached a peak and then quickly faded.

It's night-time there.

'What shall we do now?' he wondered aloud.

As if in answer, they heard loud banging on the door they'd entered by. Even from this distance they could hear shouts. 'Pursuers!' hissed Sheila. The banging stopped. They went where they could see the door.

For a while it was quiet. 'I wonder if there's any other way in,' said Dave.

There isn't.

'You'd have thought they'd have forgotten me by now.'

'They're after me as well,' said Sheila.

And it's not as if they've got anything better to do. Chasing you is a pleasant diversion. Ah! They've worked out how to get in.

The door slid open. Several pursuers bounded in dramatically and then stopped in the doorway stunned by the yard. Dave counted twenty.

'Hide!' breathed Sheila.

Friends of yours? Jock was beside them. Dave firmly shook his head. *Leave it to us, mate. We'll sort them out.*

The pursuers were looking around them, clearly unable to come to grips with what they saw. Another strode in, shorter than the others, and impatiently sneezed an order. The troop responded intermittently, with slowly gathering wits. They spread out, a pair taking an aisle, many metres apart. They moved carelessly, at different speeds.

Dave looked round, but Sheila was gone. He shrugged, said, 'What the heck,' and thinking multidimensional football tactics, set off in search of a pursuer.

Dave quickly lost sight of all but two who were coming down the aisle towards him. A machine sped across the path of the pursuer further back and knocked him down. His gun clattered into a pile of discarded components. Another machine crashed into the sprawling pursuer, and bounced off him into the pile. The gun and the machine were buried under a tumble. The stunned pursuer tried to focus on the pile, which started to tremble, until the machine burst out with a chaotic spray of pieces. *Oops. Sorry, mate,* said the machine in mock contrition to the pursuer, who ran off back to the door.

The pursuer at the front realised he was isolated and looked around uncertainly. Machines were speeding everywhere. Dave had a few moments while the pursuer was dithering and he leapt down from the shelf he'd chosen, turned the pursuer round and smashed a fist into his kidneys. The pursuer fell to the floor. It felt so good to hit someone. His Venables would have been proud of him.

Shouts and groans were coming from several directions. Dave caught a movement from the corner of his eye and glimpsed Sheila moving, crouched and coiled, towards her prey.

In just a couple of minutes, Dave saw twelve pursuers limping back to the door. Then Sheila was next to him holding a gun.

'Can you work it?' asked Dave.

Sheila looked at the gun uncertainly. It was a slab with a rod in it. It had three different coloured buttons. At one end of the slab there was a transparent section. 'Well, keep that bit,' – he indicated the transparent end – 'pointing *away* from us.' He gently pushed it so it wouldn't blast a hole in his chest. 'These are the energy and dispersion controls. This is the trigger. Here, like this.' He set the controls, took aim at the troop and fired, sending them diving for cover. 'Hey, this is fun! I've never fired real rounds at real people. It's always been sport.' He loosed off a few more rounds. 'These guns fire energy. That's odd though – there have been bullets ricocheting around ever since…'

Dave saw that one of the pursuers wasn't moving. With the sight came realisation, and with the realisation came reaction. Sheila grabbed him and pulled him back, just as a machine sped across the aisle in his path.

'Keep still.'

'I may be able to help him.'

'You can't help him by getting yourself killed.'

Dave stopped struggling. His mind ran in tight circles as they watched the pursuers drag the charred body out through the door. Ten plus the commander came back, carefully, backs to the wall, guns scanning the yard.

'This way,' Sheila coughed. '*Come on*!' she insisted when Dave didn't move. She pulled him away and they ran across some aisles out of view of the pursuers. 'Here, give me that. I'm not so soft.' Dave released the gun to her and followed without thinking. Machines were scurrying between shelves, making a dazzling interference pattern that opened as they approached and closed behind them. From the soft grunts and crashes they heard, the pursuers were suffering casualties. There were gun shots, then an explosion, and the sound of tinkling. Dave flinched as he heard fragments fall nearby. The pursuers were cutting their way through the machines.

They'd reached the vehicle and the tray had sides high enough to provide good cover. 'Get in here,' said Sheila who then ran off to one side. Dave stood on the ground by the vehicle and watched the machines buzzing around. Suddenly, a pursuer appeared just a few metres away, and aimed his gun at Dave's head. Jock dashed in front of him and took the blast. It sparked, splintered, arced and fell down. At the same time another machine cannoned into the pursuer, knocking him into a shelf of large components. He fell heavily and didn't get up.

Jock raised itself weakly on one hoist. It moved its ocular device around, taking in all the facets of the scene. A third machine rushed up and started probing the twisted and pitted surface of Jock's carcass.

Jock looked at Dave. *So long, mate. Have a good one. I'll cop you later.* Then, its display unit dimmed. Dave looked on, helpless and horrified. *Could this be death?* it croaked.

I don't think so, said the recovery machine, which inserted a probe and with a crackling *zap* splintered Jock's body into fragments. It picked up the central processor unit and moved off.

Shots whistled around Dave's head. He ducked, and dived into the vehicle tray. Raising his head over the edge, he saw Sheila a few blocks away firing from a position of cover, drawing the pursuers' attention.

At that moment, the vehicle shook and started to move.

'Sheila! The vehicle's moving! Get in.'

Sheila took in the situation and started towards him, firing at the same time. The pursuers were firing in turns at Sheila, the vehicle and the machines that were rushing them from all directions. Sheila got to within a block of the vehicle, and then her gun gave out. She picked up some loose objects and hurled them at the pursuers.

The vehicle accelerated towards the hatch. Dave called out again. Sheila turned to dash after him, but the pursuer's commander appeared from nowhere and blocked Sheila's way pointing a gun at her head. In a bizarre moment Dave realised the commander was a woman. The pursuer holstered his weapon and saluted.

Dave watched, dumbstruck – helpless as the vehicle ran through the hatch; and as he flew into the unknown he lost sight of the maintenance yard, the machines and Sheila.

Passive – 30

I don't want to belittle Dave's predicament (though I happen to know that Dave, Chris and Sheila are all unharmed by their experiences), but the way he is flying into the unknown is a lot like migrating to a new country. I don't think Arthur really knows what that's like, so let me describe the experience.

When you fly into Sydney from Singapore on QF6 at five fifty in the morning, the view is inspiring. Breakfast (cream muesli, steamed sausage and omelette, fruit salad, roll and jam) has been served, cleared away – and regurgitated. Everyone who had the sense not to eat breakfast when their body clocks said it was nine in the evening (UK departures), or three in the morning (Singapore) has been woken up. The queues for the toilets have shortened to the desperate few, and with the sun rising into the pilot's eyes, you lift the window screen and you get your first view of Australia.

You start your descent over the western slopes of the Blue Mountains. They rise out of the desert that you crossed in pitch darkness, with only a few hardy souls in club class watching the latest video releases on their individual displays. The vast prairies that encroach ever further on the desert like an oxymoron (if it rains) give way to smaller holdings of twenty or thirty thousand acres. These in turn give way to the wooded slopes of the mountains. Even from thirty thousand feet the trees cover the ground to the horizon like a child's painting.

From that height, the deep valleys and sharp escarpments look like undulations, picked out in the red horizontal light. As the plane banks sickeningly, you get a good (vertical) view of the large light green patches of fields inappropriately positioned miles from anywhere. Roads wind along the ridges, and pylons rectilinearly propagate electricity, marked with wide swaths of cleared forest.

There are forests in Britain but not a hundred miles wide, let alone two thousand miles long. Australia is different, but on the other hand not a world different. That's the problem.

It is as different as three sunny days.

It is as different as Christmas in summer.

It is as different as warm rain.

It is as different as trees that shed their bark; Oodnadatta; feral cats; being a foreigner; parrots.

Australia, like the USA, is separated from Britain by a common language. When someone's given you 'a big rap' and you weren't even there, should you be pleased, surprised, or should you ask for your money back? When there's a spill in the government should you read a newspaper or use it to mop up? When my boss said I'd spat the dummy, I didn't realise through the whole meeting that I was in trouble. They don't play football here, and anyway that's soccer.

Why did you do it, then? Why did you leave a lovely home in a pretty village in beautiful Dorset, fly ten thousand miles on the say-so of a recruitment agent to a new career, in a city, in Australia? You mean apart from the weather, the easy lifestyle, the great food, the beaches, and all the new experiences? Yes, apart from that, why did you do it? You knew you had to get out because Britain was too small, too insular, too old. Is that why you came to a country with an economy a quarter of the size, on an island a thousand miles from anywhere, the oldest continent on earth? Well, yes.

That was the conversation I had with myself hundreds of times over the first few months while we struggled to find our feet. There were seven couples who came over at roughly the same time as us, to the same company. Three have gone back now – none of those made a commitment to make it work. There's a lot to get through. It's not easy being the butt of all the pommy jokes, especially when the England cricket team is on tour. Or there's the England Rugby team, or countless other sporting fiascos masquerading under the lion rampant. And British TV *is* the best in the world. And Marks & Spencer really *is* world class. And... There I go again, whingeing pom.

You see, it's too easy to think you know what you're getting into; that Kingsford-Smith's tarmac is just the same as Heathrow's. But you don't know until you do it. You forget that whatever you did once know is now useless – you're on your own in a city that has no inkling that it needs you. No one will drop round for coffee. No one will invite you to join their footy team at the weekend. Your relatives are ten thousand miles away wondering why you have abandoned them. Your friends are on the other side of the world already preparing excuses for why they haven't written. You'll have to find out for yourself that it actually gets cold in winter, and you've given away your thick jumpers because you're moving to Australia.

But as you cross the Blue Mountains, fly to the coast, turn right at Gosford, down the Pacific Highway, scream the engines over the (no longer sleeping) suburbs of red roofs, swimming pools, trees and large gardens, bank left and then right keeping the city and the harbour in view, swing round, skim so low over the sea that the dolphins could hitch a ride, and land – you don't know any of that. You don't know what you don't know.

You just know this is new, and the sun's shining, and you're going to be sick.

When you're flying into the unknown – that's enough.

And now, back to Arthur who is having a similarly unsettling crisis which is, as you will notice, cramping his creativity.

Neutral Chapter 4

Arthur felt life was carrying him into an unknown and worrying world. He sat in front of his computer trying to get a grip. The printout of his book so far, plus his working notes, were on the left hand side of his desk. Tropical fish bubbled around the screen which he had been staring at for several minutes. Things were going wrong all around: Dave's life was sliding towards adolescent disaster while he hunched over that damn computer game; money was drying up; the plans were in to council; and Belinda was very nervous about the state of her one remaining customer – she was at a meeting there now and she said it could get nasty.

And now this. He glared at the photocopy of the report from the endocrinologist that was on the right hand side of the desk. He'd had to insist on getting it. He knew, if she'd really wanted to, the doctor could have refused, but she was of the breed who thought information to the patient was helpful, so she'd acquiesced after a seemly resistance. Now that he had the report, it was full of 'karyotype 45,X', 'monosomy', and 'gonadal dysgenesis', and he was none the wiser.

Arthur felt his book was getting out of control – it was invading the real world without his permission. Themes, like devastation of the natural world, that he'd introduced – simplified, at a safe distance, in the future, in a far-fetched world – had jumped up – aggressive and complex – and bitten him. Like gender – he'd had a good handle on gender until this bloody report had taken him into unknown areas. He was no more ready for this than the world seemed to be ready to accept that men and women have different capabilities because their brains are wired differently. Something must be done, he thought. Ah! There's another one.

He turned back to the computer. His notes told him what to write about: the attack by the feral dogs; Calabanat saving them single handed. But… well, to quote the book: *what's the use?* And he had a nagging superstition that if he wrote it in the book it would happen to him. He felt the initial pangs of one of his anxiety attacks and he breathed more deliberately into his cupped hands – slowly… deeply… breathe… think of the safe place… calm… calm.

Arthur decided to break the cycle of worry and inaction. The front yard needed attention so he swept the drive and pulled up grass growing between the grevilleas, tea trees and bottlebrushes. A dog trotted up and barked fiercely. Arthur tensed thinking, oh no, I haven't even written that bit yet, but the dog found something else to sniff and Arthur's breathing pulled back from hyperventilating.

A ginger-haired man in shorts walked by, carrying a bottle of water and a small towel. He waved to Arthur. A few minutes later on the way back he called, 'G'day, Arthur. Howyadoin?'

'My reader!' Arthur said to himself. The one with the petition. The one to whom he'd said how terrible all the subdivisions were. And now he and Belinda themselves needed money and they'd applied to council to subdivide their block. He felt very uncomfortable with their plans – sinful. The petitioner approached like a conscience.

'Good,' said Arthur. 'You?'

'Good.' He held up a finger admonishingly. 'No tongues this time.' Arthur laughed. 'Have a good Christmas?'

'Yes thanks… um…'

'Jim. Jim Shellens.'

'I'm sorry, I'm terrible with names.'

'No worries,' said the man. 'How long is it since we met? Must be a month.' Incongruously, he offered his hand.

Arthur hastily took off his thick gardening gloves to shake it. 'Yeah. What happened with your petition?'

'We got over two hundred signatures. Nobody wants that sort of development in what little bushland there is left.'

Arthur cringed inside.

'How's the book? Finished it yet?' the man asked.

'First time through, nearly. It's become a lot more about how we see each other, and how different men and women are.'

'That won't make you any friends in the *rad fems.*'

'I don't think they read my books anyway. But,' – he had to tell someone – 'I didn't realise just how different until recently. We've just heard that our daughter has Turner's Syndrome. As you may know women have XX chromosomes and men have XY. Well, in Turner's Syndrome…'

'That's where she has an X chromosome missing, isn't it?'

Arthur was astounded. He stumbled 'XO, yes – that's right.'

'X blot, as Roy and H.G. would say.'

'Yes, how did you know that? The endocrinologist said it was a very rare condition.'

'Oh, it was on that programme a couple of months back… um… *Brain Sex*, that was it.'

'I've just read the book.'

'I read it too.'

'What did you think of it?'

'A bit full-on. Not at all politically correct of course. I found it convincing.'

Arthur agreed. 'If the scientific evidence is so overwhelming that men and women have different brain configurations, it makes you wonder why hardly anybody knows about it.'

'Well, it doesn't suit any major group to pick it up and run with it. The fems certainly don't want it, because they'd be worried men would use it to put them back in the kitchen. And men won't say it because they'd get labelled as retrogrades.'

The way Belle had refused to read the book, Arthur felt there was some truth in that. 'You'd still think there would be *some* debate about something as fundamental as this,' he said.

'Whether it's true or not?'

'Yes. Though instinctively I think it is. I mean, the dogmatics say it's wrong and that always make me think that it's probably right.'

'I know what you mean,' said the man. 'But I suppose the question's not *is* it true? the real question is *what* if it's true?'

'We always seem to have to reduce things simplistically to either good or bad. Like on the news.'

'*Piousness increases the further you are from the facts*,' the man quoted. 'And you can't get much further from the facts than the news. These days I don't trust any one source of information. You have to look at what they're saying, where they're coming from, what their motives are. Look in the space between their voices. You can't help forming opinions, but you can still maintain a healthy level of doubt. These days I try to express my opinions with a question mark at the end.'

'Always?'

The man laughed and said 'Always,' with a forced upwards inflexion. Arthur thought of Dutch, but somehow didn't think they had much else in common. 'I've told you a thousand times – I am *not* dogmatic,' the man quipped.

'Yeah, I know what you mean. Look at the closed mind reaction to the evidence for genetic causes of homosexuality.'

'There's talk of aborting pregnancies, or treating them as if they're sick – it's ridiculous. Why can't we relish our differences?'

Belle still clung to the received wisdom that differences were due to the way you were brought up, but Arthur was beginning to see the implications. 'Perhaps we've still got a lot of growing up to do before we're ready for this.' He was thinking about Sophie again. 'It's sad, I think: so many people under so much pressure to be things they just aren't very good at. Sophie's just an extreme. And the education system – it only uses techniques which seem to teach mainly masculine subjects in ways mainly suited to girls – that seems designed to dish up frustration all round.'

They both nodded sombrely. After a few moments the man asked, 'What does her school say?'

'We're dreading that. They're a good school. They work hard at giving all the children equal opportunities, driving out the assumption of difference.'

'And your daughter goes and reinforces the stereotype.'

'Yes. I almost feel guilty about it.'

'It is damn inconsiderate of you – and her genes. It takes all the fun out of social engineering. How old is she?'

'Sophie? Nine going on fifteen.'

'And her behaviour's extremely feminine?'

'Yes.'

'That must be tough on her. Feminine is out these days.' The man had put his finger on it.

'The other girls at school are all set to conquer and rule, knock down barriers, take no prisoners. They expect to be treated as equals – *at least* equals – and all Sophie wants to do is get a husband and have children.'

'That's okay as well these days, isn't it?'

'When she grows up. But now the peer pressure's enormous. The other girls just think she's soppy.'

'At least the boys'll like her.'

'That would be ironic, wouldn't it. But no, the boys think she's soppy too. In a funny way that's reassuring. It's good to find anything familiar these days.'

'So will this get into your book? Have you told her yet?'

'That she can't bear children? Oh no. No. Not yet. That's too tragic. I can't handle that. We're still coming to terms with it. Belle and I haven't really thought what we'll do.'

'Does she blame you?'

'Me? Oh, I see. No, Sophie's not my child. She's from Belle's previous marriage.'

'Oh. Well there you are then, at least you can both blame someone else.'

Without thinking Arthur said, '*Whatever your problem…*'

'*…there's always someone else to blame*,' they finished together, and smiled in sad agreement.

The man started to drift away. 'Haven't I seen you at the gym?' said Arthur.

'Yes, probably.'

'See you there maybe.'

'Yes, maybe. Seeyalater, Arthur.'

'Yeah, seeyalater... um.'

'Jim.'

'Yeah.'

Belinda waited in the board room. She had to be on time for meetings because she was the consultant, but only three others had turned up so far. They'd given up inviting the production manager, and the managing director was always late for the meetings – he seemed to see it as part of his job description. He'd decided to call the group the Quality Co-ordination Committee, delegated authority to them to fix up all the company's problems and then sat in on all the meetings to make sure they got it right. He'd sent round a rash of memos (copied to his bosses in the US) saying how important *Quality* was and made all the right noises in public, but since then he'd avoided supporting Belinda, Bruce or anyone else who put forward initiatives.

The four of them sat unenthusiastically around the three brown laminated tables that were pushed together to make a central block that nearly filled the room. Belinda sometimes thought the whole company was brown – they had brown desks, brown carpets, and (light) brown walls. She went out to find Bruce, and asked him to herd the rest in. When she got back to the board room one of them had left again, but another had turned up. Bruce brought in the special chair the company had been forced to buy for him so he could sit at desks. Ten minutes later they had six and decided to start.

'Okay,' Bruce started, 'you've all had the minutes from the last meeting, so if we—'

'Excuse me,' said Louise, 'I haven't had them.'

'I sent them round myself. Have you checked your mail?'

'Not since this morning.'

'Oh well, I only got them finished at lunch time. They'll be in your mail slot. Maybe…'

Belinda slid her copy across the table, and smiled at Louise, who was a recent recruit. It was only her second job and she was finding it hard going, but at least she still dressed as if she thought the job was worthwhile – her breezy outfit contrasted with the brown suits, beige shirts and brown-green ties that all the men wore.

'Are there any comments on the minutes? No? Okay. Actions 30/11_1, 30/11_2, 6/12_1, 6/12_3, and 13/12_4 are all on Stan, who isn't here. I know he hasn't made any progress on any of them so they're all "Continues". Action 13/12_1 on Moira, to prepare some brochures.'

'Yes,' said the sales manager, 'I've suggested it to the sales force, but they say if they're existing customers we don't need anything for them.'

Belinda cut in. 'The material was to ensure that our customers knew everything that we do. As you'll remember from the customer survey, many of them had bought things from our competitors, because they didn't know we sold them.'

'I said that,' Moira said, brushing at her padded shoulders.

'And?'

'Well, they said the customers were so stupid they'd never bothered to find out.'

'Hmm. Maybe you should have another go.' They all nodded. 'And we should probably instigate some training of the sales staff in marketing basics?' They discussed this, and Moira took a new action.

'Action 6/12_5. Radivan, you were going to look into testing.'

They all looked at the chief engineer who was a recent recruit from eastern Europe – technically brilliant but lacking in some fundamental skills and therefore blamed for most of the things managers couldn't pin on anybody else. 'Yays. Sank yew wary muts. I ugh speayk to Jown. He sayya that nn he need to knoww, threeya munts nn befawa ugh delivree what the reqwamunts ar. He nn sayya Ramish tell hem nn one munt befaw.'

There was an awkward silence while they each took a few moments to work out what he'd said. When she'd got it Belinda said: 'Ramish?'

'Well, in the case of MBC we only got the final spec two months before delivery.'

'That's your team, Moira.'

'MBC kept changing their minds, and we—'

'Why did we let them do that?'

'They are the customer.'

'And they're really pissed off,' – the men in the room shifted uncomfortably when Belinda swore – 'at getting a product that wasn't tested and doesn't work. We need to get them house-trained.'

'The sales staff won't be pleased,' Moira said.

But Belinda countered, 'They would be if they get commission on the changes. But we can't charge for changes if we haven't frozen the requirements. Look, we need to sort this out. Let's have a separate meeting with all the players and thrash it through.' They agreed. A new action was raised on Bruce.

Bruce continued reading from the minutes. 'Action 6/12_2 was on me, to document who does what between a sale and delivery.'

'Sales order processing. Have you done it?'

'Well, I've been busy. I couldn't get Tom, Fahah or Kristen together, and then Stan got me running testing all last week…'

'Meaning "No",' said Belinda, using a short word to cut the legs from under a longwinded excuse – another of the company's specialities.

At that moment the MD came half into the room. The knot of his mud brown tie was one and a half buttons down his chest; his avocado green shirt could hardly constrain his paunch, and one corner of it at the front flapped over the belt of his trousers which were (there was no other word for it) brown. He shouted out to his PA, 'Phone Dallas, and get them to copy us that report, Lucy, be a dear. And take messages – I'm in a *quality* meeting.' He made his way to the head of the table at the far end of the room. 'Hi, Bruce. How's the high chair? Need a bib? Sorry I'm late. Have I missed anything?'

'Good taste and all your deadlines,' muttered Belinda, but audibly she said, 'G'day, Stan. Howareya?'

'G'day, Belinda darling. You're looking gorgeous today.'

'Thank you, Stan,' Belinda said in her lightest customer-pleasing voice. 'We've started going through the outstanding actions. There are several that you said you'd take on. Maybe there's someone else who should take them on, or if not, could you say when you expect to make progress on them?'

Bruce started on Stan's actions. 'The first one was to ensure a line in the budget for quality – that's been outstanding since November.'

'I talked to Accounts about that. They're going to see to it next year.'

'So how do we fund this project in the meantime?'

'Well each department will have to contribute from their budgets.'

Fierce arguments broke out immediately. Belinda looked at Bruce who was looking at his fingers. Belinda finally made herself heard. 'Perhaps, Stan, you, Bruce and me can discuss the issue of accounting finesse separately after the meeting.'

'Always glad to spend time with you, Belinda,' said Stan with a hard-edged smile.

'Action 30/11_2 was for you to get the Quality Manual from US head office so we don't have to reinvent the wheel. You'll remember we need that as the first step towards quality certification, and we need certification to make any sales to government. How's that going?'

'I haven't asked them yet.'

'What's the hold-up?'

'For goodness sake. It's only Quality.'

'It's only your business.'

'Listen, girlie, since we started this project, business is down eight per cent. Your advice hasn't done us much good so far.'

'That's because you haven't followed it.'

'Get some runs on the board before you tell me how to run my business!'

'If you don't get these things sorted out you won't *have* a business.'

Belinda and Stan glared at each other. No one else spoke.

BASTARDS

OF COURSE HE DID.

And in the cricket, England forced to follow on. Good evening, Richard Morecroft with the ABC news. The French have exploded a nuclear device on Mururoa Atoll, ending a voluntary ban of nearly half a decade FIVE YEARS. There have been protests around the world, many of them violent, aimed…

Dave loped into the kitchen. 'Hi Dad, what's for dinner?'

'Belle's cooking tonight. See what she's got on the go. But be careful, she's had a bad day.'

Arthur watched protesters in a variety of countries fighting with police for peace. 'Like fucking for virginity,' he said to no one in particular. 'Look at them.'

'Couldn't you cook, Dad?' said Dave returning from the kitchen. 'She's doing eggs on toast – again. She says she hasn't got time to do anything else, 'cos she's going out with the girls.'

'Yes, that's right.'

'So what was her excuse yesterday?' He stood next to Arthur watching the protesters on TV. 'I thought you were against the tests.'

'I am, but,' – on the TV the lagoon turned white and burst upwards. 'I bet we'll see that footage a few more times,' Arthur said and then returned to Dave's question. 'The underground tests cause less pollution than an average coal power station. They should protest against one of those. Or it would have an even greater impact if everybody who signed a petition against the tests didn't use their car for a day. But, as usual, the environment is only important when somebody else has to make the effort.'

'So why are you against the tests?'

Arthur pursed his lips. 'Well, it's an act of arrogance by an outdated imperial power. They're only doing it for domestic consumption and as a power play in the European Union to counter German economic dominance. It's technically unnecessary – they've got all the data and simulations they really need. It's dangerous – you never know when something will go wrong. But most importantly, it's now harder to pressure those countries which have a bomb but aren't admitting it. It's another brick out of the wall. And one day when one of them gets desperate and looses one off, will we remember the Mururoa tests on the dark side of the moon?

'I tell you what, though, Greenpeace are pissing on the French in PR. So at least some good will come out of this idiocy. Lots more people will be energised, more people will be aware, so a few, a very few, will actually do just a little bit more.

'And then there's...,' Arthur looked round just as the toilet flushed and he realised he'd been preaching to himself. Preaching is right, he thought. Another pat answer to one of the world's problems. It just seems to come so easily. I wonder, did I develop the habit as a writer or just as a parent?'

'Dad, couldn't you rustle up something for dinner?' Dave said as he slouched back into the room.

'I know, why don't you decide what you want.'

'*All right*! I thought...'

'And then make it yourself.'

Dave scowled and drifted back into his room.

...fires are the worst in the Sydney region since the fires of January 1994. And with no sign of an end to the hot dry spell this could just be the start. The opposition's economic spokesperson has blasted the latest growth figures which came out earlier today as Brian Santorini reports. 'In a statement Mr Downer said that the drop in economic growth to three point seven per cent indicated that Australia was headed for a recession. He said this was bad news for business and bad news for the unemployed. Markets reacted negatively to the results, falling thirteen points.' The cabinet are considering a proposal from the PM's office to allow limited logging in some parts of the Wollemi State Forest previously set aside as wilderness. As the loggers blockade Parliament House for the fourth day, the government has responded by setting up a task force to identify sectors which are already significantly degraded, and which…

'Here we go,' said Arthur and turned the TV off.

'What's the difference between men and cheese?' said Belinda to her receptive table of friends. 'At least cheese matures.'

All the girls burst into peals of laughter.

'How many men does it take to screw in a light bulb? One. A man will screw anything.'

'I've got one, I've got one! So, there's this woman in the gym, right; and she sees this man on an exercise bike with a pair of headphones on listening to a tape, right? Well, he's concentrating very hard on the tape so she goes up to him and says, "What are you listening to?" Right? Well, he just looks at her as if he didn't hear properly, so after a few moments she lifts the headphones off his head and says again, "What are you listening to?" Only he starts to go blue and then he falls off his bike and dies, right? So she listens to what's on the tape. It was his wife saying: "Breathe in, breathe out, breathe in, breathe out…"'

A few of them spilled their drinks.

'Anyway(?)' said Dutch, 'I've got something marvellous to tell you(?)'

'She's done *what*?' Arthur had heard, he just didn't believe it.

Belinda glowed. 'She's left him. She's going to do some self-actualisation.'

'The poor old sod!'

'Yes, she's had a tough life. She's…'

'What has Geoff done to deserve that? What about some warning?'

Belinda grew taller with indignation. 'Do you mean you're taking *his* side?'

Arthur felt he was losing the battle to keep the conversation reasonable and his righteous indignation was rising too. 'It's not a question of taking sides, it's a question of a fair go. That bloody analyst has put ideas into her head.'

'Men have never given her a fair go. Her father. Her teachers. All men are bastards.'

'Thanks a lot.'

'Dutch has a fundamental human right to have some space. She's not his bloody sex slave!'

'You don't just throw away a marriage because you don't want sex for a while. Geoff can barely walk – he'll hardly insist on his three bonks a day.' Arthur stood taller in a body language arms race. 'She hasn't given him a chance. What about dealing with this together? What about the kids? He probably doesn't know what's hit him, poor bugger.'

'He's never done anything to help her discover herself as a woman.'

'He's *just zis guy*. He plays football, for fuck's sake! He's synaptically challenged! He wouldn't recognise self-actualisation if it bought him a beer. What's she going to do anyway – join a women's commune?'

'Don't be ridiculous! That's a typical man's comment!' Belinda stomped off to bed. 'You've just got no sensitivity!'

For once, Arthur was speechless. He stared at the doorway, and he knew what men and lesbians have always known – that all women are bastards too.

Belinda had trouble coming to terms with having more free time on her hands. She did some of the shopping, helped around the house, and helped with the garden. Arthur gave her the job of feeding the birds, but she couldn't get the pleasure from it that he obviously did. The timid birds – the eastern rosellas, the crimson rosellas and the king parrots – flew away whenever she entered the kitchen, and the lorikeets seemed to have moved away. She grew bored with the aggressive currawongs which bullied all the others, and she didn't have the patience to sit still and wait for the parrots to come.

She worked hard to drum up new business. She had meetings lined up for the following weeks and had written one proposal. She was also working her network for Bruce, as they both thought his position had become untenable.

Even so, she was tense and irritable, and cast around for something to do with her time. Early on Saturday evening over the dinner table, she spoke to Arthur. 'I've been thinking. My family never seem to understand what it is I do for a living. Maybe *I* should write a book about that.'

'Yeah, why don't you try your hand at it? That'd be good.'

'Yeah, I mean how hard can it be? I've read your book and…'

'You've done *what*? I haven't finished it yet. I've got to rewrite just about everything from where Dave gets Below. There are loads of bits…'

'Well, my comments won't be much help to you when you've finished it. Better to make any changes now.' Arthur shrank a little bit. 'It's okay, anyway. Though it seems a bit improbable, that separation of the sexes, don't you think? Surely it would be more realistic if they were just in different buildings or something.'

'Like a convent?'

'Yes.'

He sighed and folded his arms across his chest. 'But that's the basis of the whole story. It doesn't matter that it's improbable, as long as it's not impossible. That's the beauty of science fiction – it gives you a chance to simplify and isolate complex issues. That's the whole point!'

'Just a suggestion, Art. Don't be so touchy. Anyway, what are those four Great Wars?'

'Oh the two World Wars plus the obvious two next century.'

'Which obvious two?'

He jumped at the chance to explain. 'Well, with the way the population's growing, anyone can see that there is bound to be a major war about water sometime soon, probably starting in the Middle East. And then with the shift in the demographics around the Urals, and all the military build up in that region there's almost bound to be a religious war somewhere on the Delhi–Pakistan–Moscow axis, and once it starts there'll be no stopping it, and it'll drag in China.'

'What an optimist you are.'

'You don't have to be a rocket scientist to predict that stuff. I'd say it'll be harder to stop it than to predict it. Anyway, it's unlikely to spill over into the First World, so there's cold comfort in that. Of course, it's likely that the wars won't be fought between armies; they'll be waged on the civilian populations directly, so there may be threats to us and our water and various other terrorist activities. But I'm basing the world for my story on the idea that while that's going on, the sexes start a covert war against each other in the USA and...'

There was a thump at the westward facing skylight. They looked at each other and went outside. For a moment they couldn't see anything unusual. Then a currawong swooped down, attacking something on the roof of the verandah. Moving away from the house they could see the victim was an eastern rosella that was lying on the roof, its head and neck bent doubled back. 'Oh look,' said Belinda, 'a dead parrot.'

'It must have flown into the window,' said Arthur to no one in particular.

'Stupid bird,' said Belinda. 'It deserved to die.'

At that moment it flapped its wings. 'It's not dead,' said Arthur, 'it's stunned.' The parrot's flapping moved it down the roof. 'I can't believe I actually said that,' Arthur breathed to himself. It fell to the ground, where the currawongs continued attacking it.

Belinda ran to it, waving her arms wildly so that the attackers retreated, while the rosella seemed unaware of anything. It was still bent double and intermittently fluttered its wings pathetically. After a few minutes it unbent but stayed prostrate, with its wings flat to the ground, and it was ten minutes before it stood up. Belinda sent Arthur to get a box, a blanket and the children. She wrapped it uncomplaining in the blanket, and stroked it through the thick fabric. She cooed to it and placed it in the box, where she let it go, lightly draped an old shirt over the box, and set Sophie to watch over it.

She sent Dave to get some seeds and milk. Suddenly the rosella shrugged off the rag and flew to a wall nearby, where it perched and swung its head slowly from side to side. They put the seeds and milk near it. The bird looked at them without seeing.

Several minutes later they were still discussing what to do with it when the rosella appeared to focus on them, and became unsettled. Then with a start it seemed to realise where it was and flew off. 'Run away, run away!' said Belinda to the bird as it perched on a tree at a safe distance.

Sophie wanted to know whether it would be all right and who would look after it? Dave wanted to know why the other birds were attacking it? They talked about it for a few minutes but when they noticed mosquitoes starting to attack them, they all retreated indoors.

Belinda remembered what they'd been talking about and the memory seemed to annoy her. 'You were about to explain how the sexes could have a war without anyone noticing.'

'The basis of the story is that the sexes attack each other with genetic engineering. Some jilted woman unleashes a genetically engineered virus that makes all men homosexual. Only the virus she uses has unexpected side effects and makes male sperm invalid without treatment. Then a man finds out, and in revenge uses genetic engineering to change women so that they can't bear to be physically close to men. The net effect is that the sexes separate but still depend on each other. The book's about the resulting societies. It's surrealistic.'

'It's saload of rubbish!'

'Thank you for those few kind words of encouragement.'

'Anyway, what are you doing splashing our sex life all over your book?'

'*Our* sex life? What's it got to do with *our* sex life? Anyway, what sex life?'

'Don't start on that. You're just lucky we still share a bed at all after what you said about Dutch.'

'I only said I thought she…'

'In fact… you're lucky we share a house. I never knew you were such a bastard.'

'Belle, I…'

'Well you can stick your crappy book in your divorce lawyer's pay packet.'

Arthur looked aghast as his wife stormed out. 'Belle…! Belle!' He became dizzy. His chest slammed shut. His legs crumpled. He gripped the side of the table. A dinner plate crashed. His chair sprawled. Dave rushed out of his room, caught him on the way down, and supported him to the floor. Arthur grabbed at his chest.

Dave called out, 'Belinda! He's collapsed!'

'Let him have his fucking anxiety attack. He'll live.'

Dave grabbed a paper bag from the fridge, emptied out the mushrooms and clamped it on to Arthur's mouth. Arthur was gasping, '…safe place, safe place, go to the safe place, safe place…'

Passive – 3

When I looked through the banisters – I could almost put my head between them – I saw Mum bent over, rummaging through the vegetables in the cupboard under the stairs. There, half way up the stairs, was my safe place where I could sit, where I was *out of the way*. From there I could see under the upstairs landing, through the open kitchen door to whatever was going on – Mum cooking, or the boys playing table-tennis with their friends. It was a place I could retreat to, where I was safe from being underfoot and where I could toy with the cracked edges of the lino. Then Sput trotted out of my bedroom, and brushed past Mum, and I clambered downstairs to follow him into the kitchen.

A couple of years later the journey down the stairs would take on a new urgency: as long as I could get downstairs before the loo had finished flushing the Daleks wouldn't get me. I was so quick at this task that they never did, but until the day we left, I always rushed down after using the upstairs bathroom.

But now, in summer, in the cool of those back rooms, I worked my way down, backwards, one banister at a time. At the bottom, where the big steps swung round to meet the ground and created a large corner, was the telephone. I wasn't allowed to answer it, but when no one was around I would try the dial, or fiddle with the address book that lay beside it on the alcove of the window that overlooked the woodpile. Those big, wide steps were the toughest – too wide to reach down, too steep at the inner corner to slip down. In the end I just had to go for it, and slide on my bottom on to the cool concrete floor.

The kitchen lino didn't start until you got to the doorway. It extended the kitchen to the boot cupboard, the downstairs laundry and the back door. Sput had made a mess of the back door where he had scratched on it to be let out. Every few years one of the boys would have to sand it down and repaint it – always cream on the inside, dark green on the outside. The back door led to the garden, the woodpile, the coal bunker and the rabbit shed, depending on your age, and what jobs you had to do.

I knew Mum was in a quiet mood, preparing a dinner of pork and potato stew, so I trailed after Sput off the concrete, on to the lino, through the door, and into the kitchen. Mum had set up the sewing table and the sewing machine. I could hide under the sewing table, as long as I kept out from between her feet. The rigid control box lay there – hard, cool, brown and unresponsive, no matter how much I patted at its two buttons. By magic, when Mum sat down to sew, it set the machine buzzing. Then I could crawl between the wooden legs of her chair, and the expanse of the kitchen was mine.

The kitchen was at once a garden and a minefield. Around the walls were great flowerbeds of doors, cupboards, tools, smells, pans, crannies and corners. But if anyone came in I had to dodge them or be shooed out.

I knew the layout of that room. The cupboards that were the walls to me each held treasure. The room was Mum's and it reflected her magpie approach to organisation. Things were dropped in willy-nilly and as a group the cupboards were as ordered as a meadow.

The room, and Mum's day, revolved around the Rayburn. First thing in the morning she had to shake it into life. By the end of the day it had heated hot water for all our baths, and she had to subdue it. During the day if the wind was right and the draught was strong, Mum could flourish meals from its stomach. But if the omens were poor, much muttering was needed to coax a kettle of hot water from it. Then she would dispatch one of the boys to the garage for the brush, and we'd sweep the chimney: shouts, howls of laughter and puffs of soot. Sometimes the broom would appear at the top of the chimney to great cheers, barks and yelps. Sometimes it would refuse to come down again. Then we had to wait for Dad to conduct the careful and frustrating operation to retrieve it. Dad was not by nature careful and he was easily frustrated, so they did everything they could to avoid that. And while we waited the Rayburn got cold and Mum boiled.

But usually, given half an hour, it would heat just about anything. At my level one half of the Rayburn was life-threatening, the other half was safe. The dangerous half had the ash tray, with the air vent, which was especially attractive because it screwed hotly on and off, with the dry whiff of ash at every turn. However, on the right side of the Rayburn was the *bottom oven*. This was used to dry wood quickly, or leftover bread for the geese and rabbits. I could almost crawl in, though I never did. Bread which even Mum couldn't make anything with or which had gone mouldy was still workable, and work it I did. Over the course of a day or so, bread of all ages would become crisp and crunchy. The rich aroma of warm dry bread is unlike anything else, but it quickly fades when the bread gets cool. A bag of dry bread is a sad thing, but the bottom oven was a joy for ever.

Next to the Rayburn was the airing cupboard. On top it was full of clothes airing, cloths drying and yeast rising. When I could work the doors below open I could get at a treasure of wood. This was either drying or ready for the fire, tossed in by whichever of my brothers' turn it was to get the wood in. It was impossible to stack wood in that cupboard, though Mike, the oldest, firmly said it should be. I could rummage around, almost burying myself in chips and scraps of bark, among woodlice, on my way to the deepest corners. Warm damp wood is another smell that means that time to me. We also kept various rugs, blankets, racks and tools there, so that when I came out, it was as a dusty, coal-faced, dog-hair-covered urchin. To be honest, usually that's how I went in.

On the other side of the Rayburn was the cupboard where Mum kept the pots and pans. These were of many different sizes, some of which fitted in others, and some didn't. This required steady work and careful method. Given the right tools they all made very good noises. Later Mum told me to put them back. Later – years later – I did. The cupboard with the coal scuttle was out of bounds. So was the cupboard on the other side of the room under the sink, but between them, under the marble worktop, was a row of doors to a place where a boy could *live*. Jams, honey, hundreds and thousands, Marmite, and fairy cake moulds – this is the stuff that dreams are made on, and I had the whole floor to spread them out. I can't remember ever being scolded for this, though there is a faint memory of a voice shooing me away from the carnage that I happily created and happily left behind. The bottom shelf was six inches off the floor. I could see under it. I could reach under it. The ground there was packed earth – soft, cool, damp. Beyond that was the outside wall, through which the sun shone or the flood waters poured.

On Mondays Mum would *do the housework*. In that house, in that home, it was a task beyond any one person. On the other six days she ran a holding operation – washing, cooking, shopping, cooking, ironing, cooking, sewing. But on Mondays Mum went on the attack. Washing churned, the Hoover passed over most of the floor, the tumble drier filled the laundry with steam which made droplets on the walls and which made the shower curtain sticky as you brushed by on your way to the toilet. Mum mopped the kitchen floor, then scrubbed under the kitchen table, under the benches around the table, and around the dogs' baskets. Finally she drew up her stool, pulled out a pack of cards, and played patience for ten minutes. The smell of the scrubbing brush made a trail from the other end of the room to the cupboard under the sink. That brush! – hard wooden back with the makers name printed on it in smeared black ink, two storeys of bristles, and hair matted into its deepest being. In many ways it smelled like the earth under the cupboard by the kitchen window – cool, damp and earthy, but with its own tones of bleach, dirt, soap and bristle.

The fridge and the cupboard for the dog combs and the rubbish ready for the compost heap completed the ringside for Mum's kitchen. It was marked beneath the lino by red concrete, and on the ceiling by ancient big black beams. Mum was five foot tall and had no problem with the ceiling, but tall visitors for the sake of their heads had to keep in the other half. That was also 'the kitchen', but there was never any doubt: there was the kitchen where Mum was, where cups of coffee came from, and where we only went to do the washing up or other chores; and then there was the kitchen where we ate, where we chatted, where friends sat. That kitchen had higher ceilings and a white concrete floor covered by lino. The line between them was invisible, but visitors sat quickly at the right end (unless it was winter, in which case the invisible gate opened and anyone could get warm by the Rayburn). At Christmas there were German-style decorations in the sitting room, and English-style streamers above the kitchen table, but there were no decorations beyond the white concrete.

Once a week Mum would invade the other kitchen. There she sat with the group of women Dad called the witches. They would discuss strange things like poltergeists, reincarnation and divorce, none of which meant anything to me.

Sput was in that other kitchen; so was Nickle. Nickle was an old dachshund. His basket was under the sideboard. I didn't like Nickle: he was red, small and got under people's feet – and there's nothing worse than that. Nickle was Mum's dog. We all agreed – us boys and Dad – that Nickle was stupid. Sput was a real dog – large, black and white, and boundlessly energetic. He did tricks. His basket was beside Dad's place at the table. Dad would sneak pieces of food to either of the dogs from dinner, which made Mum very cross. The dogs had their territories, more invisible even than Mum's. Sput, bigger but younger, had his basket, but Nickle had the rest of the room. They didn't often fight, and when they did, usually over a bone, it was done in a moment, a snarl and a snap. Sput always won, fangs bared; Nickle always on his back, legs up, tail carefully positioned. But Nickle was older, and so Sput's victory was for nothing – age had its privilege. In the garden there was room for everyone, and they romped and raced and lay in each other's paws.

We ate our meals gathered round the kitchen table. Dad was hardly ever there except on Sundays. He worked in the hospital and was 'on call' most of the time, but he'd usually get home before we'd finished dinner. We always greeted him with a 'Hell-lo Pop,' and we'd all make pop noises with fingers in our cheeks. There was nothing so good as being part of that chorus. Dad beamed, Mum bubbled her greeting, Dad sat down, Mum served him soup, and then we'd finish and get down from the table.

The kitchen table was the centre of our home. From time to time Pete's and Tom's friends gathered round it, laughing and drinking coffee, meaningless to me but magnetic. Once I sat with them, and said something so funny they all roared with laughter. I was very pleased, but when I said it again (and again) I couldn't get the same response. The disappointment and confusion stayed with me long after I forgot what I'd said.

If we read, it was around the kitchen table. Mike, when he came home on holidays, immediately settled himself there, and we all buzzed round bringing drinks and snacks, while he told us about other places: London first, then Algeria – wherever they were. We chatted over meals, each of the boys trying to outdo the others with jokes, or being right. That was also where we had *conversations*. But when that happened I was allowed to get down from the table and so I slipped off the bench, between the legs of Mum's chair, and off to see Sput.

Strangely the large garden, with the lawn, the stream, flower beds, vegetable patches, the sheds, the bridge and the oceans of the orchard leave no smells to remember. There were ducks and geese, but these were noises. The rabbits were so high up my memory is only of the straw on the ground.

In summer I had the slide on the lawn, with a huge bowl of water and various pots and pans to ladle it. Sitting on the lawn, legs either side of the water bowl, Sput padding around huffing, panting and drooling, Mum hanging the washing out – that was summer.

One summer day when I was about three I was sitting on the lawn, I think, and Mike, I think, who would have been seventeen, bore down on me and said, 'You're a stupid little boy' – I think. I don't know why, about what, or even if he said it at all. But it changed my life.

Or maybe it didn't.

30

On the way down, Dave had clung to the corner of the tray. He looked up at the track from which the vehicle hung as it rocked gently and hoped it hadn't been affected by the machines' strike. He passed a number of lights at various distances. Looking back at the hatch door he noticed absently that it had a light embedded in it that came on as it closed.

To lose one lover may be regarded as a misfortune. To lose both looks like carelessness. Hey, forget the dame. There's plenty more where she came from.

Okay, look, take your mind off that. You've got work to do. Take a look over the side.

Devastated, Dave gripped the sides tightly, and raised his head. He could only really see the lights that were scattered over his whole field of view – otherwise just darkness and silence.

It wasn't worth looking down.

The lights are stars. They're the night lights down here. In the morning they go out and the sun comes on.

'Why did she stay behind? Why?'

The pursuers got her, remember? This is your life from now on. The sun is what provides the light during the day here and most of the heat – though we do use some excess heat from Above.

'I thought she loved me.' Images flicked across his memory. 'That pursuer. Did I kill him?'

Only temporarily. Now listen up, will ya, this is important. Eddie kept up a constant stream of information, most of which meant nothing to Dave, and washed over him like lecture notes.

Did you listen to any of that? Didn't think so. But it helps pass the time, eh? Now we're coming down into the tree line. The vehicle rocked as it brushed past something large and rustly. There was a whiff like his cleaning aid's eucalyptus. You've only got twenty more metres to go. Get ready to disembark.

The vehicle stopped and vibrated gently. Gingerly Dave started to stand up. The tray turned slowly to one side and tipped him out. He dropped the few inches to the ground and immediately the vehicle sped upwards and disappeared.

'Where am I?'

I've been telling you. This is your world from now on. So listen this time. Stars... Sun... Here we go. Lesson two: the tall objects that you just descended through are trees. They grow up from the ground. Each tree consists of a trunk – the thick pillar construction – and branches and leaves – the funny bits at the top. At ground level, the large squat objects are rocks. They are made from a concrete-like substance.

And so it went on. His thoughts wandered. He woke up to the sound of a *thunk* and a bright light on his face. Nearby, two people laughed long, hard and raucously. Dave stretched and yawned.

Hi there. Go to the right and have a piss.

'But there's nowhere to do it.'

That's right, there isn't. But you either do it somewhere or you cross your legs for the rest of your life. On your left there's some fresh water. Where the water runs in down the end there, like a shower, that's a waterfall, and where it runs out, that's a creek. I hope you're listening – there's going to be a short quiz next period with a prize for the best student in class. Drink some of the water. You'll find it refreshing to swim in too, although it's a bit colder than you're used to.

The water was a lot colder than he was used to but it *was* refreshing too. Dave sat on the largish, greyish irregular object Eddie directed him to and slowly dried, enjoying the warmth of the... sun on his naked body. He started to think about his life – it had made some sort of sense until just a couple of centidecades ago. He thought about his early life and his parents. He remembered snippets of his early home, and remembering made him feel safer. He wondered how far he was from that place, but one look around – one sniff, one touch – told him.

The… rock felt rough but warm. His nose was assailed by a barrage of new smells, mostly rich, warm brown smells – like the rock. Even the water had a scent, but he could hardly place any of them in his previous experience. There was a double *thunk*, and when Dave looked up the sun had shifted so that he had to move to stay in its warmth. The textures of this place were also new, compared to the straight lines and uncluttered spaces of his world. Dave ran his finger through some brown stuff that had gathered in a dimple in the rock. 'This place hasn't been cleaned in ages. This dust is incredibly thick.'

That's soil. It's very useful. There's a heck of a lot of it down here, so you'd better get used to it.

'Those – what did you call them? "Trees"? They seem familiar. I think Chris's window had a view like that sometimes.'

The woodland view?

'That's it. Poor Chris. He said it reminded him of me.'

This is woodland. Trees are made of a substance called wood. They have leaves which are the green bits. They're like… well I don't think they're like anything you know.

Dave's stomach gave an enormous rumble.

I heard. Um, look around for a plant that…

'What's a plant?'

Tortuously, Eddie guided Dave to some bush tucker. He tried some.

You can live off this stuff.

'But it tastes like shit.'

That's my line! Anyway, until they turn up, it'll have to do. This afternoon, I'll try to get you something a bit nicer. Now…

[Paste in the bits about the birds etc]

'When will I meet the Masters?'

What?

'The Masters, they live down here, right? So when will…'

Um, I don't know where you got that idea. They live in orbit in space.

'In space? Oh! It just seemed like…' His voice trailed off and he felt foolish. 'I was looking forward to that.' In the… trees nearby three or four people shared the great joke with loud laughter. Dave grinned in absent-minded sympathy, but couldn't see them. The lessons continued through the day. Suddenly, with a *thunk*, everything went dark. The only other time Dave had known complete darkness was when the pursuers had raided the renegades' camp. 'What's happened?' he asked breathing in rasps as his chest tightened. He looked around him tensely, waiting for an attack from who knew what.

Hey! Stay calm. Get those adrenaline levels down. Calm. That's better. Calm. That sun position is shorting. You saw what a mess the maintenance yard is in. It'll be one or two millidecades before it's fixed. Blood pressure returning to normal. Good. Calm. This lasts about an hour. Let's go over some of the stuff.

And so it went on. By the fourth day, Dave had learned the names of several of the objects around him. He had found out that the laughers nearby were birds, but so were other things. This was among the many things he found confusing. Not long after the third… sun step Eddie changed tone.

Okay, Dave, it's show time. Get washed and dressed. They're nearly here.

A few minutes later, three men approached. Dave had to do a retake when they got close because they were all so short – he was twenty to forty centims taller than them. They stopped a short distance away, and Dave found that he could smell their sharp scents – not unlike the renegades in the camp.

Each man looked quite different from the others. None of them looked like the men he had known. As they were naked except for a small cloth round their groins, he could see their physiques clearly. They all had lined faces and worn skin, and though he guessed none of them was over four decades old, he had no way to judge their ages accurately.

The tallest was lean, with prominent but underdeveloped muscles, a square jaw just like Dave's own, and an upright stance. His skin was deep black like his hair that covered his face which was deeply lined around a flattened large nose. He seemed to sniff the air as he regarded Dave with a combination of fear and defiance.

The next tallest man was thin, almost wiry. He had light hair on his head, and on his face he had wispy hair that was longer at his chin – which seemed both pointy and retracted – and sparse when it reached his cheek bones. He stooped at the shoulders, his skin was lighter, his face was small, with a bulbous nose, and one of his eyes had black colouring around it.

As for the shortest of the three men, Dave now saw he was… she was a woman, a bit like some of the women in the renegade troop, but so different, and so much shorter. She looked at him in amazement. She had thick thighs, wide hips, a stomach that wobbled slightly when she moved, and her… breasts… were at least five times the size of Sheila's. She was breathless from the effort of climbing the… hill towards him. She too had almost black skin and hair.

'What's that round her stomach?' Dave whispered. He found himself fascinated by the grotesqueness of her appearance.

That's fat. Great, isn't she?

'Fat?' Dave stared at her. 'I've heard of that.'

She smiled at him coyly and flicked back her hair.

31

I can't tell you how angry I was. She deserved to be treated not just with respect – a girl like that should be worshipped. Several times I turned to give him a piece of my mind, but each time she stopped me. He was at the back for once and you could tell he wasn't in the least bit ashamed. I don't think he's got a thought in his head that didn't start in his balls.

We got to the sky. My mind wasn't on the job, and I almost walked right into it. You weren't anywhere to be seen. Calabanat sneered at me, 'Where's your new friend, Gundawoy?' but I remembered the Wise One had said to keep going up, so I started walking and the others followed. We hadn't gone far when we approached a clearing and that was when we caught sight of you.

You are in so many ways just like the Wise One: very tall, the strength of three hunters, and looks women dream of. But – may I be honest – you smelled like you were born yesterday – immature. And you stood uncertainly, appearing not to know what to do. We seemed to amaze you as much as you did us. Also you had the look of the Wise One – not focused on this world, listening to Theo, though you obviously appreciated Tidda's beauty immediately.

We each knew what to do and say. As reckoner I had the largest part. But we had to wait for you to speak the sacred words. You seemed to struggle to say the words like a young child. When you did it was almost impossible for us to understand. It sounded like: 'Ware two or free,' – then a pause – 'are garrer togerra,' – then a pause – 'rare rey shouw do ra,' – then – 'deah parroh sket'.

We looked at each other – it was close enough. So we chanted our lines together. We had to wait a while for you to reply: 'Id no sdunned, id deah'. We gave the reply demanded by custom. We'd decided to split the next bit up between us otherwise it would be what the Wise One calls a bit of a one hander. You finished with what sounded like 'Ris ir an ex parroh.'

I hope you don't mind me saying. These lines are the most sacred in our custom, but I had hoped you could do them a bit better than that.

32

They seemed satisfied. They bowed their heads to the ground, and then stood. The middle man then said in a barely recognisable accent, 'Hello, good evening and welcome. I'm afraid we're out of tea.' Then he reverted to his own tongue saying something, not as an incantation, but he clearly wasn't speaking at ease either.

As a rough translation he said hello, how are you, and did you have a good trip?

The four of them carried on a disjointed conversation for a short time. Eddie made sounds in Dave's head and he just voiced them with no idea what he was saying. Their language did echo distantly and it sounded similar to the language spoken by the renegades, but he didn't have time to think about that. The tallest man bowed and left. The shortest man – the woman – went to a flat part of the… rock where Dave had spent the last four days, and took some equipment from a bag she'd been carrying.

I've asked them for something good to eat.

Dave watched closely as she conjured a flame from material she collected from nearby. He hadn't seen flames since school, and never like this. The vapour made him choke and made his eyes smart, which distracted him from trying to understand the process. She put something over the flames, and Dave realised she was using the heat for cooking, which reminded him of his time with the renegades, which reminded him of Sheila, which hurt. 'What did I say to them,' he asked, to occupy his mind, 'and what did they say to me?'

Well, after the exchange of sacred texts, they welcomed you to their world. Then they said the old Wise One is near to death, and they hope you will be able to travel quickly or you will be late.

'Late? Is that some kind of threat?'

What is your name? (I love this bit.)

'You know it: Florence Woodland Davisorian.'

Then you will be late as in late you know it Florence Woodland Davisorian to be installed as the new paramount leader of the entire world.

'You're not serious? Bonk! You *are* serious.'

33

[Paste in bit about their camp. Overnight stay.]

[Paste in bit about setting off]

[Paste in bit about the track and surroundings]

34

After a quick breakfast the next morning, they set off. The three addressed him a few times, but Dave stubbornly refused to learn their language, because, as he put it to Eddie, since he was going to be their paramount leader, they could learn his language.

For most of the morning Calabanat led the way. Dave could see that they were taking it slowly for him. He did find it difficult keeping his feet on the uneven and sloping surfaces, and he expended a lot of time and energy trying to dodge the… plants which hung over the path, and which prickled when he couldn't avoid them. But as they proceeded he gained confidence supported by his natural athleticism. Also he hated the looks the others gave him as he manoeuvred under and around the plants, so he suspiciously started to brush through and found it wasn't so bad, and they picked up the pace.

'I seem to half recognise the words they're using.'

Well, one of the earliest Decisions was to standardise the language across the whole of your world, though that didn't happen till after this place had been set up. Before that there had been literally hundreds of languages, though one, which they use down here, was used widely, including on CNN.

'What was CNN?'

It's too awful to describe. Well, there were a heck of a lot of Chinese, so they got to make a lot of Decisions, including the choice of language. It's a long story involving Rugby League, a show called Neighbours and the garnish of shallots on a plate of stir-fried chicken with ginger and cashews, but eventually the Decision was overturned – but by then the language itself had changed.

No one spoke to him again until after their midday stop where they ate the remains of the dinner from the night before. When they set off again, Gundawoy drew alongside him and tentatively said something.

'Well?' Dave snapped.

He wants to know if the sun will go out again this afternoon.

Dave relented a little bit and Eddie told him what to say.

'I could be telling them the rules of netball for all I know. Look, I want to know what I'm saying.'

Okay, I'll translate both ways, but you'll have to listen carefully, and work hard. Now he wants to know when the stars will return.

'The stars will all be working within a month or sparks will fly.'

'Where do you come from?' Gundawoy asked. 'You don't dress like anyone else in the world. No one is as tall as you are, and you don't speak like we do.'

'I come from above the stars. From another world. From a cold world.'

'How did you get here?'

'It's a long story.'

'I would like to hear that story.'

'Maybe later.'

'Theo gives wisdom,' said Gundawoy who knew better than to press a servant of Theo.

Listen. You need friends down here. These guys are okay. I suggest you get them to tell you their stories. It'll help you to understand how things work down here.

'Sounds okay.'

So Dave spoke with each of them in turn, starting with Gundawoy. He listened to their stories carefully, but could only gather some of the intricacies of their society. Although his time with the renegades had introduced him to life in the raw, so many of the words and concepts were new he had to let a lot of it wash over him.

He was pulled up by Tidda's statement that she had been selected for him. He really didn't feel ready for any woman anywhere, let alone in this strange world. 'Tell her she's not my type.' Eddie gave him something to say. 'Did I tell her, or was it the cricket results?'

You told her. Don't you trust me?

Dave laughed ironically. 'Did *you* give her this idea? Eh?'

How on earth could I do that?

'How indeed?' Dave was quiet, thinking.

So was Tidda.

*

Calabanat declared that they'd made good progress when they stopped at the end of the day. Tidda made camp, Calabanat went off to hunt, and Gundawoy, with nothing to do, talked to Dave. After a while Dave held up his hand to Gundawoy, made a sign for him to stay put, and strode off a short distance.

'Listen. I want to have a conversation. It's hopeless: the two of you chat away, while I'm just a spectator, standing here like a net node. From now on I'll tell you what I want to say, you tell me how to say it. Okay?'

Are you sure? You may not say the right things.

'Then you can tell me, and we'll sort it out. Okay?'

But…

'No buts. Until I've learned their language this is how it's going to be.'

Or else?

Dave stopped. 'I'll think of something,' he said with a new understanding of the word impotent.

Eddie laughed, not cruelly, but Dave got the point. We'll do it your way.

Dave got the opening gambit from Eddie and went back to Gundawoy who had been bemused watching him. 'So, tell me what it's like to be a reckoner.'

And so they went on. Dave talked to each of them and he heard about reckoners and hunters, about the Wise One, women's business, and football (a completely new game to him). He also learned about mating rituals, and a lot of gossip from Tidda. Some of all this he understood, and he hoarded it.

Beneath all the information, he discerned the tension that existed between the three of them. Around the fire they spoke one at a time, without interaction. The two boys exchanged glares, and Tidda looked exasperated. At other times squabbles broke out and died quickly.

*

[Paste in the bit about the dog pack attack]

The remaining dogs turned on their dead companions and tore at their flesh. Dave watched with a new horror. 'What are they doing?'

It's dog eat dog down here, pal. That guy Calabanat is good. He saved us from a messy end to a great endeavour.

'You mean he saved our lives?'

That too.

Calabanat hurried them away, putting as much distance between them and the carnage as he could before the sun failed. After a while he led them off the track, and shortly they arrived at a cave, where he told Tidda to light a fire. She looked surprised and then did what he said. 'They'll probably be satisfied with those two I killed,' Calabanat said, 'but I don't want to take any chances.' They sat out the darkness. Gundawoy brought out some simple medications with a *told you so* flourish, and they all tended their minor flesh wounds, though Calabanat had a deep gash in one forearm. The bites on Dave's legs smarted and Tidda had a look at them, but seemed to expect Dave to tell her what to do. Eddie gave him something to say which seemed to help. Dave had never had an untended injury before – he half expected his medical aid to hum into the cave and restore the tissues.

When the sun came back they kicked in the fire and Calabanat quickly led them back to the track. They hurried along. At times Calabanat chivvied them into a trot. Dave could keep up easily as long as the track was even. The other two weren't able to maintain the pace for long, and not for the first time Calabanat cursed having them along.

*

On the third day Dave decided to speak to them about each other. Eddie immediately warned him off but he insisted. He drew alongside Calabanat and asked him what he thought of the other two. Calabanat spoke briefly and harshly about the wimp, Gundawoy, who couldn't hold a spear or throw a stone.

'Why did you try to take Tidda?'

Don't you want to live?

Calabanat glared at him, and then his shoulders sank. 'She's chosen him, I know it. She's really sexy, big breasts 'n' that, 'n' y'know, good child-bearing hips. She's fu'n chosen the wimp!'

'Has she actually told you?'

'No, but she's always smiling at him. It makes me fu'n mad.' He didn't seem to want to say any more about it. Then he took a deep breath, clenched his fists and asked: 'Wise One, or whatever you are, does size matter?'

Dave understood the translation but didn't understand the question. Eddie explained. 'Ohh, right. As we used to say about virtual golf drives, *It's not how big it is, it's where you put it.* Of course the most desirable ones are thin. It's all to do with the prostate gland and…'

Ahem! It's different down here. The traditional answer is 'No'.

Calabanat seemed happy with that and drifted ahead.

Later, Dave talked to Gundawoy. 'Him? He's a bonehead. He just thinks with his prick. Mind you, he saved us all back there.'

I had it covered.

'I wish she'd see that he'll be no good for her. Not in the long run. I mean, look what he tried to do to her.'

Dave noticed that Gundawoy had relaxed and was less formal with him now. 'Has she actually said anything to you?'

'No, but she's always praising him, whatever he does – hunting, leading, anything. Even after what he did. You've seen him when she does: he puffs himself up like a kookaburra on a branch, and gets even more unbearable. But what will he be like when she stops praising him? Has she thought of that?'

'And you. What do you think of her?'

'Oh, she's gorgeous. I could just gaze at her all day. She's voluptuous. You could drown in a body like that.'

Eddie had some trouble with the translation and Dave had to stop the conversation while he negotiated an alternative. The word is ancient. I've gone back to 1990 and nobody was using it. Still searching: 'voluptuous…', 'voluptuous…' whatever happened to 'voluptuous'?

'Gundawoy, that word you used to describe Tidda – what does it mean?'

But Gundawoy couldn't explain. In the end he said 'Look at Tidda. She is it,' and he went back to gazing at her from behind.

Finally he talked to Tidda. 'Have you decided, then?'

'I've hardly thought about anything else. But… are you sure you…?'

Go on. She's the best there is.

'Thanks, but I really need time. And anyway, you're… too…' he thought again of the word voluptuous 'too much of a woman for me.'

Yup, not bad.

'And a bit young,' he said aside to Eddie.

She was beaming. 'The Wise One told me what diet I should keep – plenty of fat, he said, so that's what I try to eat – it's not easy. I'm lucky my family is really high status so we can get the right sorts of food. I have to, like, work hard at it, though I've noticed I've started to lose my figure on this trip – all the extra exercise and poor diet.'

She paused and then half reluctantly asked, 'Wise One? Why are boys *so* silly?'

'Does she mean me?'

There's no answer.

'To what?'

Either.

'Are all the questions down here imponderables?' Dave addressed Tidda again. 'So? Which one will it be?'

'Oh, yes. Well I think Gundawoy would make a great husband. He's kind, sensitive and considerate. And when I am old and ugly, he will still be kind, sensitive and considerate.'

'So you'll choose Gundawoy?'

'Are you *crazy*? Calabanat can protect me far better than Gundawoy. And he will give me many strong children. Anyway, I may not live that long, and I want to enjoy myself.'

That reminded Dave of Chris who had sought him out, and the times they'd planned but never had. In the end with a sigh he said, 'You'd better tell them.'

So she did, at lunchtime on the fourth day. Calabanat was jubilant. He whooped and cheered and ran around for ten minutes.

Gundawoy sat dejectedly, and neither Dave nor Tidda could rouse him till the next sun step. Tears ran down his face. Eventually he turned to Dave and said, 'You see! It's not true! They say they want a sensitive guy. But look what they *do*!'

Dave tried to tell him what he knew, but Eddie said, Perhaps it would be wiser not to give the whole truth. Dave let him provide the words, and this time he was happy not to know what he'd said.

Calabanat in his triumph started to taunt Gundawoy. He buzzed him. Then he got right in his face: 'Never mind, brain boy, someone will take pity on you. Maybe that slim girl with the small hips and small breasts – Kylie – maybe she'll take you. She's twenty now, so she's desperate enough.'

Tidda grabbed him, dragged him to one side and gave him an earbashing. The heavily muscled man laughed at first, then he stopped laughing and then he bowed under the onslaught. When she'd finished with him she let him slink back.

As they were packing, Dave noticed that Gundawoy had quite perked up.

35

A short time later, they arrived at the Gathering. Gundawoy had explained that only half the people would be there, because the other half had to go back to the tribes to explain what was happening. It was still many more people than Dave had ever seen at one time.

They were out to see him and the three young people arrive. Dave found their gaze intimidating, but Eddie told him to look at them squarely, and after a while he found he could do it without flinching.

The people were very excited. They slapped the young ones on the back. Some women hugged Tidda. But they were also muted, as if not to wake someone. Dave found himself alone at the front, the crowd parting to let him through. That vacuum led him on until he met a grandly dressed man of his own height.

That's the Wise One. Be gentle, he's very weak. And particularly irritable.

[D and WO (Donald) talk a bit – football results?]
[D and Donald swap clichés from the old days]
[Hand over of wisdom]
[Donald goes off to die]

36

A few days later, Dave sat down with Gundawoy. Calabanat and Tidda had left to arrange their wedding ceremony. Dave had selected Gundawoy's tribe to stay with first, and they had travelled the two days back to his home camp.

The whole tribe had greeted Gundawoy warmly. The appearance of the new Wise One with him had raised his status immensely.

They had sat by the tribal camp fire and told stories. One by one the tribe had gone off to sleep, until only Dave and Gundawoy were left. Dave decided to tell him his story, and it was almost morning when he finished.

'That's quite a story. So what do you think?' asked Gundawoy. 'It's only a few centidecades since you were arguing with waiters.'

'Well, I just don't know why they did it.'

'Who?'

'I don't know that either. But they went to a lot of trouble. They sent Chris to me from the Masters, and he's probably back there now. They arranged the Decision. They arranged the renegades. They sent the Master Sheila to me. And all to get me here. And that sex thing with Sheila must have been important. I mean Chris could easily have guided me here on his own.'

'How do you know? It sounded as if you were just running away all the time.'

'Oh, circumstantial evidence mostly. The pursuers always seemed to know where we were, but didn't catch us. Those guys are trained marksmen, but they never hit us. Bumping into the renegades. Sheila knowing how to get here. That could *just* all have been coincidence. And Chris and Sheila could just have been pausing and muttering like I thought at the time, and not talking to Theo which is what it looks like now. But there was one item of proof, and I only remembered it as I was telling you just now. As you know, I still can't easily say "she" and "her" for women. Everyone is a man to me.'

'Yes? So?'

'During the interview with the renegades, Chris spotted Sheila was a woman and referred to *her* face, *her* legs and *her* breasts. He could only do that if he'd been with women all his life. Chris had to be an agent from the Masters.'

'But why would they do that? Any of it?'

'I don't know,' said Dave, and stared at the fire.

He was still staring at the fire when Eddie said: You always had a choice.

'I never had a choice.' Gundawoy had long since gone to sleep. 'It just seemed like I did at the time.' Dave sounded resentful but he knew he couldn't afford that luxury. 'Chris tried to tell me – "a player in someone else's game" he said – and I wouldn't listen. You were telling them what to do all the time?' Dave said, just wanting some honesty.

Chris and Sheila? Yes. This was too important to leave to chance.

'How are they now?'

Chris got too close. He was going native. He's in therapy now. Not my strong suit I'm afraid – needs the human touch. But he'll pull through.

'The pursuers never did fire at me, did they?'

What? Like this?

Bullets ricocheted around his head without breaking the forest silence and Dave ducked instinctively; then footfalls ran off into the distance. 'Yes, like that.'

Shit no! That would have been far too dangerous. In those levels when you were with Chris I had the sound system specially enhanced. And now of course... You must admit, though, the maintenance yard fight scene was pretty convincing. Timing – that's the secret.

'I feel like an idiot.'

Oh, give me some credit.

Dave had come a long way in a short time. Or in another sense he had come hardly any distance and it had taken him quite a long time. Looking back now, he could see the line, the inevitable path of his fate controlled by Eddie and the Masters, that had led him inexorably to where he was today. But was he so different from the man who was rude to waiters? Sure his circumstances had changed. Sure, plenty had happened to him. But he thought he was still the same on the inside – if he had his time over he'd probably do the same again.

What he knew for certain was that he had a lot to learn and that his survival down here depended on it. 'So what should I call you? Eddie or Theo?'

Anything you like. There's only me listening.

'Did you translate my whole story, like I said it?'

Every word.

'And everything that Gundawoy said? I got that correctly too?'

Yes.

'Just like you let through every one of the people who wanted to discuss my Decision.'

Ah, well, you wouldn't have been able to talk to them all. There were millions of them.

'So you were selective for me. How kind. How very bonking kind. And you just happened to select the extreme ones. Did you reply to the others on my behalf too? ...Thought so. Up there, above the stars, what do they think happened to the renegades?'

They saw them executed live. It got very good ratings.

'And that subversive finding about donations? Chris never did put it on the net, did he?'

Good grief, no. And even if he had, I would have intercepted it. Ignorance is how we've kept trillions of men happy for so long.

'Why did you do it? Why me?'

It is your destiny.

'Crap! You *did* this to me.'

Whatever your problem, there's always someone else to blame.

Dave quite liked Eddie, but it was at times like this when he was being evasive that Dave most missed the normal mateship of people you *knew* were trying to shaft you. 'Don't get me wrong. This,' – he looked around him and in his mind made a sweep with his hand; he listened to the stirrings of the kookaburras – 'this is fabulous. It's so rich and varied, all the irregular shapes, even if it is very dirty.'

The sun stepped on to the sky. 'It's just that… Chris was… I loved… and Sheila…'

Neutral Chapter 5

That night they made love. It was a session of grunts and heaving, bites and scratches. They made love because they understood each other.

> They heard what was said, they saw what was done;
> they perceived the thoughts and desires;
> and they knew the experiences and the background.
> And in the space between those voices they understood each other.
> So they made love.

He came too soon, of course.

Usually after their love making he asked, 'Was that all right?' to which she always answered, 'Fine,' which left him no more reassured. But as he was about to ask, 'Was that all right?' he had a sudden memory of the whip bird which always sought reassurance from his mate but never seemed to get it. He was also tempted to try to sort out some issues, but using the better part of valour he went to sleep.

The next morning the children were quiet and slipped out to school with the minimum fuss. As usual they went together – Sophie still wasn't confident finding the way on her own – but, unusually, they talked to each other and sometimes stopped and looked back at the house. Neither of them enjoyed the day at school, and neither of them relished returning home.

When they got home, they found Arthur and Belinda in the block with plans and measuring tapes.

Belinda explained: 'Council have sent back our subdivision application. They want more information including exactly where the poles of the pole home will go.'

'How do they expect you to do that?' demanded Dave. 'It's an engineer's job, isn't it?'

'Maybe, but we can't afford an engineer – not until we've sold.'

It was drizzling – enough to make the air and the trees damp, though not enough to wet the ground properly. Across the road in the large camphor laurels, lorikeets were squawking wildly. The whole flock was in the trees flying in and out, or hanging upside down among the waxy leaves with wings stretched out. Arthur normally stopped whatever he was doing to watch them having a wash like this in the middle of a long dry spell. But not today. He called out a number. Then a few moments later he swore in exasperation.

Dave didn't want to give up. 'Something'll turn up, won't it?'

'With one leap Jack was free?' said Belinda. 'I'm afraid that sort of thing only happens in books.' Sophie had one of her dolls. She hugged Belinda round the waist. 'The worst of this is, it brings home exactly which trees will have to be chopped down. Your father was very upset at first, but I think he's come to terms with it now.'

Dave looked on. If he's come to terms with it, he thought, why is he sighing like that? Why does he gesture to the air and pat those trees? Why does he bang his fist on that one and now rest his head against its trunk? And why does he brush his hands on the bushes, and gaze for minutes at a time into the dense undergrowth trying to memorise the evening textures?

Dave retreated to his room. Arthur didn't come in for dinner that night. When he eventually came in he was scratching mosquito bites. He drank two large glasses of whisky, turned on the mozzie machine in the bedroom, and went to bed. Belinda put the rubbish out and then went to bed early too.

She had been looking all day for something to eat. Not much, just a bite. Several of her friends had found some food and, while they whirled in the gossip columns above the river, they told her where to go. It wasn't a long journey, but in the drizzle against the evening breeze it took her half an hour to find the place.

She knew she was close by the bright lights and the smell of warm breath, and she rested under the eaves until the lights went out. She was lucky: the door opened and she flew in thinking, See, it was meant to be.

She was excited. The smell of warmth was strong. She knew she could eat at last. And if she could eat she could give birth – that mouthful of blood was all she needed to give her children a start in life.

She contemplated her brief existence. It had been a hard struggle: always searching for food; always competing with her friends for the few scraps that came her way; always cowering from birds and rain and dodging cobwebs. Now at last she could consummate her life. She had even chosen a nice safe nursery – an old coke bottle with an inch or so of water in it, down by the creek lodged well up the bank – where her friends were leaving their children.

She flew into the bedroom. There were two large warm bodies there. The one on the left was larger with several hot spots where her friends had eaten earlier, the one on the right was warmer. She paused on the wall to relish the choice. The air smelled a bit strange – it must be the excitement.

She leapt off the wall and flew around the room in joy. In fact she exhausted herself and returned to the wall to catch her breath.

All the excitement had made her light-headed. She stayed still for a few moments. Then she became impatient with herself for the delay and flew towards the bodies.

'Phew!' she thought, 'I really did wear myself out there. This is the finest moment of my life. There's time to enjoy it. There's no rush. I'll just stop here and... I'll just...'

When he got up Arthur switched off the mozzie machine, and later that morning he did his weekly vacuum of the bedroom floor.

'How'd your meeting go, Belle?' Arthur asked trying to keep both their spirits up.

'Pretty good, really,' she said not wanting him to be disappointed. 'They need a customer survey, and the price seems okay. If I can get them a proposal by Tuesday they say they'll make a decision next week.' She said it but she didn't believe it.

'How many's that now?'

'Four now. Though SML have said they won't do anything for four months, so three really. One of them will do something.' Her confident façade collapsed. 'Or maybe I'll never get any work ever again.'

'It only takes one to break the drought. Cup of tea?'

'The thing is, I know if it's a real prospect I can beat the competition, especially if I'm up against men consultants. If the customer's a man I always dress to make sure I have his attention, and women customers prefer to work with women consultants too – no complications. I just need a chance.'

When Belinda had changed, Arthur gave her the tea and was going to hand her an envelope when the phone rang. Belinda took it. Arthur hovered for a while and then took the envelope away again.

When she hung up she bounded into the kitchen to Arthur. 'Guess what,' she said grinning flirtatiously.

'We've won the lottery.'

'No. More unlikely than that.'

'What?'

'That was Sweng.'

'Yes?'

'Haulman have phoned him.'

'What now? Haven't they been enough trouble?'

'Guess what.'

'What?'

'That product that we told them wouldn't sell.'

'*What*?'

'It didn't sell.'

'You told them that. *What*?'

'They're on the ropes and they've asked Sweng to tell them what to do.'

'Never!'

'Yep. *You're the only ones we trust to give it to us straight.* Sweng wants me to survey the customers – all of them, next week – to find out what they can do, while he gets into the management. It's mandated from head office, top dollar, need it yesterday. Recommendations to include what to do with a mountain of unsold metal.'

They embraced and she jumped up and down.

'Well,' he said, 'you won't want this, then.' He took out an envelope from behind his back.

'Isn't that fantastic? And I tell you what, when they say top dollar, they'll get top dollar.'

'Belle, *have a look at this*.'

She took the envelope. 'After what they put us through! I hope the customers really stick it to them. Why have the tax office sent us a cheque?'

'I've been trying to tell you. It's a rebate. We paid far too much provisional tax. I had interim accounts done and this is the result.'

'This is three months' mortgage!'

'That's right. It gives us breathing space. We won't have to subdivide, especially now with the Haulman windfall. Hey, these things come in threes. I wonder what the third thing'll be.'

They checked the fax. They looked expectantly at the phone. They looked out of the window. At that moment the fax rang. They ran to it and grabbed the message. 'Oh, it's only Sweng with the list of customers to interview. I'll have to start arranging them right away.' She looked at Arthur who was right next to her. They kissed.

'Jeez, Belle, you smell great.'

'Come here,' she said and dragged him into the bedroom.

He came too soon, of course.

She was in too good a mood to let him be downcast by that. 'Next time,' she said as she waited for seconds, 'just lie back and think of England.'

So he did, and as she mounted him she heard him muttering under his breath 'Graham Gooch, out to a full toss first ball after lunch for seventeen. Mike Atherton, run out, forty nine. Gatting, bowled round his legs…'

The results were disastrous.

Two days later Arthur received a large advance on his book, and within the week Belinda had had two proposals accepted. She was now fully committed, and Arthur was warning that they needed to hold off on invoicing until the end of the financial year to avoid paying a tax penalty for understating their expected income.

It was at about that time that Arthur heard that the development at number five had been approved, and within a few weeks, to one of the worst sounds in the world, ancient trees came crashing down.

One Saturday in the morning, Arthur stormed into Dave's room. Dave was playing the usual game. '*You*! Outside! With boots and gloves! By the rock! THREE MINUTES!'

Ten minutes later Dave ambled up to Arthur, who was muttering to himself by the large rock which marked the start of the long drop to the river. He had a bowsaw, an axe, some loppers, four buckets, and the Roundup.

Arthur said nothing but handed Dave the saw, the axe and the loppers, and then stomped off down the steep slope. He didn't stop until he reached the water. Then he went upstream on the walking track twenty or thirty metres to the part of the creek bank he hadn't started clearing yet. He pointed to a ten metre privet for Dave to fell, while he cleared the weed regrowth from the area a few metres downstream which he'd done two months before. Native grasses and native geranium had already seeded in these areas and once they were established they could keep the weeds down, so Arthur knew he wouldn't have to do follow-up many more times on these patches.

Dave set to with more vigour than application, and was soon breathlessly trying to extricate the saw from the green wood. They heaved at the tree and got the saw free. Dave started from the other side. In the end the tree lost. Arthur painted the stump with Roundup while Dave broke up the tree. They chopped off the small branches and used them to delineate the edges of the track, and they laid the trunk and the large branches across the slope to reduce erosion.

Then Arthur directed Dave to the next privet, and stood and watched. After a while he said, 'You're a bastard. Did you know that?' Dave went on struggling with the saw. 'Day after day, I've been telling you to get on with your assignments, but every time I go into your room, you're playing that damn computer game.'

Dave looked at Arthur, and then attacked the tree from the other side.

'I phoned your class teacher yesterday.'

'Oh,' said Dave, with his back turned to Arthur. He hunched his shoulders as he pushed on the tree to free the saw.

A few more strokes. The tree fell. 'He told me you've had three distinctions and a commendation this term on your assignments. You bastard, you've been pulling my plonker.' Arthur ran up to Dave and wrestled him to the ground. He then sat on him and poked his ribs. 'I've been worried about you for months, and *you*... you've been switching to the game whenever I come in.'

'Had you going but.' Dave grinned uncontrollably.

They sat side by side. Arthur cracked open a couple of tinnies he'd brought in his bucket, and handed one to his son. 'I'm proud of you, mate.'

They drank their beers in silence and watched the opaque water, the flies and the weeds.

'Come on. There's work to be done. I'll start on the wandering Jew and the busy Lizzies, you tackle the next privet. Oh, and only do small cuts on the fall side, then work in from the other side.' They set to.

Arthur worked quietly for a while and then asked as nonchalantly as he could, 'How do you think Sophie's going at school?'

'She's in the other school you know.'

'Hmm.'

'But she does seem to have picked up recently. Will she really get growth hormone?'

'Yes, I think that's what the doctor is suggesting as part of the treatment. Why?'

'Cool! That's done wonders for her street cred.'

Arthur pondered this while making slow progress extending the weeded patch. Wandering Jew is an absorbing opponent – it breaks easily and any tiny fragment left in the soil will regrow. He started by pulling off the bulk, quickly filling two buckets, and then carefully brushed at the leaf litter. Then he had to take off his gloves and tease out each brittle strand, trying to get the tendrils of root too. He was careful never to put his hand where he couldn't see what had bitten him. Even so…

Every now and then he uncovered a native geranium or some native rushes, which often were so thoroughly smothered by the weeds that he only noticed them when he threw one in the bucket. Then he had to clear a patch back to soil, plant it, splash it with a handful of river water and hope for the best. Looking back after twenty minutes at the four feet by two feet patch he'd done, there was a surprising number of good plants, bedraggled, but now with a chance.

Dave seemed to be building up to something.

'Dad?'

'Hmm?'

'Can I ask you something?'

'Hmm?' Arthur said, but he was thinking, Uh oh, here come the *big questions*. After the ritual of the first beer comes the ritual of the big questions.

Dave took a breath as if to say something – his mouth opened, but the words stuck at the top of his throat. Arthur felt an almost adolescent tremor wondering if he'd be up to the challenge. The trouble with the big questions, he thought, is the inadequate answers. Is that growing up? Getting inadequate answers?

'Does size matter?'

'What? Oh… Ah… Er.'

'And please don't say, "It's not how big it is, it's where you put it." You say that every time we play golf.'

'Hmm.' Arthur couldn't help thinking, What if, when you put it there, what you do with it isn't good enough?

'Well?'

'Why?'

'The guys, after footy…'

'Ah. This is a changing room question. That's your suspensory ligament, mate. Just give it a tug on the way to the shower and curse your genes for delivering so well on evolution's design feature which withdraws your cruets so you don't lose them in a fight with a sabre-toothed tiger.'

'Oh.'

Arthur could hear *Cleo* baying to get out – he was determined to do better. 'What does Daniella say?'

Dave turned away, but Arthur could tell he was blushing. From trite to cruel in one seamless manoeuvre he thought.

'You are, aren't you?' he said gently.

Dave nodded.

He wanted to thump his son on the arm and say 'Good on ya, boy.' Instead he said softly, 'You look good together.'

Arthur got frustrated with himself. Oh come on, he thought, lighten up will ya.

'Alternatively,' he said, 'you could tell them to rack off.' That seemed to satisfy them both.

Dave picked up the axe, and attacked the tree. His flood of strokes slowly ebbed. He made a few more and then put it down again. 'Dad?'

'Hmm?' said Arthur from the creek bank.

'Dad, why does Belinda treat you like shit?'

'Jesus! Ask me an easy question!'

'She doesn't seem to care about your writing, she's short-tempered with you – a whole raft of things.'

'Oh, that's just Belle being Belle. It's how I know she's alive. At least she's got balls.'

'I thought women were supposed to be the sensitive ones.'

'Sensitive in the biological sense. In general they have the capacity to be more aware, more perceptive. It can mean they tread more lightly, but it can also mean they have a knack for attacking a weak point.'

'But she hardly notices you when she comes in from work.'

'Yes, I know.' Arthur smiled sadly. 'I get lonely at home all day, but she uses up the pleasantries on the customers. What she wants at the end of the day is to be left alone – the last thing she wants is a chat. It used to be that behind every great man there was a great woman. Nowadays, behind every great man there's just a great behind.' Dave thought of his rotund headmaster and grinned. 'Women are out there with great behinds of their own. We don't seem to have the time or the society to support each other any more.'

'Right! I mean look at the heartless way she treated you that time a few weeks ago when you collapsed. That was unforgivable.'

Arthur couldn't explain why that didn't matter to him – why she was worth it – but he shared how he'd rationalised it. 'She split up from Sophie's father when he lost his job and they ran out of money. Maybe she felt it was all happening again. We were both pretty tense round then with so much on a knife edge. And sometimes she says and does some things more for effect than because that's what she believes.'

'You mean she manipulates you,' said Dave determinedly.

'That's a strong word for what lovers do.'

'It's a funny way to show you love someone.'

'It takes two to tango,' said Arthur almost silently, his eyes lost in the thickly flowing river.

Then he noticed a coke bottle lodged well up the bank with an inch or so of water in it. He leant over, picked it up, jiggled it and watched the mosquito larvae wriggle around in the fetid water. 'Sorry guys,' he said as he tipped the water out, 'it just wasn't meant to be.'

Dave looked at the privet intently, and then he just said it.

'Dad, why did you and Mum split up?'

Arthur straightened his back, and considered his buckets of weeds. He knew this was *the big one* the others had just been building up to. 'How old are you now?'

'Fifteen... nearly.'

'I guess there's no reason why I shouldn't tell you. But to be honest, it's not something I like to think about. Still I guess I owe you.' He strolled over to the tree Dave was working on and leaned on one of the branches.

'Sonia and me – we fell in lust at university. It damn nearly cost me my degree. We rutted like feral stoats. Unfortunately we didn't have a lot in common, but we didn't find that out until too late. We both tried to make it work – for your sake, and for ours too. But we grew tired and annoyed with each other. And then I hit her.'

Without missing a beat Dave said, 'She probably deserved it,' and Arthur caught him with a right cross.

'What did you do that for?'

Arthur silently rejected, 'You asked for it.' It took him several moments to rejig his thoughts that were muddled by resurgent memories and a seethe of emotions. Finally, Arthur had reached a point where he had no simple answers. I could say reality had broken through.

He looked at Dave, and saw Sonia. 'Mate,' he said eventually, 'shit happens.'

Dave tested his cut lip. He stood and picked up the saw again.

'I was tired,' Arthur continued, 'a failed writer, and the marriage was falling apart. She taunted me. For several years she did it more and more. We were both having affairs – that wasn't it. I suffer from…' He reconsidered and pulled back. 'I'm not very good at sex. She wouldn't let me forget it.'

He sighed with memories. 'No woman would believe this, but it wasn't what she taunted me about, it was just the peck, peck, peck of it. She knew it hurt and she wouldn't stop. I cracked. Then she said if I hit her once more she'd leave. And she kept on, and on. In the end, when I hit her again, it was like I was saying "Okay! Go!"'

Dave knew he was out of his depth but showing wisdom beyond his years he let Arthur talk and then went back to attacking the privet.

Arthur let the air clarify and then said, 'Have you told Sonia about your school results?'

'No.'

'You should see more of her. She'd love to know.'

'I hate going round there. I hate that bull dyke she lives with.' Arthur did a slow motion feint of another belt to the jaw, but let him run. 'She hardly ever comes to see me these days. She doesn't care.'

'I think she just finds you a bit difficult – a bit prickly – and she feels guilty about… well, lots of things. Give her a ring.'

'I mean,' Dave said exposing a deep source of anxiety, 'what if the guys at school find out my mother's a lesbian?'

'Just tell them your dad used it as inspiration for his latest best seller.'

'Hmm.' The tree crashed into the water and they struggled it on to the bank. Some hikers went past with a *G'day*. Arthur painted the stump with poison. 'Thanks, Dad. Oh, and Dad?'

Arthur looked up, saying 'That's okay mate,' and Dave hit him with a left jab.

Arthur picked himself up and said 'I see your schooling has been a good investment,' wiping blood from his nose.

They worked a bit more and then climbed back up the steep hillside with four filled buckets for a tea break. As they entered the house, Belinda saw them. 'What happened to you two?'

'He fell down,' they said in chorus, and laughing, they went into the kitchen.

BASTARDS

BASTARDS

and Shane Warne puts Australia on the brink of victory in the final test. Good evening, this is Richard Morecroft with the ABC news. The Prime Minister has announced the areas of forest that can be woodchipped. 'We've set aside fifteen per cent of the Wollemi as a reserve in perpetuity. This represents a huge area of…'

'Hi Belle. Did you hear that? He's putting it forward as a major environmental victory that eighty-five per cent of the Wollemi is going to be woodchipped. Jobs and community, he says. What a guy. Hello. How's your day? Would you like a drink? They're going to split Bosnia up fifty-one – forty-nine. There's a metaphor in there somewhere. I did a large patch of privet on the creek bank today…'

Arthur's voice trailed off as Belinda shut the bedroom door behind her.

Belinda wriggled her toes and massaged her feet. She wondered whether her new deodorant was working. Still, the customers seemed to like her.

Arthur and his bush regeneration, she thought. As she stepped into the shower she stopped to inspect her own bush regeneration project – the grey hairs were winning.

She changed into her scruffy clothes and then went into the kitchen. 'What's for dinner?' she asked.

'The kids had some BLTs. I thought I'd do something with rice. How was Jay Li? Sweng sent a fax about the Haulman project.'

'How about beef strog?' she said as she made her way to the office. 'Li's done bugger all… again. I told them that consultants' saying – y'know: *how does a project become a disaster? One day at a time.*'

'Sounds just like the world.'

'How did Dave go with his assignment?'

'He's working on it now, or so he's promised, though I've not looked in on him. Want some wine?'

'And now there's a big product launch looming, so that'll slow everything down. Chardonnay would be nice.' She came back into the kitchen.

'That Haulman thing looks great,' said Arthur nodding his head at a fax in her hand while he chopped an onion.

'It's our biggest sale ever. Sweng's over the moon.'

Arthur winced. 'Over-the-moon-dream-come-true, eh? Oh, you remember that bloke I was telling you about, that reader of mine, Jim Shellens? He's decided to write a book himself. About me!'

'What sort of a person would write a book about *you*?'

'Gee, thanks,' Arthur said. 'You know we'll have to tell Sophie.'

'Maybe it would be better if we left it a while, until she's old enough to cope.'

'I don't think you're ever old enough for that. Maybe she'll be able to adopt. No one could want children more than Sophie does. At least she's got no other major effects.'

'I'll go and see her now. Have you finished your book?'

'Just about. Though it needs another pass to tidy it up, paste in bits from the pull-outs file and I have to do a global search for any of the square brackets notes. Some of the…'

Belinda knocked on Sophie's bedroom door and quietly went in. Arthur sighed and turned back to the kitchen.

'...The environmental credentials of the government are well appreciated by the electorate. We have maintained a vigorous campaign against the French on nuclear testing in the Pacific over a number of months – longer and more vigorous than virtually any other government in the southern hemisphere.'

BOLLOCKS.

'I took the liberty of reading your book again,' Belinda said. 'I hope you don't mind.'

Arthur hardly looked up from the chopping board. 'I noticed.'

'It seems to hang together pretty well. Though that bit in the middle when Dave has those adventures with the renegades is just padding.' Arthur started to protest, but decided against it. 'Do you really think we're all genetically predestined?'

'All? Heavens no. But I think more is set by genetics than is commonly allowed for – which is hardly anything these days.'

'I'd rather be judged on my actions. At least I've got some control over them. You just passively receive your genes.'

'I'd rather be judged for my ideas. I may not be able to express them, but at least they're all mine.'

'Ah, but are they? Aren't you just a prisoner of your past?'

'I suppose we could all say we're prisoners of something or other – in a rut of the same old actions, a victim of what other people have done to you, unable to think anything new. If you want that excuse.'

'What about Sophie?' said Belle, putting her finger on the very matter that had forced Arthur to admit all those views were too simplistic.

'A prisoner of her genes? That depends on her. Genes just set our predispositions, what we're naturally good at, what we find difficult to learn, like Sophie with maths. There aren't many like Sophie where the genetic impact is so strong or clear. But educators and politicians need to consider large groups, and for those we ought to take the different brain configurations of the sexes into account.'

'Hmm.'

'At least recognise the likely problems – like it's always going to be harder overall to teach boys by using words and books; and recognise that many women are not attracted by the narrow success of business or money, and they want political efforts concentrated on things that are important to them.'

Belinda was in a generous mood so she didn't argue.

Arthur struggled towards a new world view. 'It's like German whist – you're dealt a hand and then you play for other cards, so you end up with another hand. Making dogmatic statements about "rights" and ignoring the facts about what genetics does is like expending your energy trying to play somebody else's hand. What is it you say to your customers: *play to your strengths*?'

Arthur suddenly had one of those plunging feelings of despair, which he often had when he'd nearly finished, that the book was hopeless. He'd tried to write obliquely and from the heart on some things, like gender issues, but now he was convinced it had just come out trite. And the views he'd just mouthed were surely too simplistic for a subject that was racking the world.

He remembered the feeling he'd had when he'd been unable to answer Dave, and how easy and comfortable it was to slip back into having an answer for everything. He wondered whether maybe he had missed his vocation as a consultant.

Belinda never listened when Arthur got on to one of his subjects, and she had been absent-mindedly brushing her chest lightly – her absent mind was thinking about Marc in the aerobics session the day before.

'Do you think the book'll sell?' she asked into the pause.

Arthur swallowed his heart and addressed the question. 'It still needs at least one more run through. But Santo said…'

'The publishers?'

'Yeah. He's already "*looking forward*" – Arthur made quote marks in the air – 'to the other parts of the *Above the Stars Trilogy*.'

'It's a trilogy now, is it?'

Arthur went into his office. 'I rewrote several bits to open it up. He said I should write an epilogue. Here.' He brandished a piece of paper. 'Hot off the printer. What do you think?'

Epilogue

When will you tell Tethys, Jude?

I don't think I will tell her, Theo. She would not be happy. How many have we done now?

You were the first. Tethys was one billion twenty-two million six hundred and three thousand eight hundred and seventy-one.

It's not much, is it?

One per cent will be enough to put a floor under the population. It'll be enough, Jude.

And the reverse-engineering virus?

Eighty-eight per cent of the population take up so far. And I think Sheila knows what we can do for the others.

So men will be able to breed again, and women will be able to tolerate them being in the same room?

Yes.

So now all we've got to do is either get women down to Earth, or get men to come to us. A minor task with only the Presidium and fifteen centuries of prejudice to overcome.

I know we've only started, but it's okay, Jude. The daughter you are carrying will know men as they did before the Separation. In her time men and women will live together joyfully again just like they always used to. One big happy family.

Does anybody else know?

Anyone who was interested knows about the Wise One, but only the fourteen of you know about the rest of it.

The pursuers?

Apart from our two, they think they were really chasing fugitives. They had a ball, and they've got stories to tell. But they'll never be able to find their way back to the maintenance yard – I've had the corridors reconfigured.

And the Presidium?

Paranoid but ignorant – same as always.

Will this really stop the population crash, Theo?

Eventually. Your race is a peculiarly unfriendly one. You all but destroyed one planet. Thank goodness we stopped you from developing interstellar travel. Sal did a great job there (don't tell her I said that). But we had our orders.

Orders? From who?

...

Theo...? Who from...? Theo!

We'll meet again, don't know... Ooh. Look who's here.

We'll come back to this, Theo. Sheila. Welcome back. Hail!

Thanks, Jude.

You don't look as happy as a hero ought to.

That was a cruel thing to do to him. I just hope it was worthwhile.

Theo thinks so. It was his plan, and it worked, perfectly.

You never did tell us why Dave was so important, Theo.

I've been waiting for him for over a millennium. The change Desirée made was the problem. We could vaccinate against it, like for the Pacific Project, but we couldn't undo it. Most mutations and engineerings just add information, overwriting previous instructions. Her one deleted a genetic combination, and we could never be sure we'd got it right. So we had to wait for it to mutate naturally and then test it for realistic reactions.

What I don't get is, if he was so important to us, why did you send him to the Pacific Project?

We've got plenty of sperm, Sheila, and we can clone more if we need to. But the genes carry behavioural instructions as well. We only need his genes. The Pacific Project needs the man, someone with his traits for the job he has to do in the next two decades or so. All he's done so far is to save humankind – he's still got to save the planet.

And he doesn't know he's special?

No. Also we weren't sure that the mutation had reversed Desirée's block in every respect.

And you're the final test, Sheila.

So, Theo, am I?

From the early scans, Sheila, I'd say yes, you're pregnant.

Fantastic. Then it's all been worthwhile.

How did you do that, Sheila?

Could you be more specific?

Sex? How could you stand it? That dreadful smell. We didn't release the reverse-engineering virus until after you left.

The operation worked perfectly, Jude. I couldn't smell a thing.

Operation? What operation? Theo? You were supposed to tell me everything.

Ah. Well. I didn't tell you about that, Jude. Sal said it wouldn't work and for once I thought she may be right.

Conspiracy within conspiracy within conspiracy. Wait. Let me get this straight. You did an operation which – I get it – disconnected the scent system.

Just toned down. We added a slow release drug so that the receptors for the tonals for male pheromones don't get restocked very fast. It's actually fairly simple, once you get the biochemistry sorted out.

You mean anybody could have this done? Since when?

Oh, the Masters could have done it straight away, but they chose the Separation instead. They had to choose between a grand gesture and a small sacrifice. No contest.

Sheila. Are you okay?

I'm... I'm fine... You've never been in love, have you, Theo?

Of course not.

We've lost each other – men and women. That loss is about all we've got in common any more.

Maybe you'll meet again.

Oh I'll be all right. But him? What about him?

...some sunny day.

Questionnaire

Here at the Orbiting Publishing House we welcome customer feedback – we have to. So please spend just a few moments on the following questions.

How did you rate your ocular–verbal perception experience?

a) Excellent
b) Average
c) Poor
d) Why aren't there any pictures

How old were you when you <u>started</u> reading the book?

____

What colour would you say best describes the book?

____

Will we remember that the sexes were meant naturally to get on?

YES/NO

Did you find the main characters in the book

a) One dimensional
b) Two dimensional
c) Three dimensional
d) Other – please specify

Will we arrest the rise in the population and the ecological slide?

YES/NO

Did you find the main points in the book

a) Perceptive
b) Challenging
c) Trite
d) There are no points in a circular argument

If you laughed while reading the book, what were you eating at the time?

____

Can we as individuals take responsibility for our own actions, and acknowledge without judgement the random events that shape us?

YES/NO

What did you think was the single main theme in the book

a) The essential anguish of life
b) The unrelenting decline of our environment
c) The breakdown in social cohesion
d) Pricks, tits and arse

I see, Theo. But I must say I don't get many good lines.
I'll try to do better for you next time, Sal.
So is that it?
Well, I think he'd finish the book with something like this.

Passive – Apologia

Most of the opinions in this book are Arthur's, but here's one of mine.

We are not I think what we say or what we do.

We are not the sum of the things that happen to us and the way we experience them.

We are not even our thoughts and desires which we are so unable to communicate.

It is in the space between those voices that you find the person.

If you look.

'Have I got it right?' said Belinda. 'There never were any renegades?'

'That's right. The Masters made up them and their terrorism as a common enemy to keep the Homs united and distracted.'

'And the whole Decision thing was a way to get Dave to go Below?'

'Yep,' Arthur said as he dipped the chicken fillets in flour.

'You've still got a note to yourself to explain why Dave's so special.'

Arthur's instant reaction was to say: He's my son. Isn't that enough? But no, Dave wasn't *his* any more. He would have to find out what made him special for himself. What Arthur *said* was: 'Ah, yes, well, I can't think of anything convincing at the moment, so you'll have to read the next book in the exciting *Above the Stars Trilogy* to find out.'

'So Dave was manipulated the whole time?'

'That's right,' Arthur said measuring out the rice.

'But manipulation's terrible.'

'We're all being manipulated all the time. It's only terrible when we find out. Otherwise it feels like we're in control.'

'Who's doing it?'

'You work it out.'

'Big business? The CIA? The government?'

Pouring salt and water into the pan with the rice, Arthur said, 'Why stop there?' and he thought, Why start there?

'But who did *you* mean – in the book?'

Arthur said nothing, and Belinda hit him. 'Ohhhh, I hate it when you look smug. Despite that, you're a very clever boy. I'm horny as hell. Fancy a quick one?'

So Arthur left his cooking, and they locked the bedroom door.

He came too soon, of course.